Where Love Leads

KC LUCK

This book is a work of fiction. Names, characters, places, and incidents are products of the author's imagination and/or are used fictitiously. Any resemblance to actual events, locales or persons either living or dead is entirely coincidental.

Copyright © 2022 KC Luck Media

All rights reserved, including the right to reproduce this book or portions thereof in any form whatsoever.

Chapter One

Taking a flute of the sparkling champagne from the tray the waiter offered, Melanie Sotheby gave a longing look at the stuffed, green pimento olives pierced with a toothpick. Even though the glass would be her fourth of the evening, she had yet to eat. Going without meals was a long-established habit, and she gave the man a slight shake of her head, letting him disappear into the crowd. Sipping the drink, Melanie let the expensive bubbly slide over her tongue as she looked around the ballroom at all the men and women in expensive clothing. As in very expensive—Versace suits and Vera Wang dresses, Cartier jewelry or at least good imitations. Dressed to match in sleek, black Dolce and Gabbana, with her long blonde hair in an expensive updo, Melanie fit right in. All in accordance with the blockbuster movie premiere event she was forced to sit through, only to be followed by the pretentious afterparty. The film had too much violence, too many explosions, and far too many frequent saliva-dripping alien monsters for her taste, but at least the main character was a woman who kicked everyone's ass in the end. Of course, the film was a sequel to a sequel to a sequel, but audiences loved the movies, so Hollywood would milk it until things became absolutely ridiculous. *They never know when to stop,* she thought, starting to sip again when she noticed her flute was close to empty. *Well, shit. How did that happen already?*

"Looks like you need another one, doll," a man said as he sidled up beside her in a cloud of cologne. One glance and Melanie had to force herself not to roll her eyes when he gave her a wink. Alan Forrest, a B-list movie star too old to hope of rising any higher. It was clear he was using his good looks, and a lame attempt at charm to... *Do what exactly?* she wondered. *I'm married to one of the wealthiest men in the room. Surely, he's not that stupid. Besides, he's well past his prime to be trying to use his smooth playboy moves on anyone, let alone me.* Not that at fifty-three she was a spring chicken herself, but then she was never an actress, only a swimsuit model with a minuscule shelf life. After the fashion industry stopped calling, Melanie had wisely married up to the wealthiest bachelor she could find. Or husband number one as she called him. Considering she was on husband number three, it was easier to think of them that way.

Which makes me wonder where husband number three, Mr. Monty Sotheby, has wandered off to, she thought. "I don't suppose you've seen my husband?" she asked Alan, glad she hadn't brushed him off yet. At least he could help her find Monty. Suddenly looking in any direction but at her, Alan appeared ready to bolt back into the sea of Hollywood somebodies. Melanie put a hand on his tuxedo jacket sleeve to keep him in place. "Is that a hard question to answer?"

"Uh, no, it's not," he said before clearing his throat. "I just assumed that since he was...um, busy, you might need company."

Melanie narrowed her blue eyes. "Busy?"

Obviously unwilling to answer, Alan waved at a person in

the crowd, or at least pretended to, after all he was an actor, and started to move away. "I need to go talk to someone," he said, but Melanie took a firmer hold on his arm.

She watched him lick his lips and swallow hard and didn't need him to explain any more than that. "Where?" she hissed under her breath, not wanting to make a scene but tired of being made to look like a fool while her husband philandered. He at least kept it private in the past, but lately, the rules appeared to have changed. For a moment, she considered turning the tables and returning Alan's pitiful advances. Maybe even sleep with him, but quickly discarded the idea. Suffering through him pawing all over her to get back at Monty wasn't worth it. *And it is possible husband number three won't care,* she thought, feeling unsure of what to do for the first time in a long time. At least until the waiter came by again and offered more champagne. Melanie gratefully took another glass. Getting drunk seemed like a good enough answer.

Driving the forklift loaded with a pallet of fifty-pound bags of dog food, Elizabeth Milo followed the yellow line painted on the concrete floor of the giant warehouse. She moved through the towering shelves of pet food from dozens of different brands, all waiting to enter the complex American supply chain network. It was one of the most sophisticated material goods transport systems in the world, but she never gave any of that much thought. By her reasoning, in the greater scheme, she was the tiniest of cogs in a series of intricate wheels, and besides, they didn't pay her to think. They paid her because she worked hard, didn't cause trouble, and was never late for her shift.

After placing her load on the designated shelf and raising the forks high for safety, she drove back to the front of the building. It was almost quitting time on a Friday, and although she didn't have any particular place to be, especially at eleven o'clock at night, there was something special about finishing a workweek and heading into the weekend.

"Hey, Milo," she heard someone yell after she parked the forklift in its designated spot and shut off the engine. The voice was her shift supervisor, and Milo had half a mind to pretend she didn't hear him and head for the locker room. Rarely did he have anything good to say. Still, he was her immediate boss, and dodging him would likely make the news worse in the end.

Pulling off her yellow hardhat with Milo stenciled on the back, she turned to him. "What's up?" she asked, and he smiled as he approached. She hated the man's smile. Not only because he had a mouthful of yellow-stained teeth from decades of smoking, but the look always meant he wanted something. Before he said a word, she could guess what it was, and although she would say yes, it frustrated her. There were a half dozen other workers in the warehouse with less seniority than she had, but that didn't stop him from constantly coming to her.

"Milo, here's the thing," he started. "I need you to come in and work the afternoon shift tomorrow." Not saying anything but holding his stare, Milo made the man sweat for a beat. Saturday and Sunday were her designated days off, and although working the weekend would result in overtime, something she always wanted, it was the principle of the thing. His smile faltering, he coughed into his hand. "And no one else can do it."

Bullshit, Milo thought, wondering if he even bothered to ask anyone else. She considered being a hardass and turning him down for a second, but that didn't align with her master plan. Making money was priority number one, and even though she had hoped for a lazy weekend of working out and finishing the book she was reading, she would say yes. Every penny counted. "I'll be here," she finally said, and the man's ugly smile returned.

"I knew I could count on you," he said, looking ready to give her a collegial slap on the back before he caught her stare. Milo had no interest in being touched, particularly by her shift supervisor, and it showed in the hard lines of her face. Instead, the man dropped his hand and backed away. "You'll be covering for Mitch. His kid's having an afternoon birthday party, so I'm sure he'll appreciate it."

Milo nodded. "I see," she said, not the least bit interested in the details. Not that Mitch was a bad guy, but she wouldn't call him a friend. Although a few tried, she had no interest in becoming close to any of her coworkers. To her, work was work, and tomorrow she would clock in to get the extra pay. Nothing more.

Staring out the tinted window in the back of the limousine, Melanie explored her emotions. Angry, or perhaps furious was a better word, and embarrassed topped the list, but there was hurt there too. As much as she liked to pretend she had steeled herself against reacting to her husband's exploits, for some reason tonight felt like a dagger. To make matters worse, Monty appeared oblivious and was in an excellent mood as he talked into his cellphone to some mogul or another. *Of course he is,* Melanie thought. *He just got off thanks to the no doubt practiced skills of some wannabe starlet.* That fact pissed her off too. She couldn't remember the last time she had an orgasm or even sex, for that matter. Husband number three was never particularly interested after the first few months, and Melanie didn't complain. In her opinion, sex was highly overrated.

"I could use a drink," Monty said after ending his last call. "Make me something. You know what I like."

Turning from the window, Melanie was not sure who he talked to, especially considering it was only the two of them, plus the driver, in the limo. "What did you say?"

"A drink," he answered, sounding surprised by her reaction. "You used to do it for me all the time." He snorted a laugh. "But then, you used to do many things though you seem to have forgotten." Still completely taken off-guard, but registering the dig at their lack of intimacy, Melanie only glared at him. The man frowned. "What? It's not like you don't want one yourself." Another dig, but that time more accurate. She had been drinking a lot more lately. Still, even after champagne all night, she didn't feel intoxicated enough, and the pain seeped in.

Melanie returned to looking at the passing buildings as the limo rolled by. "Get it yourself," she murmured.

There was a pause of silence, even the sounds of traffic muted by the luxury vehicle. "I know I didn't hear you correctly," Monty finally growled. "And if I did, you're on very thin ice."

Melanie whirled to face him. "Am I?" she spat. "What? Someone blows you in the coatroom, and now you think you can threaten me?" She watched as his face flushed scarlet and, for a moment, she did think about reconsidering her tone. The last thing she wanted was another divorce, especially considering their ironclad prenup, but enough was enough. Her dignity mattered for something.

Slowly, Monty lifted his hand, and for a nanosecond, she thought he might strike her, but instead he pointed at the minibar. "You have ten seconds to make me that drink," he said, the stone coldness in his voice unsettling her more than anything else he could have done. "Or you can walk to the airport."

Narrowing her eyes, Melanie measured his statement. Even if he did kick her out, she could always take a taxi and join him at the Los Angeles International Airport. His private jet waited to fly them home to their mansion on Long Island. Monty refused to buy in California, claiming that even the most extravagant properties were 'overpriced trash' so instead they would sleep in luxury at forty-thousand feet. No matter how angry he was with her, she knew he wouldn't fly off and leave her.

Melanie lifted her chin as the limo rolled to a stop at a red light. "Well, then I guess I'll walk," she said, calling his bluff as she opened the car door. "Make your own stupid drink."

When the man didn't move to stop her but instead let a smile creep across his face, Melanie realized she calculated wrong. Still, backing down would prove he owned her, and at that, she drew the line. Stepping onto the curb, she didn't bother to say another word but instead slammed the door with all the strength she could muster. Waiting to see what would happen next, she was more than a little stunned when the light changed to green, and the limousine sped away into the night.

Chapter Two

Cycling to the neighborhood corner market, Milo coasted her secondhand blue Schwinn to a stop beside the light pole in front of the store. In the bright light filtering down, she dialed the number 0801 to open the lock on the thick chain wrapped around the bike's frame. Although she would only be in the shop for five minutes max, attaching her property to the pole wasn't optional. Or at least not if she wanted it to be still there when she came out.

Although Milo didn't live in the worst part of Los Angeles by a long stretch, some of the neighborhoods east of the airport were rough. Primarily filled with low-end apartment buildings built in the sixties when the area knew better times, the community had changed, and crime was now all too familiar. Even though there was often car window glass littering the gutters, elaborate graffiti tags on nearly every surface, and at least one domestic dispute in the area every week, Milo put up with the risks. It wasn't like she lived there for the hospitality. Her six-hundred square foot one bedroom was affordable and within bike riding distance of work. Plus, the area had everything she needed—a no-nonsense gym down the street, a public library a short bike ride away, and the little grocery store for the essentials.

While she focused on securing her bike, she heard tennis shoes scuffing along the sidewalk. Glancing up from her work, she registered two guys walking in the dim light, headed in her direction. Although dressed in baggy boardshorts and yellow and gold sports jerseys like half the young men in the neighborhood, they weren't familiar looking. *Hardly even men,* she thought, taking a closer look at their faces as they got nearer. Both appeared to be trying to grow facial hair, but it was coming in uneven and patchy. *If they're old enough to buy beer, I'll be surprised, which is probably why they are here.* Unfortunately for them, Mr. Nguyen was not one to sell minors alcohol. Not in the mood for any hassle, Milo considered unlocking her bike and going home. The milk would wait, even if it meant no cornflakes for an easy breakfast. Before she decided, one of the pair slowed as he reached her. "Nice bike," he said before cackling out a laugh. "Let me guess. A DUI, and they won't let you drive?"

His friend joined in on the merriment. "Yeah," he said. "Loser."

Milo didn't bother to respond as the two disappeared through the glass double doors and was even more convinced going home was the right idea. Then, a thought occurred to her, and she paused. Most late nights, Mr. Nguyen's adult son was behind the counter with him, but not always. If the store was empty, and the two guys got angry over being turned down, there could be trouble. Although there was a thick sheet of plexiglass between Mr. Nguyen and his customers, the strangers could still decide to trash the place. *And what will I do about it if they do?* she asked herself. In reality, the situation wasn't her business, and there was no need for her to play the hero. Closing her eyes, Milo tried to convince herself to simply let it go and leave, but after a beat, she knew she couldn't. She probably worried for nothing, and everything was fine in the store. *But what will it hurt to go get my milk and check?*

Already cursing at herself for being stupid, Milo pushed through the double doors. As she predicted, the two strangers were at the counter with a case of cheap beer. Mr. Nguyen was behind the counter and holding up an ID to study the picture. "This is not you," he said before dropping it back into the tray that fit under the plexiglass. "Go away."

"What the hell?" one of the smartasses from the sidewalk snarled. "Listen to me, old man. We are leaving with this beer."

Milo stepped closer until they registered her presence. "Try someplace else, guys," she said in a soft voice.

The two men looked at each other and laughed. "You're seriously butting in on this?"

With a sigh, Milo nodded. "Yeah." The laughing stopped, and she watched the pair's faces turn angry again. Any second, things were going to get out of hand, and she let her weight shift to the balls of her feet to be ready for any attack.

Then a noise came from the back of the small store. "How about you take her advice?" Milo heard Mr. Nguyen's son say from between the rows of food and household items. All eyes turned in that direction, and Milo felt her body relax when she saw him appear with a baseball bat resting against his hip. "And go try somewhere else."

Clearly no longer liking the odds, one of the guys pushed on his friend's shoulder. "Come on," he said. "This isn't worth it."

The other spat a glob of phlegm onto the floor before starting for the exit. As he walked past Milo, he glared into her face. "You should have stayed out of it," he said a moment before the two of them pushed through the doors and were gone.

. . .

It took approximately sixty seconds before Melanie realized her purse was still in the limousine. Not only was her cellphone stashed in the small clutch, but so were her New York driver's license and all her credit cards. Standing on the street corner in the near dark, with only streetlamp lights glowing orange above her, Melanie had nothing but what she wore—a black, faux fur coat, a black cocktail dress, and four-inch matching black heels. Feeling a wave of panic, she looked in the direction Monty and the limo had gone, praying he had pulled over after her dramatic exit. From what she could see, he hadn't. Only empty cars parked along the curb were on the side of the street. Some traffic passed in both directions, but there wasn't much considering the time of night. *And it's not like I'm going to step out into the road to flag a stranger down,* she thought. *Especially dressed like this.*

A glance around at the stores with bars on the windows confirmed she was not in the best neighborhood, and with no other options, she started to walk along the sidewalk in the direction the limo had driven.. There was no way her husband would desert her in such a dangerous situation, and she expected to see them returning at any second. Yet, after six blocks, with the high heels already killing her feet, she felt the panic again. There was no sign of Monty coming to rescue her. Stopping, she slipped off her shoes and surveyed her surroundings. She had wandered into a more residential area. Worn-out apartment buildings filled the neighborhood, and the cars parked on the street were older models. None left her a clue about where she was other than a street sign saying Century Boulevard. Feeling tears burn her eyes, more from fury than anything at that point, she wiped them away and started walking again.

Finally, out of the night, an illuminated sign glowed in the distance—a small grocery store on the corner with a blue bicycle chained to the light pole in front. Feeling some hope at last, she picked up her pace and was almost to the doors when someone in a dark denim jacket and matching pants came out. Everything about the stranger screamed blue-collar worker, and she hesitated to approach the store while the person stood there with a small plastic bag of groceries in hand. She was especially glad she paused when she heard the person swear while looking at the bike. Following the stranger's gaze, she understood the problem. Not only were the tires flat, but someone had kicked the front wheel, bending the frame. As the person gazed skyward as if asking the heavens for a break, Melanie realized she was a woman with dark, close-cropped hair. Moving slowly into the shadow of the building, Melanie hid while the stranger unfastened the chain holding her bike against the light pole and hoisted it to her shoulder as if it weighed nothing.

Not sure what she would do if the woman started walking in her direction, Melanie was relieved when she carried her bike the opposite way. After letting her disappear into the night, Melanie hurried into the grocery store and finally felt relieved when she saw two men sitting behind the counter. "Oh, thank God," she said, moving to the plexiglass. "I'm stranded, and I need to use your phone."

When the men stared at her for a second and didn't answer, Melanie worried they would refuse. Undoubtedly, they were not used to women dressed for a cocktail party wandering into their store in the middle of the night. Before she could explain further, the younger of the two nodded. "You can use mine," he said, taking the cellphone from his pants pocket to slide it into the metal tray. Snatching the thing up, Melanie didn't even waste time thanking him. She had to reach Monty before he got further away. Dialing the number, Melanie was already rehearsing the angry earful she intended to give him for his antics tonight. There was only one problem. Monty didn't answer.

. . .

Carrying her bike up two flights of stairs, Milo mentally kicked herself for butting in at the grocery store. She knew better. *No good deed goes unpunished*, she thought, fishing for her keys in her front pocket. When they failed to cooperate, staying snagged on the fabric of her work pants, she growled but still set the bike down as quietly as she could. The doors and walls in the apartments around her were cheap construction, and sound carried. Unlike some buildings Milo had lived in, everyone here tried to respect each other's privacy. That included not banging around at one o'clock in the morning no matter how pissed off she was at the state of things.

Finally able to work the three deadbolts open, she pushed inside the small but tidy apartment. There was nothing fancy about Milo's space as she saw no need to spend a lot of money on furniture simply because of who made it. Comfortable and functional were her criteria, which meant buying things like her secondhand couch, colored bright burnt orange. Not that it mattered, because it wasn't like she expected any visitors, so putting on a fancy interior design show was pointless.

Leaning the bike against the wall and making sure to re-engage all the door locks, Milo walked to the kitchen to set the groceries on the table before stripping off her jacket to hang it on a peg. Dark navy blue denim, it matched her pants and was part of the uniform sold to employees at the warehouse where she worked. Underneath was another piece of the required clothing. A light blue, short-sleeved button-up with "Milo" stenciled above the breast pocket. As a teenager, the idea of wearing a uniform like that never crossed her mind. Her aspirations were higher, but now at twenty-eight she was simply thankful for the job.

Putting away the milk, a cold beer on the top shelf called her name. Beer was the one thing she felt warranted spending a little extra money. Although Budweiser and Miller Lite filled most of the coolers at Mr. Nguyen's grocery store, Milo picked the microbrews. One of her favorite hobbies was trying new brands, and Mr. Nguyen was kind enough to order her some variety. Tonight, she would pass. Although usually Friday night required celebration with a cold one, she would be running the forklift again tomorrow afternoon. Not that she would still be feeling the effects of the alcohol, but Milo was sharper at work when she skipped drinking the night before.

With a sigh, she closed the refrigerator door only to hear the soft meow of a cat. Glancing out the small window over the kitchen sink, she saw one of her friends walking on the roofline of the neighboring building. No doubt the tomcat was out causing havoc earlier but guessed Milo would likely be home to put out a can of wet food so had stopped for a visit. Reaching into the grocery sack, Milo pulled out three cans of Friskies pate to set on the counter. She knew spending money to feed the neighborhood strays wasn't a part of her master money savings plan, but she couldn't help herself. They weren't allowed to have pets of any kind, so helping the homeless ones was the best she could do. However, there was one downside to the late-night feeding. Putting out the food would mean another trip downstairs and going into the alley to set out the can. *Best get it done,* she thought, glad she hadn't taken off her boots yet. Picking up one of the cans, she headed for the door.

Chapter Three

After leaving her third scathing voicemail for Monty without a response, Melanie finally gave back the phone. The two men behind the plexiglass continued to stare at her, only this time she guessed it was more because of the language she used on the phone than her expensive clothing. Feeling completely abandoned, she had never in her life been more upset. Moving closer to the plexiglass, Melanie forced a smile. "Do either of you have a car?" she asked. "I need a ride to the airport."

"No. You can Uber," the older man said, but Melanie knew that was not an option without her phone and no credit cards.

She shook her head. "I can't," she said, hoping she could win over their sympathy and get a ride. "We were on the way to the airport, and I left my purse in the limousine when I got out, so now I—"

"Why were you in a limo?" the older man interrupted. "You a hooker?"

Blinking with surprise at the outlandish statement,

Melanie forced herself not to be offended. "What? No," she answered. "Of course not."

"Dad," the younger man said. "That's not nice." He turned his attention to Melanie. "It does sound like a problem, but we don't keep a car parked near here. Too risky."

Melanie frowned. "Well, then what am I supposed to do?"

The two men glanced at each other and then shrugged, looking so much alike that Melanie would have laughed if things weren't so screwed up. "Walk?" the older man said, making Melanie gasp at the thought of going any further on foot. Her feet had blisters from the blocks she had walked already.

She held up her high heeled shoes for them to see. "In these?"

Suddenly, the older man laughed. "Good luck," he said, and his son put a hand on his shoulder.

"Dad, no laughing," he said, and the old man quieted but by the twinkle in his eyes he was still clearly amused.

Melanie, however, was not in the least entertained by the idea. "How far is it?" she asked, thinking if it weren't too many more blocks, maybe she would say screw them and actually walk.

"Two miles," the son answered. "But it's a straight shot if you stay on Century Boulevard, so you shouldn't get lost."

Melanie shook her head, unable to fathom the idea of walking two miles anywhere. "You're serious?" she said. "You want me to walk?"

The younger man held up his hands. "I'd have suggested the bus, but they stop running this route at midnight." Melanie forced herself not to shudder at the idea of riding with a group of strangers in such a germ ridden vehicle. *Still, it would have been better than walking*, she thought. *I can't believe it's come down to this.*

"There's no other option you can think of?" she asked,

and the son shook his head as he opened the gate in the counter to join her.

"I'm afraid not," he answered. "Let me show you which direction you should go." Not having any other choice, Melanie followed the younger man out to the sidewalk. "I'm sorry we can't be more useful, but my dad is a little funny about helping strangers." He pointed west. "Go that way, and it will eventually reach the airport." He turned to go but then hesitated. "Be careful."

Snorting a laugh, Melanie started to walk. "Yeah, right," she said, not bothering to look back at him once she started. *I can do this*, she thought, and while still carrying her shoes, the first four blocks weren't so bad. She began to think she would be fine and contemplated ways to make Monty pay for what he did. Once she found him at the airport, a slap across his face felt like a worthy start.

By the seventh block, an earlier blister made by her shoe started to ache. *This is unbelievable,* she thought, not imaging how anything could be worse than what she was suffering. At least until she saw the two young men in sports jerseys and baggy boardshorts step out of the shadows to block her path.

Milo ran a hand over the back of the gray tabby as he eagerly ate the wet food. The fur was thick, but she could feel rough spots and scars from previous catfights underneath. "Slow down, Ranger," she said softly. "No one's going to take the food away from you." That was part of the ritual. Milo always stayed with him until he finished, usually half a can, and then he wandered away into the night. She would leave the rest for whoever else came along, knowing there were many more strays in the neighborhood. The can was always licked clean by the next time she checked again.

Finally, he lifted his head, licking his whiskers to look at her. His unspoken thanks was clear in the light reflecting in his green eyes, and Milo gave him a final pet before standing. With a yawn, she watched him saunter off into the shadows. Ready to hit the sack, Milo started toward the stairs to her apartment when a scream pierced the night. She froze in place. The sound came from a woman, of that she was sure, but she didn't know from what direction the way it bounced around the buildings. *And even if I could tell, what then?* she asked herself. *I've heard plenty of screams in the night in this neighborhood. More than likely it is only another domestic dispute.* When there were no more sounds, Milo started walking again, faster this time. All she wanted was to go to bed.

"Somebody, help me," came the cry of a woman's voice, making Milo stop again. Though she didn't know why, the yell for help sounded different than usual. More desperate, less angry. Not like two adults fighting after too many drinks. It was someone in real trouble. *And again, what am I supposed to do about it?* she wondered, hoping there would be no more sounds as she made it to the stairs. Then, the cackling laugh of a young man drifted to her ears, and she remembered it. The punk from the grocery store. The one who bashed her bike.

Stopping to listen harder, the night grew quiet, and Milo thought it was too late to find them until there was another much louder scream. She turned toward the sound and realized it was coming from a block or two west. Breaking into a jog, she scooped up a broken two-by-four lying in the dirt. The men's laughing grew louder, and they didn't see or hear her coming up on them. She watched as they shoved a woman with long blonde hair and dressed in clothes that seemed so out of place, Milo was confused for a second. *A prostitute?* she wondered but couldn't quite believe it. The coat and dress were too... She tried to think of a word. *Classy?*

"This is our lucky night after all," one of the men said as he wrapped his arms around the woman, who kicked and struggled, trying to fight back, but Milo guessed she was lucky if she was more than five foot two.

"Yeah," said the one Milo recognized as the guy who threatened her at Mr. Nguyen's grocery store and most likely busted her bike. "And here I thought we were shit out of luck over the beer."

Milo stepped out of the shadows. "Actually, you still are shit out of luck," she said, and before either could react, she brought the board around to catch the punk behind the knees. As he toppled, she spun on the other guy who still held the woman. "Let her go and get out of here."

"What the hell? You again?" the man said, but Milo was glad to see he started to release his grip. Things looked like they might be handled easier than she expected, and she lowered the board. A beat later, Milo felt the impact of someone tackling her from behind.

When Melanie saw the flash of movement coming out of the darkness, she didn't have time to register where the person came from or how. All she knew was someone was there to help her. The first of her attackers fell with a yelp of pain, and then the stranger stood threatening the man holding her against him. "What the hell? You again?" he said but started to let go. As soon as she felt the release of tension, Melanie tried to wriggle free. Before she was successful, her rescuer was bowled over by the man who seemed to be the instigator of everything. The board went flying, and the two crashed to the ground. Seeing her opportunity to escape quickly diminishing, Melanie tried harder to get free from the man's grasp.

"Oh no you don't," he said, pulling her even tighter against him. "This will be over in a second, and then we can get back to our business."

Not liking the sound of that, Melanie turned her head to

see the other two thrashing on the ground. Rolling around in the dirt and gravel, no one seemed to be winning until her rescuer finally got on the man's back. Wrapping an arm around his neck, the stranger squeezed, and in another second, the man started to thrash as if unable to breathe. Whoever had come to help Melanie was close to winning. "Son of a bitch," the man holding Melanie said, releasing her so suddenly she stumbled. He hurried to help his friend, jumping into the fray, and sending the trio rolling in the dirt again. Suddenly, the fight was two-on-one, and even though every instinct in Melanie was to run for her own safety, she hesitated. The person who came to help her was suddenly the one in trouble. *But what can I do?* she thought, knowing riding her stationary bike for forty-five minutes every day did not translate to much physical strength. Plus, at one hundred and twenty pounds, she could hardly pull one of the men off the stranger.

Looking around, her eyes landed on the broken two-by-four. With no other option and a sudden unwillingness to be the selfish brat she usually was, Melanie picked it up. Not exactly sure what to do next, but in one look realizing she had to hurry, she moved. Her two attackers were on top of the stranger and punching their victim's face. Brandishing the board like a club, Melanie rushed in. "You piece of shit," she yelled at the top of her lungs as she swung the two by four with all her strength at the closest man's head. Never being a softball player or anything along that line, the board missed where she aimed but landed near enough. Bouncing off his shoulder and then into his face with a crunch, the guy grabbed his nose, letting out a cry of pain, and scrabbled away. Distracted by the new attack, the second man lost his advantage and was bucked off. As he sprawled in the dirt, Melanie's rescuer jumped up and delivered a hard kick to his groin.

Suddenly, the tables had turned, and both men were on

the ground in pain while Melanie and her new best friend stood side by side.

"Are you okay?" the stranger next to Melanie asked, and it suddenly clicked that her rescuer was not only a woman but the one she saw with the broken bike at the grocery store.

"Not really," Melanie said, realizing that, although she was no longer under attack, she was still in a horrible spot. Continuing to walk another mile and a half alone at night was impossible. Having the stranger help her might be her last hope. "Here's the thing," she said, looking into the woman's battered face. "I'm kind of in a bad situation."

"Worse than this?"

Melanie bit her lip and glanced at the two men on the ground. "Not exactly, but unfortunately, I kind of still need your help."

Chapter Four

Staring into the beautiful woman's face, Milo wasn't sure what to do. As the two men writhed on the ground, she was certain standing in an alley in the middle of the night having a discussion with the woman while they recovered was a bad idea. Yet, she was already more involved than she ever wanted to be and needed to find a way to explain that. Even though saving the woman was the right thing to do, Milo was ready to be done with all of it. Obviously, the woman had a story considering she was in their less-than-optimal neighborhood at night while dressed as if she had come from a fancy party, but Milo didn't want to know any of the details. She didn't like drama and wanted no part of any trouble. Plus, the swelling around her left eye was starting to be a real problem. If she didn't get ice on it soon, the thing was liable to close all the way. Going into the warehouse with a black eye and bloody lip would not look good but calling in sick because she couldn't see would be worse.

Her regrets about butting in continued to grow, and the fact she got unnecessarily involved in things twice in the same night frustrated her, yet when one of the men started to show signs of recovering, Milo decided. Knowing she couldn't leave the woman in the alley, she sighed, turning in the direction of her apartment. "Follow me."

"Wait," the woman said, and Milo glanced back to see her gathering her black high heels from the gravel. "I need my shoes. I can't walk on this."

Milo shook her head, still having trouble reconciling the time and place with the woman's outfit. "That's all you have?"

Evidently, something in her tone offended the stranger because she glared at Milo. "Yes, this is all I have. It's not like I intended to be hiking across Los Angeles tonight," she said. "I am not doing this for fun, trust me."

Trying to keep her frustration at bay while the woman slipped on the shoes, Milo noticed the man she kicked in the groin getting to his feet. *Great*, she thought, not eager to use the two-by-four again. "Can you hurry it along?" she asked while the woman started to wobble slowly toward her in the heels. *Oh, you have got to be kidding me.*

The punk made it up. "I'm going to kill you," he growled, although he was still bent at the waist. Milo had seen enough and picked up the woman without bothering to ask permission.

Throwing her over her shoulder in a fireman's carry, Milo heard the woman let out a screech. "What the hell are you doing?"

"Getting us out of here," Milo said, not wasting another moment as she started to jog in the direction of her apartment building.

"Like this?" the woman cried, and Milo didn't see any point in answering. Being carried ass up was never fun, but they were in a hurry, and she didn't want to take time discussing the options. The woman slapped her on the back. "Put me down."

Milo slowed to a walk as they turned a corner and out of

sight of the attackers. "If I put you down, I'm leaving you behind," she said. "What do you want to do?"

After a beat, the woman groaned. "All right," she said. "Keep going, but can you at least tell me our destination?"

"My apartment," Milo answered, starting back into a trot. She wasn't thrilled with the idea of taking a stranger there, mainly since everything about the situation screamed unnecessary drama. Hopefully they would arrive, and the woman could make a phone call to have someone come pick her up. And that better be soon, because the longer Milo was involved, the more uneasy she felt. Her life was simple, with a straightforward plan to get her to where she wanted to be. Unfortunately, the closer they got to her home, the more Milo worried the woman would somehow mess up everything.

When Melanie didn't think she could take much more of the bouncing over the woman's shoulder, she set her down at the bottom of some stairs. They were in front of a run-down apartment building that, even in the dark, looked like it badly needed a new coat of paint. "You can take off your shoes and climb the stairs yourself," the stranger said, winded from the jog. Still, Melanie was impressed. Even though she didn't weigh a lot, and the distance was only a few blocks, the effort took a lot of strength and endurance. She couldn't think of many other women she knew who could pull it off, but it helped that her rescuer looked especially fit. At least half a foot taller, if not more than Melanie, she had broad shoulders and thick arms.

The woman started up the stairs without her. "Wait," Melanie said, slipping off her shoes and following the still climbing stranger. "We're not all superwoman here."

The stranger paused at the landing, looking at her. "Superwoman?"

Joining her, Melanie nodded. "What you did was super in my mind," she said. "And I'll be eternally grateful." A thought struck her. "Plus, I will ensure you are appropriately compensated for your trouble."

"I see," the woman said, starting to move again, and Melanie wasn't quite sure what to make of the reaction. Most people, particularly those who lived in low-end housing like the one they were at, were anxious to get their hands on rewards. *But I get a strong sense this woman is not like most people*, she thought as she watched the three deadbolts being unlocked and the door opening.

"Come in and have a seat," her rescuer said, holding the door to let Melanie pass before closing it and re-engaging the locks. "I need to get ice on my eye." A lamp was on, letting Melanie get a clear look at the woman's face. She cringed at the damage, noticing not only swelling and cuts but that a lot of blood had dripped onto the woman's shirt. Her eyes landed on the name stitched in the fabric above the pocket. Milo.

Moving out of the way to let the woman go to what Melanie assumed was the tiny kitchen, she looked around the living area. "Do you go by Milo?" she asked as her eyes fell on the world's ugliest couch. It looked clean and possibly comfortable, but she wasn't sure she could sit on something so obnoxious and pulled out one of two wooden chairs from the small table in the corner. "I'm Melanie Sotheby."

She heard a freezer door closing and a hiss of pain before Milo reappeared with a bag of frozen peas against her eye. "Yeah, calling me Milo is fine," she said. "Do you have someone you can call or something?"

A little surprised at the woman's bluntness but realizing she had no reason to care, Melanie nodded. "Yes, actually I do," she said in a less friendly tone. "But I don't have a phone." A lot of time had passed since Monty deserted her. *He will have calmed down enough to answer a phone call by now,* she thought. "I need to borrow yours."

Without hesitating, Milo pulled an iPhone from her back pocket, only to frown when she looked at the screen. "Shit," she muttered before sighing. Sliding the phone across the table to Melanie, Milo pulled out the other chair and sat down. "It's not going to work."

"What?" Melanie said, grabbing the phone to look at the front. The screen was black and entirely smashed. Feeling a mixture of anger and panic, Melanie closed her eyes and held back a scream of frustration. "And you don't have another one?"

"No," Milo said. "And nothing is open until morning."

The woman's face was momentarily unreadable as she sat at the table with her eyes closed. *Her name is Melanie*, Milo reminded herself. *What the hell is her situation, so I can fix it and go to sleep?*

Melanie opened her eyes. "I'm going to guess you don't have a car," she said. "And your bike is busted."

Frowning, the random statement confused Milo. "You're right," she said. "I don't have a car, but how do you know about my bike?"

"I saw you outside the little grocery store," she answered with a shrug. "The two men there tried to be helpful once I explained I didn't have my purse, but my husband wouldn't answer his stupid phone." She shook her head. "I bet he's sorry as hell. Frantic now that he can't find me."

Milo didn't want to ask for more details, although hearing Melanie lost her purse explained a lot. Still, she didn't want to become more engaged. Melanie, however, didn't seem to notice and kept talking, suddenly perking up. "I bet the police are looking for me. Where's the closest police station?"

Milo shook her head. "Nothing nearby. You'd have to go down to Hawthorne," she said, wondering if that was feasible. Considering the shoe situation, it didn't seem likely, but she would try anything to move things along. "What size shoes do you wear?"

"Six and a half," Melanie answered, tossing her head in a way that made Milo think she was offended by the question. "I highly doubt we wear the same size, and besides, I would never wear someone else's used shoes."

Raising the eyebrow over her good eye, once again Milo didn't know what to make of the stranger in her apartment. She acted like everything was beneath her. "Well, you're lucky then because I wear a nine," she said. "But you need to remember beggars can't be choosers."

Melanie glared at her. "I will never be a beggar," she snapped. "It's clear we haven't fully introduced ourselves. Like I said, I'm Melanie Sotheby, as in I'm married to Monty Sotheby. Billionaire."

Tired, Milo wasn't sure she registered what the woman said properly. "You're who?"

The woman threw up her hands. "You're kidding?" She shook her head. "The real question is, who are you?" she asked. "No car? And I don't see a television. In fact, it's pretty barebones in here."

Feeling heat rise to her cheeks, Milo checked her temper. She didn't have time for giving any explanations about how she lived. Although her work shift wasn't until noon, her window for sleeping was getting smaller and smaller. "Listen," she said in an even tone. "Who I am doesn't matter, and I honestly don't care who you are, but I need to go to bed." She sighed, not wanting to say the next thing, but there seemed like there was no other alternative. "You can sleep on my couch, and in the morning, I'll walk to the grocery store to buy one of their throwaway phones. You can use it to call your husband."

The woman's eyes drifted past her to the orange couch. "You can't be serious," she said. "If I have to sleep on that hideous thing, I'll have nightmares."

"Well, you're not sleeping with me. Remember what I said about beggars can't be choosers?" Milo said, standing to get an extra sheet, pillow, and blanket. "Unless you want to walk to the nearest Ritz Hotel, you're bunking on it." Melanie mumbled something that Milo couldn't hear. "What?"

"I said I wish I could pay for a hotel," she shot back. "At least the people there wouldn't be rude."

Setting her jaw, Milo left the room to go to the bathroom closet. *Well, at least I'm not a spoiled brat,* she thought, wanting to say the words, but the last thing she needed was an argument. In the morning, she would get the phone from Mr. Nguyen's store, and Melanie Sotheby would be on her way out of Milo's life.

Chapter Five

Slowly coming awake at the sound of something sizzling, Melanie opened her eyes only to see a room she didn't recognize. Nothing looked or felt right. Even the smell was wrong. Her oversized bedroom was normally filled with the light scents of lavender and vanilla, but there was something very different in the air—bacon and coffee. Becoming more disoriented by the second, she raised on an elbow only to see the burnt orange couch beneath her. As she grimaced at the horrible color, it triggered her memory, and all the events of the night before rushed back. Fighting in the limo with Monty, leaving her purse behind, being accosted by the two men on the street, and then... *I was rescued,* she thought. *By a stranger named Milo.*

With a shudder at the idea of what could have happened, Melanie sat, pulling the blanket around her. "Milo?" she called, guessing from the sounds and smells coming from the kitchen the woman was there.

After a beat, Milo poked her head into the doorway. "Good, you're awake," she said. "I bought a phone, and it's on the table so you can make your call." Surprised by the blunt statement and unsure how a phone suddenly materialized, Melanie blinked.

She also noticed the damage to Milo's face—badly bruised and swollen. "My God, your face," she said, and the woman frowned.

"It is what it is," she said in a matter-of-fact tone before disappearing again. "Make your call."

Furrowing her brow, Melanie didn't make a move for the phone. "I'm not sure why you're mad at me," she said. "I didn't do that to your face."

"Just call," Milo said from the kitchen.

Feeling her temper rise at the treatment she got from the woman, making a call to get out of there sounded like a fabulous idea. "Fine," she said, standing to grab the phone. It was a cheap throwaway thing that a person paid for minutes in advance. *They call it a burner phone*, she thought remembering all the law and order dramas she loved to watch and wondered again where it came from. "Whose phone is this?"

Milo reappeared in the doorway. "I went out this morning and bought it," she said, making Melanie raise her eyebrows.

"You came and went without waking me up?"

With a shrug, Milo lifted a mug to her mouth to take a sip. "I've learned to be very quiet," she said. "I'm having coffee. Do you want some? Before you ask, I only have skim milk to put in it." Not sure what circumstances Milo would have been in to need to be stealthy, she considered asking and then hesitated. Offering coffee was the first relatively friendly thing the woman had done since Melanie woke and pushing for details about her life felt like a bad idea. The woman seemed very unwilling to reveal anything. *Besides, why do I care?* she wondered. *One call to Monty, and I'll be out of here in the next ten minutes. And then I can have a double expresso laced with coconut milk.*

Melanie shook her head. "No," she said, dialing the phone.

"I don't need it." After three rings, a hint of anxiety crept into her stomach. *Oh, don't you dare not answer this, Monty Sotheby,* she thought, only to hear the phone make a connection.

"Let me guess. Melanie?" Monty said in a cheerful voice mixed with... Melanie frowned. *Amusement?* she wondered. *That bastard.*

"Oh, you think this is funny?" she snapped, trying to quash the hurt inside her that he didn't sound the slightest bit worried about her. "Do you know what almost happened to me? Because of your stunt?"

"My stunt?" her husband shot back. "You're the one who got out of the car. Whatever happened is what you deserved."

Her mouth dropping open, Melanie couldn't believe what she heard. "What I deserved?" she said, fury building. "What about what you deserved? Screwing around at the party. Do you know how embarrassing that is?" When Monty laughed, Melanie felt a mixture of emotions course through her. Astonishment, fury, and a growing feeling of panic. "Why are you laughing?"

"A man has needs," he said, suddenly serious. "And you stopped fulfilling them years ago. Guess what, Melanie? I've put up with you long enough, and I'm filing for divorce."

"What?" Melanie cried. "You can't do that."

"Oh yes, my dear, I definitely can," Monty said, and the line went dead.

Jogging the three miles to work, Milo couldn't believe the strange direction her life had suddenly taken. Yesterday, everything was simple. Today, it was a nightmare. Melanie hadn't left, and Milo's banged-up face hurt with every bounce in her step. *It's going to be a very long day,* she thought, finally arriving. The timing of working on Saturday could not be worse, and she hoped no one would pay attention to her face. *At least I can see out of both eyes. Sort of.* Her left one was still swollen, but she could open it enough to drive a forklift for twelve hours. Besides, she didn't have a choice. Bailing on a shift at the last minute was always bad, but unacceptable when a person was covering for someone else. Milo needed the job so she would suffer through it.

"Holy crap, what happened to you?" one of her coworkers said the minute Milo walked into the locker room.

She went straight to her locker without looking at anyone. "It's nothing," she mumbled, dialing the door's combination. "Fell off my bike."

"Right," the coworker said, dragging out the word. "Your bike."

Grabbing her hard hat, Milo headed for the exit. She didn't have time for a conversation about her life with anyone, especially people she hardly knew and cared nothing about. *And what would I say anyway?* she thought. *I got in a fight saving a woman in a cocktail dress and heels with no place to go. They will think I helped a hooker.* Milo paused. Melanie was definitely not a prostitute, but Milo still wasn't clear on exactly who she was. After the woman finished her call with her husband, she set down the phone and burst into tears. It was the last thing Milo knew how to deal with, and it took ten minutes before Melanie could even explain why she was upset.

"I can't believe this is happening to me. I've put up with his shit for years," she said with venom in her tone that let Milo realize the tears were not from sorrow but fury. "And now he has the balls to say he is divorcing me?" Milo didn't figure she wanted an answer, so she waited while she sipped her coffee. Over the years, she had learned sometimes a person simply needed to vent. "And then he hung up on me." She started to redial the phone. "That son of a bitch. I'm not through with him."

All the rest of Melanie's calls went unanswered. The voicemails she left the man were enough to make Milo worry the woman wouldn't be leaving her apartment anytime soon. If the husband wouldn't help her, Melanie was still as stuck as she was the night before. As the hours ticked by until Milo had to leave for work, Melanie made no headway on her situation. Milo heard her call her attorney and then some supposed friends, but none seemed ready to help. Finally, Melanie tossed the phone onto the table and leaned back in her chair, arms crossed. "Well, this is just fantastic," she said as Milo came back into the living room. She had been in the bathroom, where she had done the best she could to clean up her face. "Either they can't or won't help me."

"And what does that mean exactly?" Milo asked, sure she didn't want to hear the answer. Melanie had boasted hours before she would be 'gone in ten minutes' yet there she sat at Milo's table.

Melanie threw up her hands. "Hell if I know," she said. "They are all afraid of Monty, so won't do a damn thing." The woman had stared at the ceiling for a beat. "I'm going to kill him for this."

Confused, Milo frowned. "So, you don't think he's really divorcing you?"

"Of course not," Melanie shot back. "I'm the perfect trophy wife. He's just being an asshole." None of that made sense to Milo. In her short relationship before her life turned upside down, she appreciated the woman she was with. Being so horrible to another person sounded crazy.

In the end, Milo left Melanie at her apartment with the phone. The deal was the woman would find a solution to her problem while Milo was at work. She hated leaving Melanie there among her stuff but putting her out on the curb wasn't something Milo could do in good conscience. So, she was about to start work with no idea what was happening at her apartment. *I just took her at her word that she was this supposedly rich woman,* she thought, ready to kick herself. *What am I thinking? She could be a total con artist!* Before she walked onto the warehouse floor, she turned to her coworker. "Hey, can you google something on your phone for me?"

"Where's your phone?" he asked, and Milo blew out a frustrated breath.

"I broke it."

The man laughed. "With your face?" he asked, and Milo started walking again. She wasn't in the mood to deal with bullshit, but the man put a hand on her arm.

"Hey," he said. "Sorry. I'll look it up. What do you want to know?"

Milo paused. "Search for Melanie Sotheby for me and show me a picture."

Her coworker fiddled with his phone for a second and then held it so Milo could see the screen. Staring back at her was the radiant and incredibly beautiful face of the woman in her apartment.

Sitting with her hands clasped in front of her on the table, Melanie stared at the ceiling. Like the rest of the apartment, it was outdated with off-white, popcorn texturing. *Or it was once white,* she thought and wondered how long it had been since anyone bothered to paint it. Then, she barked out a laugh. *Why in the hell am I sitting here thinking something so random when my world is falling apart?* She had called everyone whose phone number she could remember, but it was a short list. There were a few other wives of rich men like herself, but when she explained her situation, they said they couldn't help her. They didn't dare step out of line if Monty was involved. Otherwise, without the internet available, contacting people was next to impossible. *And even then, who would I call?*

The only other phone number she considered calling might be her sister, but she had been estranged from her decades ago. Although she had a good idea where her sister lived because she doubted the woman would ever pull up stakes and leave the small town where they grew up, they did not communicate. When Melanie was seventeen, she left home, never looked back, and resentment built. She had no doubt her sister would take great pleasure in her miserable situation.

"So, what am I going to do?" she said to the empty room. Dropping her gaze, she took in the space around her. She was so caught up in her mess that everything else had gone unnoticed. A quick assessment and Melanie guessed three things about Milo—she was clean, smart, and poor. Whatever job she went to earlier apparently didn't pay much because the woman's living space looked beyond sparse. No television. No computer. Pretty much no material things that went beyond those necessary to live, except for books. Lots of books. Milo had a tall bookshelf crammed full.

Getting up to examine the contents more closely, Melanie was impressed with the eclectic mix of fiction and non-fiction. A broad range of authors and subjects also, including a disproportionate number of travel books, some of them about places where Melanie had vacationed with one husband or another. She leaned toward tropical settings with cabana boys rushing her umbrella drinks, but there were books of places Melanie hadn't even considered. *Agra?* she wondered, pulling the book out enough to see a picture of the Taj Mahal Palace on the cover. *Pretty sure no cabana boys serve drinks there.*

Running a finger over another of the book spines, she frowned, unable to remember when she had last taken time to read a book. Especially a paperback that she had to hold in her hand. Everything was electronic in her world—modern and cutting edge. *About as far from my current situation as a person can get*, Melanie thought, not missing the irony of her predicament. *Of all the people on the planet to come to my rescue...* With a shake of her head, she moved to the hideous couch and sat. There was nothing more she could think to try as far as getting help, and she wondered how Milo would take the news when she found out she had a roommate a little longer.

Chapter Six

By the time the mid-shift break finally came, Milo's head ached, and her left eye would not stop watering. Six more hours before she could jog home and lay down felt daunting. Unfortunately, there wasn't any choice, so she parked the forklift and headed to the breakroom to eat her dinner. As she walked in, the conversations in the room stopped, and Milo didn't have to guess what everyone was talking about. Her black eye and fat lip were a walking billboard for the recent trouble in her life. *They all want to know what kind*, she thought. *Mugged? Trouble at home?* Those were certainly possible given the population of people in the neighborhood. Still, Milo had never mentioned a spouse or even a girlfriend. It was part of her distancing from her coworkers. While they all chitchatted their days away recounting family drama and bragging about fantastic weekend excursions, Milo kept her head down and did what she came there for—to work and earn money. *And now they have no clues to try and build a story about my face.* It was hard to suppress a smug smile as she went to the breakroom's fridge to grab her food.

"Hey, Milo," one of the men sitting at a table with three other workers said. Since this wasn't her usual shift, Milo didn't know his name. "Come sit with us." Lunchbox in hand, she turned from the refrigerator and looked him over. *Randy* was stitched over his pocket, and although he grinned, Milo wasn't convinced she could trust him. Considering how well she had honed her instinct for sniffing out trouble, she didn't rush to sit.

Moving to one of the other unoccupied tables, Milo shook her head. "No thanks," she said, popping open the container containing a bacon, lettuce, and tomato sandwich on wheat bread. On top of it was a paperback book, and she held it up for Randy to see. "I'm really into this story and want to read the next chapter."

Randy squinted his eyes as he tilted his head, looking at the book's cover. "Into the Wild?" he said before shrugging. "Never heard of it." For a split second, Milo considered explaining to Randy that the story was of a young man's tragic quest to find meaning in his life. She had read it before, but parts truly spoke to her, and lately, she used it as a reminder to not give up on her dreams.

Then, she caught herself. "Yeah," she said. "It's a little obscure."

"Obscure?" Randy repeated, starting to laugh. "Well, isn't that a fancy word. Aren't you a smart one." A few of the other people in the breakroom chuckled.

Not wanting to talk anymore, Milo dropped her gaze to her sandwich and started to unwrap it. The fact she had a college degree in English Literature would probably blow Randy's mind. It was part of the reason she liked to read anything she could get her hands on, and if she had to name anyone as a friend, it would be the old woman who ran the neighborhood library—none of which Randy needed or even deserved to know.

As she prepared to take a bite, a thought of Melanie crossed her mind. *Did she eat the sandwich I made and left in the fridge for her?* she wondered. When Milo told her about it, Melanie waved it off, claiming she never ate and besides she would be ordering room service soon enough. *I wonder how that worked out?* If she had her way, Melanie would be long gone when Milo got home, and her life could return to normal.

She hadn't even taken a bite when the shift supervisor walked into the breakroom, looking around for someone. His eyes landed on Milo. "You," he said. "In my office." She didn't even get a chance to ask him what was happening before he vanished again.

"Oooohhhh," Randy said. "Someone's in trouble."

That made no sense to Milo, but she quickly packed her stuff and headed toward the warehouse's main office. The door to the man's office was open, but she knocked on the doorjamb anyway. "You wanted to see me?"

Sitting behind his desk, the shift supervisor picked up a white envelope and held it toward her. "Take this," he said. "Your last paycheck. Includes today's six hours too."

Milo blinked. "What?" she asked. "I don't understand."

The man leaned back in his chair. "We run a tight ship around here. People come in with a busted-up face, and it's clear they are not a good fit for our company."

"But—"

Shaking his head, he waved toward the exit. "No buts. We have standards, so go clean out your locker," he said, leveling his gaze at her. "Don't make this difficult."

After an unsuccessful check through the cupboards in Milo's tiny kitchen hoping to see if the woman had any hard liquor stashed, Melanie was about bored to death. There was no one left to call for help, and Monty wouldn't answer no matter what kind of voicemail she left him. Even when she broke down and started to beg him to at least call her back to talk, her phone didn't ring. Of course, then she reverted to telling the man how much of an asshole he was, and no surprise, but he didn't call her then either.

At least Milo was considerate enough to leave her a bacon, lettuce, and tomato sandwich that, although Melanie didn't plan to eat it initially, turned out to be delicious. Having not eaten for over twenty-four hours, she was starving. As she munched the food, she tried to remember the last time she ate a simple homemade sandwich. Her and Monty's private chef would faint if he ever caught her in his kitchen frying up bacon to make herself lunch. The image made her smile— Melanie in a thousand-dollar dress with a skillet in hand. *Never happen*, she thought. Even growing up, she hated to cook, and now that she was rich, there was either someone to prepare food for her or she ordered food brought in.

With nothing else to do, Melanie resorted to scanning the book titles again. *Not a lot of fluffy love stories here*, she thought with a slight laugh. Even though she barely knew Milo, the woman did not seem the type to read romance. She came across as rough around the edges, which worked out for her, considering Melanie needed to be rescued. Still, she wondered what might hide beneath Milo's 'still waters run deep' persona. It took a certain kind of person to come out in the middle of the night and fight off punks to save a stranger. *I sure wouldn't have done it. That's what the police are for, thank you very much.* Pausing, she considered that thought for a second. Milo's phone still worked at that point, so she could have called the police rather than intervene alone. *And get her face so messed up.*

Even more intrigued about what Milo's story might be, she scanned the bookshelf more closely. This time, she really read the titles to learn what she liked and came across a manilla folder slipped between two of the taller travel books. The thing was at least a quarter inch thick, clearly stuffed with papers of some kind, and Melanie's hand paused over it. Looking at what was inside could be a huge invasion of privacy. *Or it's just a bunch of cooking recipes cut out of magazines and no big deal*, she reasoned, and because Melanie had a bad habit of doing exactly what she wanted regardless of the consequences, she pulled the folder free. A cursory glance inside confirmed two things—it was not cooking recipes, and Melanie wanted to keep looking.

There was page after page of maps. Some of entire continents, others of countries, and many of different cities around the world. Circles in colored pens marked specific areas, lines connected the circles, and everywhere were numbers. At first, she thought they were distances but looking closer, she realized they were estimated costs to go from place to place. When she paged through to the folded-up world map, she didn't dare open the large piece of paper and risk being unable to refold the thing. But that wasn't necessary because Melanie had a good guess what everything added to—Milo dreamed of traveling around the world. *Is that why she lives as she does?* she wondered, repacking the folder to put it away. *To save money for a grand trip?*

She slid the intriguing pile of papers back onto the shelf at the same moment the lock started to turn on the door. Whirling around, feeling guilty but knowing she hadn't been caught quite red-handed, Melanie hurried to sit on the edge of the couch. As she sat, a glance at the clock on the windowsill made her pause. Milo said she would be home after midnight, but the time was only seven o'clock.

. . .

With a black plastic bag from Mr. Nguyen's grocery store in one hand, Milo used her key to unlock the door's simple lock. When the door didn't budge, the fact the deadbolts were still engaged made her frown, knowing it could only mean one thing. Melanie had not left. She was supposed to lock the single door handle on her way out, leaving Milo's apartment with little security, but there wasn't an alternative. Evidently, she had nothing to worry about because the door was still secure from the inside. Frustrated, she leaned her forehead against the wood for a moment. Her day was shit, and all she wanted to do was open the pint of Jack Daniels she bought, along with the six-pack of beer, and get a little drunk. With a bit of luck, she would forget all about how bad things had gone for her over the last twenty-four hours. More importantly, she could put the high maintenance, yet admittedly attractive, Melanie Sotheby behind her.

After a few deep breaths, she finished opening the door and walked in to see the woman sitting on the ugly, orange couch, still wearing her short, black cocktail dress. *I should have loaned her clothes*, she thought, although they would be huge on her. *But the plan was for her to be long gone back to her high society life by now.* "Hi," Melanie said, a little more cheerful than Milo expected. *Like she missed me or something.* She shook her head at the crazy thought. *Or she's just bored out of her mind, and grateful I came back.*

"Why are you still here?" she asked, knowing the words sounded gruff but not in the mood for cheerful no matter what the reason.

Melanie held up her hands in mock surrender. "I know," she said. "This was not the plan, but things are going a little slower than I expected."

Narrowing her eyes, Milo already didn't like the sound of the situation. "What does that mean?"

"I couldn't get ahold of anyone."

That was enough to make Milo stomp past her to the kitchen. "Great," she growled, eager to get a drink poured.

As she unpacked the sack, setting the bourbon and beer on the counter, Melanie appeared in the doorway. "Oh, that's the best news I've had all day," she said, and Milo glanced to see the woman staring at the alcohol.

Milo shook her head. "Glad I could make you happy," she said, taking down her only two glasses from the cupboard. "I assume that means you want to have a drink with me." When she didn't answer, Milo looked again, but Melanie stared at her. "What?"

"Why are you home early?" she asked. "And with alcohol?"

For a minute, Milo considered telling Melanie the details were none of her business but then reconsidered, thinking everything was her fault anyway. "I got fired," she said, pouring a healthy portion of the bourbon into each glass. "Because they didn't like my face being banged up."

"What?" Melanie cried, moving closer and laying a hand on Milo's bare arm. The touch was warm and strangely comforting. "I'm so sorry. I won't let them get away with this."

Not sure what to make of Melanie's reaction, or even her own response to the touch, Milo held one of the glasses out toward her. "It is what it is," she said, and after the woman accepted the drink, lifted her own. In one swift toss of her wrist, the liquid was gone down her throat, burning a path to her empty stomach.

After a beat, Melanie did the same, coughing as she swallowed. "My God, that's horrible stuff," she said, waving at the Jack Daniels bottle. "I can't believe you can drink this."

Starting to pour herself another, Milo snorted a laugh. "Pretty sure I can't afford whatever the hell you like," she said, then motioned the bottle at Melanie's glass. "Does that mean you don't want more of it?"

"Oh, no, I didn't say that," she replied, giving Milo a smile so radiant and beautiful she paused. If she was being honest, Melanie Sotheby was by far the most physically attractive woman she had ever shared a drink with. *And the most spoiled,* she thought. *Plus, still in my apartment, screwing up my life.* As Melanie held out her glass for a refill, Milo poured and wondered what in the world they were going to do next.

Chapter Seven

Taking the second drink a little slower, Melanie tried to hold back the wash of guilt rolling over her. Milo was fired for one reason—she chose to help. *I am going to make all of this up to her*, she thought, already trying to decide the dollar figure to assign to cover the damages. In Melanie's world, throwing money at something solved all problems. *It would certainly help right now. I could get out of this poor woman's life, which I am sure she wants more than anything at this point and go back to New York like this never happened.*

Leaning against the kitchen counter, holding her drink, she studied Milo. The woman stared into the glass in her hand, clearly lost in thought and not noticing Melanie's attention. It gave her a minute to really see her, something she had not taken the time to do since they met. Close-cropped dark hair, olive skin. *Aside from the black eye, her face has great lines, excellent symmetry,* she thought, imagining that Milo photographed well. She wouldn't classify her as beautiful necessarily, but she had an intriguing face. Unique. *Perhaps handsome is a better word.* The idea made her pause. *I wonder if she's gay.* Not that it mattered, but she was curious. Melanie didn't have any close gay friends, so wasn't sure about the protocol around asking a person. *And this is probably not a great time to be bringing up her sexuality, especially considering she likely hates me over this mess.*

Milo sighed before suddenly tossing back the refill and setting the glass on the counter. She met Melanie's gaze. "I'm switching to beer," she said. "Do you want one?"

Melanie raised her eyebrows. "You're kidding?" she asked. "I don't drink beer."

"Why not?" Milo asked as she pulled one of the bottles from the six-pack before opening a drawer to take out an opener.

"Because I just don't."

"So, you don't like the taste? Because it's not champagne?" Milo said, a hint of mocking in her tone that Melanie didn't care for, and she lifted her chin.

"I am proud to say I've never tried a beer," she said. "I don't even like the smell."

With a shrug, Milo opened her bottle and held it out to Melanie. "This is one of my favorite breweries," she said. "Not some swill like the big guys make. Taste it." Not sure what to make of the generous offer, she stared at the bottle in Milo's hand. Her eyes noticed the woman's long fingers and somehow knew she would have strong, capable hands. *Like the rest of her*, she thought, flicking her eyes back to the woman's face only to see her smirking. "I dare you."

Never one to give in to a dare, Melanie set down her drink. "You're not even going to put it in a glass for me?"

"I don't have any more glasses," Milo replied, still holding out the beer. "Toughen up for a second and take a drink from the bottle." The woman chuckled. "I think it will do you good."

Toughen up? she thought, caught off guard by the word

choice as well as Milo's sudden amusement. "Oh, I can be tough," she blurted, taking the bottle, unwilling to give this near stranger anything else to mock her about. "I'll have you know I grew up on a farm in the middle of nowhere. And guess what, Milo. I've even milked a cow." When Milo blinked, clearly surprised, it was Melanie's turn to laugh. "See? I'm not necessarily what you think I am." Then, she sipped. The flavor was rich, surprisingly citrus-like, but almost piney too, and she was shocked she didn't hate the taste.

"Well?" Milo asked, and Melanie sipped again, wanting to be fair in her analysis.

She handed the bottle back to Milo. "I can see how it could grow on you," she admitted, retrieving her glass of bourbon. "Certainly, better than this other stuff you're offering." Milo smiled, and the look lightened her face, making it more open and inviting and confirming what Melanie surmised. The camera would love her. "You should smile more often."

Instantly, Milo's face turned to a scowl. "I will when there's something worth smiling about," she said and without warning, brushed past Melanie to stomp out of the kitchen.

Dropping onto the couch, Milo could not believe the nerve of the woman in her kitchen. *Smile?* she thought and regretted that she even had the beer conversation with her. *What am I doing? Trying to be buddies?* Knowing better, she shook her head before taking a long pull on the bottle of beer in her hand. With her head swimming from the two glasses of bourbon, Milo knew she needed to slow down or suffer a hell of a hangover tomorrow, but the dizziness felt good. Dulled the reality around her. *The reality where I got fired from a shitty, low-paying job today. And God knows where I'll find another one.* Some of her wanted to scream at the outrage, but she held the emotions. She learned long ago that moaning about a problem wouldn't fix it. *I guess that should be 'problems'. As in plural. There's certainly more than one.*

As she contemplated her choices, her biggest problem walked into the room and sat on the other end of the couch. Considering she was still wearing the same little cocktail dress, Milo had a great view of Melanie's shapely legs as she crossed them. Between the liquor and natural instinct, she couldn't help but feel a tug of attraction. *Oh, hell no,* she thought, slamming the lid on that line of thinking. *My life is challenging enough without going down a dead-end path by getting interested in this woman.* After a beat, Melanie cleared her throat. "I can see you're upset," she said, and Milo barked out a laugh.

"Yeah," she said. "A little."

Melanie pursed her lips. "I know my still being here isn't making you happy but are you that upset about your job?" she asked. "I mean, I didn't get the sense you were doing anything…" She stopped, making Milo look at her. "…you know…"

"No, I don't know," Milo said, but in a way, she did. Because of how she lived and what she wore to work, that she had no car, or other material possessions, Melanie was judging her. For a second, Milo fantasized about telling Melanie to get the hell out of her apartment. Get out of her life. *Let her find her own damn way home,* she thought with a growl, but deep down, she couldn't. Even after twenty-four hours, she knew she had never met anyone more helpless when it came to the real world. The woman might have grown up on a farm in some small town like she said, but her street smarts were apparently zero. *And because I can't leave well enough alone, I'm stuck with her.* Taking another drink, she turned her gaze to study the bookcase. Crammed full of titles with dozens of travel books that were a part of her plans. Paris. Rome. Cairo. *Plans that will have to wait a little longer.* She shook her head.

"Someone like you can't understand what that job meant to me."

They sat in silence for a minute, and Milo thought they might be able to enjoy a nice quiet evening of drinking before Melanie continued. "Listen. What I said came out wrong," she explained. "It's just, you seem like a smart person to me, especially with all of the books I imagine you've read cover to cover, so there must be lots of good jobs out there for you."

Milo narrowed her eyes, tired of the conversation and ready to end it. "Yeah, you'd think that," she said. "But you're wrong. I needed that job," After draining her beer, she turned to glare at the woman. Milo had enough. "Guess what, Melanie Sotheby? You're sitting here next to a felon." Melanie's eyes widened, and Milo took some satisfaction in making her react. "Yeah, that's right. And because I have a record, no one will hire me."

Letting the words sink in, Melanie wasn't sure how to react. It wasn't like she didn't know people who had been to prison, but that was for insider trading, and those weren't felonies. *And I doubt the white collar facilities were the same as Milo experienced*, she thought. *That could explain some things though.* "Is that how you learned to fight and move so quietly?"

The woman rested her head against the back of the couch and closed her eyes. "Yeah," she said. "Among other things."

"I see," was all Melanie could think to say, her mind going a hundred different directions after that bombshell statement. One thing was clear, though, learning Milo was once in jail did not change how she felt about her. Her first impression that the woman was the strong, silent type with a generous heart still stood. *No matter how gruff she gets with me*, she thought. *I cannot believe she is a bad person.* Her actions certainly proved otherwise. Some people would have shown Melanie the door by this point. Surely there was a reasonable explanation for all of it. "Can I ask what you did?"

Without hesitation, Milo shook her head against the cushion. "No," she said. "You can't."

"I see," Melanie murmured again. "Well, if you think by telling me I will run screaming into the night, I have bad news for you. I'm not leaving.

With a sigh, Milo rolled her head so their eyes met. "I would never be so lucky," she said, but there was a touch of playfulness to the tone. "At least now you'll stop talking about jobs, right?"

Crossing her heart, Melanie smiled. "Promise," she said. "That's not my business."

"Good," the woman answered, closing her eyes again. "You need to spend your energy figuring out how to get out of here." She frowned. "When was the last time you called your husband?" Rolling her eyes, thinking about Monty was the last thing Melanie wanted to do. The bastard had not returned any of her calls, and the last time she tried him, the number went straight to voicemail. A glance at the clock on Milo's wall and she realized it was after nine, making it midnight in New York.

She shook her head. "It's no good," she said. "He's being a complete bully. I need to see him face to face to sort this divorce nonsense out. He can't be serious."

Milo rubbed a hand over her face. "Well, that's a very long walk," she said. "You'll need better shoes."

Leveling her with a cool look at her poor attempt at humor, Melanie tried to keep hiding the anxiety she felt about getting back to New York. All joking aside, walking was not a practical option. Unfortunately, without identification, flying commercial was out even if she could get a plane ticket. *I need a car*, she thought. *Then I could drive there.* Considering how much she hated to drive, the idea of traveling over three thousand miles sounded impossible. Then, there was the problem of where she would eat and sleep along the multi-day journey if she had no way to pay. Logistically, the idea felt impossible, and things were beginning to seem hopeless. *What am I going to do?* Biting her lip, she wasn't willing to admit defeat and kept turning over the problem, only the answer always came back to driving. Then, as she heard the low sound of Milo starting to snore on the couch beside her, the only solution became clear. Somehow, they would get their hands on a car, and Melanie would pay Milo to drive her. Looking into the relaxed face of her rescuer, she was more and more certain her idea was the right one. *Now all I have to do is convince her.*

Chapter Eight

It was the kink in her neck that first woke Milo, but the sensation of something on her lap was what made her eyes open. She stared at the ceiling of her crappy apartment for a moment, trying to recall why she had been asleep on the couch, and then looked to see Melanie's blonde head in her lap. The beautiful woman was fast asleep, and Milo didn't move while she took a second to look at her face. Relaxed, it made her look younger, softer. *More innocent?* she wondered and had to suppress a little laugh. *I already have a sense Mrs. Sotheby is far from innocent. Grew up on a farm in the middle of nowhere yet ended up married to one of the wealthiest men Milo had ever heard of?* There was an interesting story there for certain, but Milo couldn't decide if she cared to know it or not. *Let's hope her husband calls back today. Then it won't matter and this whole fiasco can be over.*

As if the universe had read her thoughts, the phone on the table started to ring. Melanie shot upright, and Milo watched her blink her big blue eyes, clearly disoriented. "Phone's ringing," Milo said, and the woman pushed off the couch, launching herself at the thing. Snatching it up, she put it to her ear. "Hello," Melanie said, and after a beat, she yanked the phone away and angrily hung up. "Son of a bitch. Nothing but a damn telemarketer trying to sell an extended warranty." With a grimace, the woman shook her head. "If only we had a car to worry about."

We? Milo thought, raising her eyebrows. *Since when is there a 'we' in this situation?* At that exact moment, Melanie leveled her gaze at her. "And there's no way you can get your hands on a car?"

Furrowing her brow, Milo wasn't even sure how to respond. Not only did she not have any options readily available, but there was no reason she should want to try and find one. "No," she said. "There's not unless I were to rent or buy one, and I don't plan to do that."

A smile crossed Melanie's face, reminding Milo how attractive the woman truly was, even in two-day-old make-up and the same wrinkled clothes. "Well, right before you fell asleep," she said, "I had a perfect idea."

Already not liking the sound of whatever the woman was thinking, Milo started to stand. "I have a feeling I don't even want to hear it," she said, noticing the world was still dark outside her front window. There was time for more sleep. "I'm going to bed."

"Don't be like that," Melanie said, sliding back onto the couch. "Hear me out. It can solve both our problems."

After a beat, Milo settled back onto the couch again. "Let's hear it," she said with a yawn, skeptical but a little curious. Solving her problems sounded good, as improbable as whatever idea the woman had seemed.

From the sly smile still on Melanie's face, she was obviously about to launch into a heck of a sales pitch. Even though Milo was pretty confident she would say no, she was ready to be entertained by the presentation. "We are going to drive to

New York," Melanie announced, sounding so satisfied with her idea, Milo almost smiled. Almost.

"Drive to New York?" she repeated, making sure she heard the woman correctly.

"Well," Melanie said. "You will do the driving because I hate it, but that can get me home, and then I can pay you."

Not quite sure how to respond or even how she felt about the offer, Milo paused before pointing out the obvious. "All good, but we don't have a car."

Melanie averted her eyes, suddenly plucking at a loose string in the couch cushion. "Well," she started, hesitating before meeting Milo's eyes again. "This is rude, and I know it, but Milo, do you have any money saved that we could use?"

Initially, Melanie had been so excited about her idea to drive across the country, she had considered waking Milo to explain. Still, while she had watched the woman finally relax after what had to be a horrible day, she knew any conversation could wait until morning. There would be a lot of logistics to figure out, foremost, how to get their hands on a vehicle. Instead, Melanie tried to decide if she wanted more of the bourbon that was slowly growing on her the more she drank or if she wanted to try to sleep. The latter would be difficult with Milo taking up an entire end of the couch. *Although I could just lean over a little,* she had thought, and the next thing she knew, the phone was ringing, and she was halfway into Milo's lap. "Phone's ringing," Milo had said, and that was enough to throw Melanie into action. Monty called her back at last.

Grabbing up the phone, ready for the apology she was sure her husband was about to give, the droning recorded voice surprised her. Realizing it was a telemarketer, she all but threw the phone against the wall but then saw the irony in the call. The last thing she remembered before going to sleep was that they needed a car. *Maybe it's a sign*, she thought before letting Milo know the caller was a damn telemarketer. The only good thing about the phone call was it gave Melanie the opportunity she needed to talk about her vision.

Amazingly, Milo didn't immediately reject the drive across the country idea, giving Melanie hope, only to have it crash down when she made the mistake of asking Milo about money. "Oh, hell no," Milo said, standing abruptly. "I'm mixed up in this way more than I want to be. I'm not making it worse." Melanie wasn't ready to give up so quickly but guessed begging or badgering the woman would only make it worse.

Instead, she took a civil approach. "Milo, please sit down," she said softly. "I don't know your history, but I have figured out you're both reasonable and very intelligent. Let's discuss my proposal. I'm sure you want to hear it."

"Really?" Milo asked, still standing but not walking away. "You have me figured out already, do you?"

Melanie nodded. "I think so," she said, letting the details of her idea form in her mind as she spoke. Although she hadn't taken the time to think through all the specifics until right that second, the plan taking shape continued to get better. "Think of it strictly as a business arrangement."

At that, Milo slipped back onto the sofa. "I'm listening."

"Good," Melanie said, pausing while Milo gave her attention. Starting to reach for Milo's arm, ready to deploy a flirtation tactic she used on different men over the years, she paused. It was one of the ways she always got what she wanted. But before she moved, Melanie hesitated. *But is this how I want to handle this conversation?* she wondered. Although she thought it might work, for some reason, she wanted to earn Milo's agreement on the plan's merits and not use some damsel in distress ploy. Something about the woman's quiet strength inspired Melanie to stand up for herself. She rested her hands in her lap. "Thank you for listening. From my perspective, we both have a problem the other can help fix." When Milo did nothing but stare, an encouraged Melanie continued. "I need to get to New York, and you need a job."

At that, Milo narrowed her eyes. "You're saying you're offering me a job?" she asked. "Basically, hiring me to drive you over three thousand miles?"

"Exactly," she replied. "And for your trouble, I will pay you one hundred thousand dollars once we arrive." She held up a finger. "But you are responsible for all the details of getting me there—vehicle, lodging, food." If the dollar figure impressed Milo, Melanie couldn't read it on her face. "Well?"

"I'll think about it," Milo said, getting up from the couch and disappearing into the bedroom without a look back.

Sitting on the end of her narrow twin bed, Milo stared at her scratched, secondhand dresser drawers and tried to imagine having a hundred thousand dollars in her bank account. The number seemed a little unrealistic for the simple task of driving across the country. Still, Melanie was rich. *Or at least her husband is,* she thought. *However, he doesn't seem particularly cooperative. What if she can't get the money for me?* Then Milo would be out of whatever she invested, which was unacceptable. She hadn't busted her ass at minimum wage jobs to blow it on an empty promise. *Still, if she can pay me back, I might be able to start over and maybe even take my backpacking trip around the world.* It all came down to what Milo would be willing to risk.

Even if she said yes, traveling with Melanie would be no picnic, but Milo had put up with worse. During her two years in jail, different bunkmates came and went. Some were decent, others a nightmare, but the lack of privacy bothered her the most. She was never alone. Driving would require being with

Melanie a lot of hours nonstop. *Can I deal with that?* she wondered. *For a hundred thousand bucks?*

As she continued to visualize the drive, some parts were attractive. Although the trip east would be nothing but hard driving to get there as fast as they could, the way back would be an excellent opportunity to visit parts of the United States she always wanted to see. Even something as simple as standing on the shore of the mighty Mississippi river would be thrilling. *Maybe even find a place that offers authentic steamboat rides*, she thought, remembering the books she read where Samuel Clemens and other famous figures used the trips for inspiration. Suddenly, she wanted to look at her maps stuck in the bookshelf in the other room. *I wonder if Melanie is asleep yet, and I could sneak past her.*

The other option was for her to try and sleep for the few hours remaining before daylight, then making an informed decision in the morning when she was fully awake. She grinned, knowing she was too excited at the possibilities to wait. All she would do was toss and turn, trying to decide if she should risk her nest egg for the chance to accelerate her dreams. Calculating the actual distances and estimating how much it might cost would help.

Going to the door, Milo listened, and hearing nothing, decided to chance it. Unfortunately, she was only halfway across the living room when Melanie busted her from where she lay on the couch. "Can't sleep either?" she asked, sitting up with the blanket wrapped around her. "I'll take that as a good sign."

Reaching the bookcase, Milo took out her folder. "Not necessarily," she said. "I need to check some things."

"Like what?"

Milo sighed, not wanting to discuss it but not seeing a reason to lie. "My maps."

A smile crossed Melanie's face. "Can I look too?" she

asked. "I have no idea the way we need to take." Resigning herself to having to share, Milo sat in a chair at the table, opening the folder to find the map of the United States.

Blanket and all, Melanie joined her as Milo spread the colorful map out on the table. "Since there might be snow already, to avoid the Rockies, I think we take Interstate 10," she said, tracing the blue line out of Los Angeles. "Then veer northeast once we know we are clear of bad weather."

"If you think that's best, I'm all for it," Melanie said, excitement in her voice. "Thank you so much for this. I promise I will make it very worthwhile for you."

I guess that means I've agreed to go, Milo thought, not realizing quite how it happened. "You better," she said, keeping any enthusiasm out of her voice. *She doesn't need to know how much this can mean to me.* "I'll go find a car in the morning."

"And clothes," Melanie added, opening the blanket enough Milo could see the top of the black dress. "I can't wear this the whole way."

She had a point. "Fine," Milo said. "Tomorrow, we will go shopping too."

Chapter Nine

From the depths of sleep, Melanie heard someone calling her name. "It's time to rise and shine," Milo was saying as Melanie fluttered her eyes open. The woman stood over her, smiling mischievously. "The day is wasting. We have things to do and places to be."

Slowly, Melanie sat up with a groan. "What time is it?" she said, guessing the cheap bourbon the night before was one reason she felt foggy-headed.

"It's actually past eight," she said. "I let you sleep in."

Melanie yawned, not ready to admit she usually stayed in bed until well past ten. "Thanks, I guess," she said. "Although we were up kind of late looking at maps."

With a chuckle, Milo started toward the kitchen. "No excuses," she said. "Want some coffee?" The idea of coffee sounded fabulous, but more than anything Melanie was surprised by the change in Milo. *She seems almost...happy,* she thought. *Is she that excited about getting rid of me? Or is it the idea of earning money?*

She hoped it was the latter but guessed the answer was

probably both were true. "Coffee would be wonderful," Melanie answered. "Can I have milk in it at least?"

"You can even have sugar," Milo called from the kitchen and Melanie shook her head. It was as if, over the last few hours while she slept, the woman found a new, much more positive perspective on the plan to drive across the country. Considering Milo's attitude the night before, Melanie decided not to ask questions and instead be glad about the change. Running her hand through her hair, she was horrified at how tangled it felt. She hadn't taken the time to look closely in a mirror since she ended up at Milo's apartment and could only imagine her appearance. *Hideous is likely the best word,* she thought with a shiver. Suddenly she had the strongest desire to be clean again. "Milo, do you mind if I take a shower?"

Milo popped her head into the doorway from the kitchen and looked her up and down before nodding. "Probably a good idea."

"Thanks a lot," Melanie said with a frown. "I don't suppose you have any clothing that's not going to be way too big for me?"

Rubbing her chin, Milo hummed. "That may be a problem," she said. "I guess you could wear one of my T-shirts and a pair of gym shorts that tie around the waist."

Hating the idea of how she would look but knowing there was little else to do, she sighed. "Fine," she said. "And do you have flip-flops or something? I can't very well wear my heels with that ensemble."

Laughing, Milo disappeared into the kitchen again. "I do," she said. "Can't wait to see the final product."

"Ha ha," Melanie said, wishing the coffee would hurry up. "What is the plan this morning? You seem very focused."

Milo returned with two cups of coffee and handed one to her before settling in a chair around the table. "Pretty simple. I'm going to talk to Mr. Nguyen about borrowing a car."

Melanie raised her eyebrows. "Borrow?"

"Yes," Milo replied, blowing on her cup. "I'll pay him, but I see no reason to spend unnecessary money purchasing a car when I only need it for two weeks."

"Two weeks?" Melanie asked with a frown. Last night when they were looking at the map, it seemed like an incredibly long distance to travel. They hadn't talked about how long it would take.

Milo nodded. "Two should be enough," she answered. "I ran the numbers in my head, and we should be able to make it to New York in forty hours. If things go smoothy, that translates to approximately three and a half days at the most before I drop you off."

Numbers were not a problem for Melanie, and she quickly did the math. "Wait a minute," she said. "That sounds insane. You can't expect me to ride in a car for twelve hours each day."

"What were you expecting?" Milo asked, taking a sip. "That this is a scenic trip?"

"Well, I wasn't expecting that either," Melanie shot back. "But I don't want to be miserable every single second."

Milo narrowed her eyes. "Then we have a serious disconnect," she said, her good humor disappearing. "Because stopping takes time and money, and I don't plan to waste either."

Milo didn't like the direction the conversation was going. Melanie seemed to think they were on some joyride when all she wanted was to drop the woman off and collect her money. Then she could take her leisurely time heading back across the US, visiting places she earmarked on her mental map. *There are lots of amazing things between California and New York*, she thought. But first, she had to drive Melanie home. "I'm going to go see about our car," Milo announced, standing. It was time to end the conversation. Melanie would do things her way or the deal was off. "Let me find you some sweats, and you can take your shower while I'm gone."

"Sounds lovely," Melanie snapped. "I can't wait to see how that makes me look."

Ignoring the woman's tone, Milo strode across the room to her bedroom, grabbing some clothing from the drawer before tossing them on the counter in the bathroom. "I'll be back in an hour," she said on her way out the door. She didn't have time to worry about the feelings of a diva. "Then we can buy you what you need for the trip."

"Well, find us something decent. I don't want to ride in a junker," Melanie called to Milo's back as she walked out the door. Hitting the stairs, Milo grit her teeth. She had thought they were on the same page after the discussion last night. But suddenly, it sounded like Melanie had different expectations of what the next few days would be like. It was not that Milo looked forward to hard traveling over three thousand miles in a car, especially considering she would be doing all the driving. *Sometimes you have to hunker down and get things done*, she thought. In the end, the reward will be worth it. *Melanie is just cargo, and I need to remember that.* Yet, as Milo walked along the sidewalk toward the grocery store, she knew that wasn't true. Although part of her frustration was about the trip, there was more.

Last night while she was in bed imagining what the trip would be like, Milo let her mind wander into dangerous territory. Something about Melanie grew on her, and she didn't want the feelings developing inside her. *It's not like we will ever be friends or even interact after these next few days*, she had thought, but that didn't stop her from staring up at the ceiling and fantasizing about Melanie as more than a friend. In her defense, it was impossible not to be attracted to the beautiful woman. Even though she was high maintenance and had no street smarts, a certain charisma about her sucked a person in. Milo was not immune to the allure.

Thinking about it, Milo shook her head as she reached the grocery store. *No doubt that's how she managed to snare her husbands*, Milo thought. *And I'm not going to be a sucker. I'm in this for the money.* Ducking inside, Milo was disappointed to find only Mrs. Nguyen at the counter. "Good morning," Milo said. "I don't suppose Mr. Nguyen is available? I have a question for him."

"He's sleeping," the woman replied. "But will be here around noon."

"I see," Milo said, trying to hide her frustration. "How about your son?"

Mrs. Nguyen smiled. "He is in the back," the woman answered. "You can go through the swinging doors and find him in the office."

"Thank you," Milo said, heading in that direction and after a minute knocked on the door frame of a little office filled with a desk and two filing cabinets. There was barely room for Mr. Nguyen's son as he sat tapping the keys on a computer.

He looked at her. "Can I help you?"

"Sorry to barge in," Milo said. "But I'm looking to borrow a car for two weeks, and I was wondering if you had one available that I could negotiate."

The man leaned back in his chair. "Why don't you just rent from Enterprise?"

"I'd rather do something under the table," Milo said, not interested in giving details about her dislike of using credit cards when she didn't have to. "I'm willing to pay cash."

The man grinned. "I like the sound of that. I want two thousand dollars cash up front," the man said without batting an eye. "You can have half of it back when you return the car in the same condition." He grinned. "I'll warn you. This thing's a classic."

"That doesn't matter to me," Milo said, reaching in her pocket to give him the money.

Like everything about Milo and her apartment, the outdated bathroom was sparse but sparkling clean. The small single-stall shower had barely enough room for Melanie to turn around in, and she wondered how the much taller and broader Milo managed. With no other choices available, she used Milo's all-in-one shampoo and conditioner combo and tried not to think about what it was doing to her hair. Luckily her stylist was amazing, and no doubt could take care of any damage once Melanie got home.

She also ended up using Milo's bodywash, and as Melanie lathered her body, she had the strongest sense of Milo. After a moment, she recognized the fragrance of the soap. Not noticing until she smelled the bubbles, she realized Milo had a distinct scent. *And it's very attractive*, Melanie thought, letting the water wash away the soap, before frowning. *That's an unexpected way to think of her.* Milo was many things, including intelligent and capable, but Melanie also found her very stubborn. *That part of her is definitely not attractive.* Thinking they could drive across the country in under four days was insanity, and she wouldn't do it. She wouldn't pay the woman a hundred thousand dollars to torture her. *I only hope whatever car Milo is arranging is comfortable.* For a moment, she had a scary image of something tiny and cramped. Even at five foot two, she did not want to feel like she was riding along the highway in a soup can.

Completely rinsed of all the shampoo and soap, she turned off the water and reached for the towel outside the curtain. As she started to use it, Milo's scent came back to her, and again she felt strangely drawn to the fragrance. *What in the hell?* she thought. *Why am I reacting this way? It's not like I am attracted to women.* Still, there was something about Milo that intrigued her. The woman wasn't like anyone she had ever met and certainly not like anyone in her social circles. *And not just because she's been in jail.* Even with the rough edges, Melanie found something about her appealing. A part of her wanted to peel back some of Milo's complex layers and learn more about her. She laughed. *I'll probably have my chance if we are stuck in a car together for days.* Surprisingly she looked forward to it.

Stepping onto the bathmat and appraising the pile of clothing on the counter, Melanie sighed. The gray shorts and dark blue t-shirt lacked anything feminine, which might be fine for Milo, but Melanie hated the clothes. Then, she made the mistake of looking in the mirror at her wet hair and face with no makeup and was ready to weep. She never went anywhere without making herself beautiful. *And I look like a drowned rat,* she thought. *I can't go on like this.* Shopping for the stuff she needed couldn't happen soon enough.

Slipping on the t-shirt and shorts, she heard a car horn honk outside the apartment. She ignored the sound for a moment, and then it registered that the driver might be Milo. Hurrying to the front, she turned the three locks before pulling open the door to see what was outside. A long, vintage, silver convertible Cadillac with white wall tires sat at the curb. Stepping onto the landing, Melanie stood with her mouth open. When she wanted luxury, a 1960s classic was not on the list. Milo stepped out, grinning from ear to ear. "Well," she said. "What do you think? Is this fancy enough for you?"

Melanie shook her head. "You're serious?"

"Oh, very serious," Milo said with a laugh. "A 1968 Cadillac Deville convertible. Mrs. Sotheby, we will be traveling in style."

Chapter Ten

The Cadillac rode as smooth as butter as they cruised down the freeway. Although it was like driving a ship considering its size, Milo knew she would happily get used to it. After a few years of not driving anything but a forklift, it felt good to be behind the wheel again. Even Melanie seemed content, which was especially nice after her initial hesitation. When Milo pointed out the car wasn't a junker as prescribed, the woman appeared to resign herself to the situation.

Driving into the parking lot of a giant supercenter, Milo scanned for a space large enough to accommodate the Cadillac. "Oh no," Melanie said from the passenger seat. Milo glanced over to see her starting to shake her head. "We are not shopping here."

Milo pulled into a parking space and shut the car off before bothering to answer. "Oh yes, we are," she said with a grin, unable to help being amused that Melanie would never be caught dead in a place like the giant building in front of them. But money was money, and she wasn't going to waste it on some designer fashions simply to make the woman happy.

If the store was good enough for Milo, it would have to be for Melanie too. "There's nothing wrong with the clothes they sell here." She started to reach for the wallet she carried in her back pocket. "And besides, I'm only giving you a hundred dollars, so you will need to be thrifty."

"What?" Melanie exclaimed. "I can't even buy a good mascara for a hundred dollars."

Milo couldn't resist continuing to grin. "I'm pretty sure they don't sell that brand here anyway," she said, pulling out five twenty dollar bills to hand to Melanie. "I'll wait in the car." The woman stared at the money in Milo's hand for a moment. Milo waved it at her. "Take it."

"No," Melanie said, crossing her arms. "I will not go into that store, and I will not settle for a hundred dollars." She looked Milo hard in the eyes. "I'm offering to give you a lot of money to drive me to New York, and I expect at least part of that money to make me comfortable." Milo thought about it for a minute. In some ways the woman had a point, but she still wasn't going to take her to some fancy shopping mall. Among other things, they did not have time for it.

She nodded. "All right, let's compromise," she said. "I will let you spend three hundred, but you still have to shop here."

The woman was quiet for a moment, and Milo almost heard the wheels turning in her head. "You are so stubborn," Melanie said, grabbing the cash from Milo's hand. "And you know I'll give in because I can't exactly wear this." She waved a hand at the baggy t-shirt and athletic shorts. Milo couldn't help but laugh. Melanie did look like a kid wearing grown-up clothing, especially without any makeup and her hair pulled back in a long ponytail. If she was being honest, Milo liked the fresh-faced appearance better. Melanie didn't need to know that though.

"Lots of people dress that way," she said, and Melanie snorted a laugh.

"Maybe in your world, but not mine. And if you're making me do this, I have one condition," Melanie said. "You have to come in the store and shop with me."

"Why?" Milo asked. "I have what I need at the apartment, and besides, I hate shopping."

Melanie tilted her head. "Oh really? I would think at least you would want some supplies for the road," she suggested. "Some bottles of water, maybe even some snacks." Milo raised an eyebrow. The woman made sense. All she had focused on was getting the trip underway but having some provisions was a good idea, especially because she had no intention of stopping except to gas up the car and maybe sleep for a few hours.

Taking off the old-fashioned seatbelt across her lap, Milo nodded. "Fair enough," she said. "Let's do this."

With four simple but colorful dresses, and some passable sandals, Melanie looked at the signs overhead to find out where she could buy some panties. As she made her way to the undergarments section of the mega superstore, Melanie tried to fight the flashbacks from her childhood. Not that anything terrible happened to her while growing up, but she still hadn't been able to wait to get away from the farm life. After she did, she never looked back. Among other things, she had vowed never to set foot in a low budget store like the one she was standing in. *Life has a funny way of circling back on itself*, she thought. *But this is just temporary.*

As she browsed through the different racks of panties, she couldn't help picking out ones that had at least a little lace. Even though she knew it wasn't necessary, Melanie always wanted to feel pretty. *And you never know*, she thought and then paused. *Never know what?* She frowned. *Why would I want something sexy between now and when I get home to my real clothes?* No clear answer came to mind, but she was beginning to question her reactions to things. Crazy thoughts kept surfacing, not to mention the very frustrating Milo was constantly popping up in her head. *I'll never forgive her for making me shop in a store like this.*

As if conjuring her with her thoughts, the woman appeared around the corner, pushing another shopping cart. It held three cases of water, one case of microbrew, and a box of power bars. "Are you about ready?"

Melanie shook her head. "Not even close," she said, pointing at the contents of the shopping cart. "Please don't tell me that's all you intend to bring on the trip."

Milo looked at what she had gathered and frowned. "Were you expecting something more?"

"Well, perhaps something I would actually want to eat," Melanie replied. "You know fruit or crackers with cheese."

Milo glared. "Do you think we are getting ready for a party?" she asked. "This is a hardcore road trip, and don't you forget it."

"Oh, I can't forget it," Melanie snapped. "Aside from you reminding me constantly, I assure you it is something I cannot wait to get over."

"That makes two of us," Milo growled. "Now, what more do you need to get?"

Melanie surveyed her selection. "Well, I have dresses, shoes, and underwear, so what I need to find now is someplace to get some decent shampoo and conditioner," she said. "Oh, and some makeup."

"Why can't you just use my shampoo?"

With a roll of her eyes, Melanie sighed. "You can't be serious," Melanie said. "I used it this morning, and I'm surprised my hair hasn't fallen out."

Milo ran a hand over her head, ruffling her short hair. "It works fine for me," she said, and Melanie shook her long mane of blonde.

"Well, it doesn't work for me," Melanie said. "Maybe it would be better if you went and found me a suitcase?" She didn't want Milo looking over her shoulder as she tried to finish shopping. Obviously, they were not aligned on what was necessary for a woman like Melanie to survive.

Turning her cart, Milo started walking in the other direction. "I'll get you a duffel bag."

"No," Melanie said, all but stomping her foot. Enough was enough. "I need a suitcase. Otherwise, everything will get wrinkled."

Glancing over her shoulder, Milo looked skeptically at what was in Melanie's cart. "I don't understand why you're getting dresses anyway," she said. "You should be getting sweatpants and t-shirts so you can relax during our twelve-hour days in the car."

"Over my dead body," Melanie said and heard Milo mutter something under her breath. "What did you say?"

Milo kept walking. "Nothing, dear," she said and disappeared around a corner, hopefully to go find a suitcase.

Melanie could be so infuriating. Milo wasn't sure how they could survive days together in a car, even in one as big as the Cadillac. *Maybe I can get her to ride in the back*, she thought as she walked down the aisle filled with suitcases. There were a lot of colors and sizes, and Milo had no idea what she was looking for since her luggage consisted of an old, green army duffle bag. Stopping at a larger black one, she made the mistake of looking at the price tag and let out a curse. The thing was almost two hundred dollars, and she once again contemplated going with something simple like maybe a backpack. "And then I will catch hell," she growled to no one in particular. *Sometimes, it's just easier to go along to get along*.

Continuing to search, she finally came across one that was

pink with white polka dots, and with a grin, she knew it would be perfect for Melanie. Not daring to look at the price, she piled the thing on top of her cart and headed in the direction of cosmetics. The fact the woman was going to spend some of her money on something that would be useless on the trip made no sense to Milo. *Besides, it's not like she needs it*, Milo thought. Although she was aware Melanie hated the baggy t-shirt and basketball shorts, there was still something sensual and sexy about her. Something that would never wash off and didn't rely on fancy dresses. *I wonder why she doesn't see it.*

As she walked the maze of aisles, Milo knew trying to figure Melanie out was a lost cause. All she could do was try and find her way to where Melanie would hopefully be waiting and get them out of the store. Unfortunately, locating her proved to be a challenge. Cosmetics wasn't a department she ever shopped in. After asking for directions, she finally came around a corner and saw Melanie ahead standing at a display case. Milo slowed her steps and took a moment to really evaluate the woman. Her long blonde hair pulled back in a ponytail halfway down her back. Her small stature. *They call it petite*, Milo thought. *The exact opposite of me.*

Suddenly, Melanie glanced over her shoulder, and their gaze met. Milo almost stopped. *It would be so easy to get lost in the depth of her blue eyes*, she thought and then grit her teeth. *What am I thinking?* Any desires for Melanie needed to stop otherwise she would end up going down a road that led to nothing but embarrassment. *And even worse, hurt.* Melanie's eyes dropped to the pink suitcase, and Milo was rewarded with a huge smile along with a little laugh. "Now that is perfect," Melanie said. "I'm surprised you were brave enough to push it around in your cart."

Milo shrugged nonchalantly. "It takes a lot to embarrass me," she said, then grinned. "Besides, if anybody asked, I would say it was for my girlfriend." Again, their eyes met, and

Milo felt heat rise to her cheeks over her unintentionally suggestive statement. "That didn't come out like I meant it to."

Melanie shrugged. "We are friends, and I am a girl," she said. "Now, come over here and tell me if you like this lipstick color."

Milo shook her head. "Why in the world are you buying lipstick?"

The woman tossed her head, giving Milo a sly look. "I have to look pretty if I'm going to be your girlfriend."

Glad they weren't bickering again, Milo enjoyed the playful banter. "Well, I think you look beautiful enough that you don't need it," she said, and, for a second, she wasn't sure if Melanie heard her until the woman blushed.

"Thank you," she said, her tone suddenly shy. "But not everybody feels that way."

Everybody should, Milo thought and tried to wait patiently while the woman continued to shop.

Chapter Eleven

Cruising down the California freeway in the Cadillac, Melanie would never admit it, but she was beginning to like the feel of riding in the classic convertible. *They simply don't make cars like this anymore*, she thought and wondered if Milo would be willing to put the top down. She frowned. *And then what? Let the wind blow through my hair as I ride along with this woman I've known for forty-eight hours?* Confused as ever, she looked at Milo's bruised profile driving beside her and again was taken aback by how unique and attractive her face was—strong chin, full lips, high cheekbones. *I really need to take pictures of her before this is over.*

As if feeling Melanie's eyes on her, Milo glanced in her direction. "How long will it take you to pack?" Milo asked, and Melanie blinked at the abrupt question. Milo might be interesting to look at, but she was still lacking in the diplomacy department.

She shrugged. "I don't know," she said, then realized what Milo might be planning. "You're not thinking we were going to leave tonight? I don't know what time it is, but from the looks of things, it's at least late afternoon."

She watched Milo look at her watch. "It's a little past four o'clock, so we have plenty of daylight left."

"You know that's not true," Melanie said. "This time of year, it'll be dark by six at the latest, and we will have to stop after only a few hours."

Setting her jaw, Milo had a look of frustration on her face. "Why are you having so much trouble understanding me," she said. "We're not going to stop. I plan for us to drive all night and well into tomorrow before we need to take a rest."

Her eyes widening at the horrible sounding plan, Melanie started shaking her head. "Absolutely not," she said. "I don't want you falling asleep at the wheel."

Milo frowned. "I'm not gonna fall asleep at the wheel," she growled. "I can drive us all night."

"When was the last time you drove for twelve hours straight through?" Melanie asked with a tilt of her head. "Because I'm not taking this lightly. One more evening here in Los Angeles will not make or break our trip." Milo didn't say anything for a minute as she stared out the windshield. Giving her time to think, Melanie turned her focus back on the passing world around them. The sun was already well into the western sky, and Melanie had the strangest temptation to go somewhere and watch it set over the ocean. *What if I asked her to take me to the beach?* Even though it was a crazy idea, she couldn't help but suggest it. "I have an idea. What if we pull over, put the top down, and cruise to Malibu to watch the sunset?"

Hearing the question, it was Milo's turn to look surprised as she glanced at Melanie again. "What are you talking about?" she asked. "You suddenly want to watch the sunset?"

Melanie smiled wide. "Yes, that's exactly what I'm saying," she said. "I've been to California a bunch of times with Monty for film stuff, but we never do anything touristy." She sighed, thinking about everything she willingly suffered through. "It's all boring dinners, premieres, and things like that, and then we fly home. He doesn't really like California." Rubbing her hand over the seat cushion between them, Melanie knew she sounded silly, but what she was about to say was the truth. "I've never seen the sunset over the Pacific, and this might be my only chance."

They cruised along in silence for a minute and Melanie watched the woman's face but couldn't read what she was thinking. Finally, she shook her head as if not believing what she was about to agree to do. "You've truly never seen the sun set over the ocean?"

"Truly," Melanie replied, waiting patiently to see what the woman would do with her request.

Milo blew out a long breath. "Okay, just this one small thing," she said. "And then it's down to business. We get home, we pack, and we leave before dawn."

Warmth filling her at the unexpected agreement, Melanie almost slid over to kiss Milo on the cheek but then checked herself. Something like that might set Milo off and she was not risking her changing her mind. "I can live with that," Melanie said. "I'm so excited."

"Good," Milo said, turning on her blinker to change lanes and take the next exit. "Let's go take the top down."

If she didn't think about all the other circumstances around her, Milo could pretend her life was complete. She was cruising along the Pacific Coast Highway on a perfect October evening with a woman who took a person's breath away. The top was down on a classic Cadillac Deville, and she felt the warm southern California wind against her face. All in all, she found it impossible not to smile. "I see you," Melanie murmured beside her, and Milo looked in the woman's direction for a moment.

"What do you see?"

Melanie's eyes twinkled. "I see you are enjoying yourself," she said with a little laugh. "This is pretty amazing, isn't it?"

Although Milo tried to scowl in response, she couldn't conjure it. The woman was right. *And why would I want to hide it?* she thought. *Melanie is not the enemy. Sure, she is a pain in the ass...* Still, Milo felt there was a good person deep down. Behind the hundred-dollar mascara and stylish dresses and shoes, there might be someone she wanted to get to know. *Maybe on this trip I will get the chance.*

Arriving at a pullout along the highway, half a dozen other cars were parked facing the ocean and awaiting the spectacular end of the day. Milo respectfully parked a few spots away, allowing everyone to keep at least a little bit of privacy. Then she shut off the engine and made herself comfortable to watch the sunset. "Thank you for this," Melanie said softly, and Milo suddenly felt the woman's hand brush her arm. "I know you wanted to start our trip this evening, but I think this is better."

Doing her best to ignore the tingle from where Melanie's fingers lingered, Milo shrugged. "I guess starting in the morning won't make a big difference."

"Exactly," Melanie said, facing Milo across the wide seat. "And maybe this will help us get to know each other better."

Milo frowned, suddenly not sure what to make of Melanie's comment. "Is that what we're doing?" she asked, unable to keep the edge out of her voice. "I was only watching the sunset."

"Don't sound so offended," Melanie said, a hint of hurt in her tone. "What is wrong with us sharing a special moment?"

Sharing a special moment? Milo thought, not ready to admit she felt the same. *I have to keep her at arm's length, or it will be a disaster.* Preparing to explain to Melanie they simply had a business arrangement, she let her eyes meet the woman's gaze, and they held. As much as Milo tried to resist, she was drawn in by the open look on Melanie's face. *How can she be getting under my skin so easily?* She took a deep breath. *Maybe watching the sunset together was a bad idea.* There was a strong possibility the decision would come back to haunt her. Their friendship would never last. Milo would never stay in her life, and there was no reason they would be in contact after she dropped her off. "This is only temporary," Milo corrected. "We are just two people watching the sunset together."

A sad look showed in Melanie's eyes. "Okay," she said in a quiet voice instead of the biting tone Milo expected, and for a second she regretted her harsh words. *But they are for the best,* she thought. *Start us off on the right foot.*

Not saying another word, Milo turned to watch the sun as it moved nearer the water's horizon. There wasn't a cloud in the sky, and the sphere started to turn into a fiery orange ball. "It's magnificent," Melanie whispered, and to that Milo had to agree. As they watched the sun move lower, she couldn't deny the moment was special.

As much as it hurt when Milo denied what they were building had meaning, Melanie understood. They came from different worlds, and they would probably never interact again after the trip. Even though she had only known the woman for a couple of days, a lot of which was spent bickering, the reality she would lose Milo eventually made Melanie sad. *I need to protect myself from being really hurt over this,* she thought. *And make myself remember Milo is right, this is a business arrangement.* Yet, as she looked out the windshield and watched the sun disappear, she had the strongest desire to reach for Milo's hand. She gave her head a slight shake. *It makes no sense.* Melanie refused to believe her confusion was because Milo was a woman. It seemed more that she would never be attracted to someone so quickly. *Especially someone so different than I am.* They could not come from further ends of the social spectrum.

Stealing a glance at Milo, there were other obvious differences. The woman was tall and strong, especially compared to Melanie, and something inside her was very attracted to it. *What would it feel like to have her put her arm around me?* she suddenly wondered and then felt herself blush. *I wonder what Milo would do if I told her that I want her to?* Trying to force herself to refocus on the spectacular sunset, Melanie couldn't help but compare Milo to Monty. Her fat-bellied, balding pompous ass of a husband would be no match for Milo.

As the memory of Milo defending her in the alley came to mind, she knew Monty would never have done something so brave. But then, he would never bother to sink low enough to have a physical fight. Instead, he would hire someone to do the dirty work. *I guess that sort of sums up the difference between them*, she thought. Milo took the challenges of life head on. The woman didn't live to manipulate others with a secret agenda. Milo was real, and as Melanie watched the sun disappear, she knew that was what she liked most.

The minute the sun vanished, Milo sat straighter. "Well, that's that," she said, starting the car as if eager to go. "Did you get what you came for?"

Melanie studied the woman for a second, wondering why she was in such a sudden rush. "I did," she said. "I will never forget this. Thank you."

Swallowing hard, Milo stared at her for a moment, her eyes searching Melanie's face. "You're welcome," she said softly. "It was a beautiful sunset." Again, the moment held, and as much as she wanted to say the right thing, Melanie could not form words that could express how she truly felt.

Her thoughts were so crazy even she could not entirely believe them. Finally, Milo turned away. "We should go."

Knowing the opportunity to say something had passed, Melanie forced down the disappointment and smiled. "Maybe we can pick up some dinner on the way home?"

Looking over her shoulder, Milo put the car in reverse and started to back out of the parking space. "What do you like?" she asked, and Melanie gave the question some thought. She didn't stop on the way home from anywhere in her day-to-day life with Monty. Considering they were always in a limo, it wasn't practical to swing through a fast food drive-in. Suddenly her options were unlimited, and although she rarely took time to concentrate on eating, she was surprised to realize she was ravenously hungry.

The strangest thing came to mind. "Tacos," she said matter-of-factly. "Is there someplace we could get really good tacos?"

Milo grinned as she pulled them onto the coast highway to head to Los Angeles. "I know just the place, and it's not too far out of the way. *Tito's Tacos* in Culver City." She laughed. "If you think the sunset was amazing, wait until you try one of these." Melanie loved the new enthusiasm in Milo's voice.

"Then, let's go," she said. "I'm ready to be impressed, but I warn you, they truly will have to be spectacular because so far, my evening has been perfect."

Chapter Twelve

After dragging all of Melanie's purchases, her suitcase, and the travel supplies Milo picked out up to the apartment, they finally settled at the table to enjoy the tacos. As Melanie tore open the bags, Milo went to the kitchen for drinks. "You want more bourbon tonight?" Milo called from the kitchen. "Or can I talk you into a beer?"

There was a long pause, and for a second, Milo thought Melanie hadn't heard her. Before she could ask again, Melanie spoke up. "I'm going to try drinking a beer," Melanie said. "But would it be okay to have it in a glass?"

Smiling at the woman's concession, Milo nodded. "I can do that," she called back. As much as she wanted to deny it, in her current frame of mind, she might be willing to do about anything for Melanie. The night had been fantastic, and although she knew in her heart the calm was all an anomaly, she would run with it. By dawn they would undoubtedly be back to their normal relationship of arguing and frustration. *I'll worry about reality tomorrow,* she thought. Five o'clock in the morning would come soon, and then they would go from there.

Walking into the living area, she set the beer bottles and the glass on the table before pulling up a chair. Melanie had a taco unwrapped in front of her. "I'm ready to be impressed," she said with a smile that Milo was already getting way too fond of seeing.

Returning the smile, Milo reached for a taco from the pile. "Go for it," she said and watched as Melanie took her first bite. Tilting her head as she chewed, the woman appeared to be genuinely savoring each flavor.

Finally, she nodded. "It's impressive," she said with a laugh, preparing to take another bite. "But to be fair, I can't think of the last time I've had a taco." Not waiting to comment, Milo took a bite of hers and was rewarded with the mixture of spiced meat, cheese, and warm corn tortilla.

Chewing the mouthful, she used the bottle opener on her keychain to pop the top on her beer and then Melanie's. "Why?" she asked after she swallowed. "You seem to like them."

As if to prove her right, Melanie finished the taco before answering and surprised Milo by reaching for another. "Because I usually only eat salads," she said, unwrapping the taco. "I would never normally do something like this."

Milo swallowed. "Like this?"

"Yes," Melanie said with a shrug. "Spontaneously eating tacos and drinking beer. We simply don't do that sort of thing."

"I see," Milo said, not sure she liked being a 'sort of thing' and took a long pull on her drink.

Clearly sensing something was wrong, Melanie stopped eating. "I'm sorry," she said. "I didn't mean for that to sound like a bad thing." When Milo didn't answer, she set down her taco and reached to touch Milo's hand. "Tonight has been wonderful, and I am grateful you let me have it." Nodding, Milo leaned back out of Melanie's reach and didn't reply but could feel the reality of their differences rushing back sooner than she anticipated. *I should have known better,* she thought. *She had a fun night slumming it, but it's not her world. This is my world. I was stupid not to remember that.*

Suddenly not as hungry, she pushed the taco aside. "I think I'm going to go to bed," she said. "I want to get on the road before dawn in the morning."

"Oh," Melanie said, a surprised look on her face. "Okay. You don't want to eat anymore?"

Standing, Milo picked up her beer and stepped away from the table. "I've lost my appetite," she said. "And I suggest you go to bed too. We need to make good time tomorrow." In one long swallow, she finished her beer, setting the bottle on the table. "And get you home."

Tossing and turning, Melanie couldn't get comfortable on the couch, making it impossible to fall asleep. She knew the discomfort wasn't the real reason she struggled. It was Milo. Something had triggered the woman earlier while they were eating, and she couldn't figure out what she said that caused it. Thinking over the conversation, all she did was tell her how grateful she was for a wonderful evening. *How is that upsetting? She's so incredibly touchy,* she thought, ending up on her back and staring at the dark ceiling only visible from the slivers of streetlight shining in around the blinds. *One moment, I catch her smiling, and as soon as she notices, I get a scowl.* The part that baffled her the most was the fact it bothered her so much. Normally, Melanie cared little about how other people around her felt. She never worried about Monty's feelings, and he definitely didn't worry about hers. But like in so many other ways, Milo was different.

Knowing she could never sleep without understanding the woman's sudden attitude change, Melanie decided to be bold. Grabbing up the blanket around her, she got off the couch and went to the closed door of Milo's bedroom. Before she could change her mind, she knocked gently. For a moment, there was no answer, and then the door was yanked open. In nothing but boxer briefs and a thin tank top, Milo stood in front of her. "What's wrong?" she asked, but Melanie couldn't form words yet. Even in the dim light, she could tell the woman's body was impressive. The loose t-shirt and jeans she wore during the day did not do her justice.

Finally dragging her eyes from exploring Milo's body, she looked into the woman's concerned face. "Nothing to be alarmed about," she said. "I wanted to talk to you."

The usual Milo scowl was back. "And it couldn't wait five hours?"

"No," Melanie said, pulling the blanket tighter around her. "It couldn't because I can't sleep until you explain to me what happened earlier."

Milo frowned. "I don't know what you're talking about."

Shaking her head, Melanie wouldn't let her blow it off. "I think you do," she said. "At dinner I said I was grateful for our wonderful evening, and then you stormed off. What was wrong with what I said?"

For a long minute, Milo didn't answer, and with the shadows, Melanie couldn't read the woman's eyes. "Let me show you something," she finally said. "Wait for a second." Before Melanie could respond, the woman disappeared into her room and returned with an old, dark green military duffle bag. She held it up for Melanie to see.

"Okay," Melanie said. "Your duffle bag. What does that mean?"

Milo gave it a shake and seemed to be getting angrier by the second. "In the morning, this is what I will be packing with my few things for the trip."

Trying to understand but quickly starting to dislike Milo's attitude, Melanie narrowed her eyes. "What is your point?"

"Come here," Milo said, taking Melanie by the elbow through the blanket and turning her around. She guided them until they stood before the large pile of things Melanie had purchased. There were a dozen plastic bags all heaped around her pretty, new suitcase. "Look at what you'll be packing." Milo looked hard into Melanie's face. "See the difference?" Furrowing her brow, Melanie was more confused than ever. *Why is my fancy suitcase making her mad?* she wondered. *She picked it out for me.*

"Honestly, Milo," she snapped. "I don't know what the problem is. If you wanted a new suitcase, why didn't you buy one?"

Throwing her hands up, Milo went back toward her bedroom, leaving Melanie standing in the middle of the room with no clearer idea of what Milo was freaking out about. "Exactly what I expected," Milo said. "Money is always your answer."

Suddenly, Melanie thought she understood, and she felt her cheeks flush with anger. "Oh, so is that it?" Melanie said. "You're poor, and I'm not, and somehow that means you can be rude to me?"

Milo stopped walking and stared at the carpet. In the dark, she couldn't see the ugly beige color or all the stains from previous tenants, but she knew they were there. A part of her overall crappy apartment, but it was all she could afford. *Is that what this is?* she wondered. *Am I bitter over her money and taking it out on her?* For a moment, she analyzed the question. Before Milo went to jail, her world was entirely different. She had a happy life with a woman she cared about, a brand new college degree, and even a little dog. *And now I don't have shit but some grand dreams that Melanie may or may not help happen.*

Trying to center herself, she let out a long breath. "That's fair," she said. "I was rude, and I'll work on that but let's keep one thing clear." She glanced over her shoulder at Melanie. "We're not friends. This is a business arrangement."

Melanie tossed her head. "You're right," she said. "I guess I forgot you're only doing this to get paid. Sorry I bothered you."

Obviously angry, she turned toward the couch but stepped on the edge of the blanket, pulling it off her shoulders. A sliver of the streetlight shined across the bare skin of her deep v-neckline with only two spaghetti straps to hold up whatever satiny-looking, beige nightgown she wore. Unable to help herself, Milo let her eyes linger on the perfect slope of the woman's shoulders, only to trail down to the lacy bow centered between her breasts. Even without Melanie trying, the look was sensual and inviting. In the next instant, Melanie regained her balance and pulled the blanket up to wrap around her again. Still, it was enough for Milo to realize that she might insist there would never be anything between them, but actually, she was playing with fire.

When Melanie wasn't angry or defensive, her attitude toward Milo bordered on... *What?* Milo thought, remembering the lingering touch on her arm while they watched the sunset and how Melanie reached for her at the table. *And she cared enough that she couldn't sleep because of me.* Unfortunately, Milo couldn't decide what all of that added up to or how to interpret it. If Melanie weren't some spoiled, filthy rich woman married to one of the wealthiest men in the world, Milo might believe there was chemistry between them. *But that's not only impossible, it's also ridiculous.* There was nothing Milo could offer her that could compare to what Melanie already had, which was pretty much everything. *All I can do is drive her safely to New York.* Making a new resolution, Milo would focus solely on that objective. No more sunsets or fun detours to buy tacos, but she wouldn't be a jerk about it either. She needed to find the right balance.

"Melanie," she said, taking on a gentler tone. "I won't lie. The money is important to me. I don't expect you to understand, but it will change my life." She took a deep breath to help her say the next sentence as honestly as possible. "I promise to try not to take things so personally going forward."

Melanie met her eyes. "Thank you," she said. "But you're wrong, Milo, I do understand how money can change your life. I'm not the person you think I am." Then she looked away. "I'm tired, and I know you'll be after me early tomorrow. So, goodnight, Milo."

Not sure what to make of Melanie's statements, Milo opened her mouth to ask more but stopped. The middle of the night was not the time to dig deeper into who the real Melanie was, and in reality, it didn't really matter. *Just a job*, Milo reminded herself again. *A business arrangement. Nothing more.* "Goodnight, Melanie," she finally said and left her alone in the living room to go to bed.

Chapter Thirteen

Waking to the sound of a shower running, Melanie peeked her eyes open. Milo had turned on a lamp on the end table, possibly to wake her but likely because, she could tell from the gap around the curtains, it was still dark outside. *God, what time is it?* she wondered, pulling the covers over her head. She felt like she could easily sleep for another twelve hours. Last night had been upsetting. Knocking on Milo's door to talk had been a mistake. Even after the woman pointed out the differences in their luggage, Melanie still didn't entirely understand how she set her off. After arguing with Milo and not understanding precisely what the problem stemmed from, falling asleep was nearly impossible. After hours of tossing and turning, she finally dozed off but had no idea when, and the hours didn't feel like enough. *But if I don't get up, she will come barging in here like some drill sergeant.* She sighed. *The last thing I want is another argument to start us off. Today will be long enough.*

Knowing no matter what she tried, Milo wouldn't take any excuses, so Melanie uncovered herself and sat up. Rubbing her eyes, she looked around the room. The leftovers from their tacos were still on the table. They had started delicious, but everything ended so unpleasantly. It made her a little sad to remember the wonderful evening watching the sunset only to have the progress erased with a random comment.

With a shake of her head, she let her gaze land on her adorable suitcase surrounded by blue plastic bags filled with items she only purchased out of necessity. She didn't really want them. Suddenly she was overwhelmed with what her life had come to in the matter of a few days. Forced to wear a cheap dress and stuck with a woman who didn't like her. The next few days on the road promised to be grueling. *Maybe I can sleep in the car all the way,* she thought at the same time as hearing the shower stop. *Oh great. Time to get growled at, but if she thinks I'm leaving without a shower too, she's got another thing coming.*

Yawning, she stood and went to the suitcase. *The least I can do is start packing*, she thought, kneeling to unzip the top. The mound of stuff felt overwhelming, and after grabbing a bunch of things she would need to get ready for the day, she threw the rest in the suitcase, plastic bags and all. The best she could do was hope that at one of their stops she would have time to organize things a little. After a minute, Milo came out of the bathroom in nothing but a long, brown terrycloth robe. "Are you taking a shower?" she asked in her usual blunt style.

Already frustrated with Milo's tone, Melanie bristled. "Yes," she snapped back. "If that's not too much of a delay."

Milo narrowed her eyes. "I'll give you fifteen minutes," she said. "And then we are hitting the road."

Standing, suddenly aware she left the blanket on the couch and was in nothing but her short nightgown, Melanie crossed her arms. Her attire didn't stop her from blasting back at Milo. "And if I'm not ready?" she said. "It's not like you can leave without me." The strangest look came over Milo's face. Melanie paused in her attack. After a moment, color rose to the woman's cheeks, and she looked at the ground. *What in the hell was that?* Melanie wondered, feeling even more self-conscious. *Is she embarrassed because I'm half naked?* She scooped up the shopping bag filled with her clothes for the day and hid behind it. "I'd like to take my shower now."

Clearing her throat, Milo nodded. "Okay, and you're right, I can't leave without you," she said in a more neutral tone. "But I would like to leave soon." Looking up, Milo met her eyes. "I think that will be the best for both of us."

Angrily shoving clothes by the handful into the duffel bag that sat on the end of her bed, Milo could not believe how she had acted when Melanie stood up wearing next to nothing. She couldn't even remember what she said before retreating to her bedroom and closing the door. Once alone, she had leaned her back against the wooden surface, closed her eyes, and tried to calm her racing heart. *I can't believe that just happened,* she thought. *What is wrong with me?* Melanie was obviously embarrassed by how Milo looked at her while she stood, exposed in her nightgown. But Milo's physical reaction was instantaneous, and she could not stop the heat that flashed through her. Melanie had looked so sexy yet vulnerable. *So desirable.* Milo rubbed her face with her hands. Apparently, every one of those thoughts and emotions showed on Milo's face because the woman had tried to hide behind a plastic shopping bag. *I've got to get myself under control before I make her even more uncomfortable.* The whole thing was ridiculous.

Even though it had been a long time since she had sex, that was no excuse to keep reacting like she was toward Melanie. Yet, as hard as she tried, something about the woman drew Milo like a moth to a flame. The situation frustrated and baffled her. *And she has no idea she is doing this to me,* Milo thought. *No doubt she would be horrified to learn how I'm feel-*

ing. The night before, as Milo lay in bed and reflected on the times Melanie touched her, she realized she was reading too much into them. Some people were huggers and touchers, and it meant nothing. Although it surprised her a little, apparently Melanie was one of those people.

With a growl, Milo zipped her duffel bag. Packed, it was time to load the cooler and make sandwiches for the road. Not only because they needed them for the trip, but she wanted the distraction. Yet when she left her bedroom, and she heard the shower running, Milo's mind tried to circle back to the smooth, almost satiny look of Melanie's soft skin. *Hell no,* she thought and mentally slammed the lid on the line of thinking. *No more. Not only is it torturing me, but it isn't fair to her. She has no idea how I feel.* Striding to the kitchen, she channeled her thoughts into making something for the trip. Yanking the bread and peanut butter from the cupboard, she started slapping sandwiches together.

After a moment, she caught herself and looked at what she made. The sandwiches were so pathetic, Milo chuckled. *I need to add jam at least,* she thought with a snort. *Not that it really matters how I make the sandwiches.* They weren't anything fancy, and she guessed Melanie would never eat one. Lowering herself to eating tacos last night was a spur of the moment decision, but a PB & J would never fly. *Unfortunately, I don't have lobster and caviar, so she'll simply have to deal with it.*

Feeling her frustration returning, Milo pulled the cooler out of the closet and began to wonder how long she should give Melanie in the shower before she knocked on the door and told her to get out. *We don't have all morning*, she thought. Then the shower suddenly turned off, and Milo raised her eyebrows. It was much shorter than she expected. Imagining Melanie was used to lavish walk-in showers with spa treatment, she expected a battle to get her to come out. *Maybe this start won't be so bad after all.*

. . .

Coming out of the bathroom with her hair still damp but in a long, blonde braid, something Melanie hadn't done since she was a teenager, she saw Milo wiping off the table. All the remains of the taco feast from last night were gone. There was also a small cooler and duffel bag near the door. The woman had been busy and looked ready to go. "How much longer?" Milo asked. "I don't want to get stuck in any LA traffic."

"I'm actually ready for the most part," Melanie answered. "If I can talk you into going through a Starbucks drive-thru so I can get some coffee. I imagine that will be faster than waiting for a pot to brew here."

Milo took the dirty paper towel into the kitchen. "We can do that," she called. "I could use some coffee myself."

Pleased they were actually on the same page for a change, Melanie smiled. "Thank you," she said, putting her few items from the bathroom into her suitcase. The contents were still a mess, and she regretted being so hasty in throwing everything inside. *My clothes will be incredibly wrinkly*, she thought with a sigh. Hopefully, they would stay someplace where there was at least an iron. Then, realizing what she was thinking, she laughed a little to herself. *Look what I've come to, braiding my hair and hoping for an iron. I might as well be in a little house on the prairie.*

"What so funny?" Milo asked, and Melanie shook her head.

"I'm just ready to go."

"Good. That makes two of us," Milo said, picking up her duffle bag. "I'm going to put everything in the car, and I'll be right back."

"Do you need help?" Melanie surprised herself by asking. She couldn't think of the last time she carried her own suitcase anywhere.

Evidently, the surprise showed on her face because Milo grinned. "Let me handle it," she said. "And don't worry, I won't expect a tip."

Just happy to see a smile, Melanie didn't take offense at Milo poking fun at her. "Since I haven't got a dime on me," Melanie said. "That's a good thing, which makes me think I should have a little allowance if I want to buy something."

Milo's smile quickly disappeared. "We'll talk about that in the car," she said as she walked out the door loaded with everything. Rolling her eyes, Melanie picked up the small handbag she had purchased at the megastore off the couch. It was cheap imitation leather and cost almost nothing compared to her least expensive purse at home, but it was black and would go with whatever she decided to wear. In reality, she didn't need it, but Melanie was used to having a place to put her lipstick and a few necessities. She had stashed the cellphone Milo purchased the morning after Melanie arrived in it. *I wonder if the batteries are dead*, she thought, realizing they hadn't used it for over twenty-four hours.

Taking the phone out, she saw that the thing had shut off. Melanie paused. If there was still power in the battery, she could turn it on and call Monty again. *Maybe he's calmed down by now*, she thought, and all the craziness could be over in a minute. Pushing the button, she started the phone. *It's the right thing to do. I'll still pay Milo but not make us suffer through her driving me to New York.* As the screen lit up, she saw there was a text message. There was only one person it could be from and with a shaking hand, Melanie pressed the screen to open the message. It was the number she suspected with a three word message.

"Call me now."

Nothing else. Only the one abrupt text. No apology or anything to say he missed her or was worried. *Just giving me an order*, she thought. *Like he can boss me around from three thou-*

sand miles away. Suddenly, she no longer wanted to call him. Instead, she powered the phone back down and stashed it in her purse just as Milo came into the apartment. "All set," she said. "Is there anything left you need to do?"

Melanie shook her head as she slung the purse strap over her shoulder. "Absolutely nothing," she said and followed Milo out the door.

Chapter Fourteen

Lasting longer than Milo thought she would, Melanie made it as far as the California border before she fell asleep. Not that Milo minded. Things were a little awkward once they were underway. Milo wasn't a talker by nature, and Melanie was especially quiet, as if lost in thought. For a little while, Milo considered asking her if she was okay but then let it go. If Melanie was upset about anything, Milo likely was the reason anyway.

Luckily their early morning start meant there was almost no traffic, and once they were beyond the outskirts of Los Angeles, the drive was smooth sailing. Considering how long her ass would be in the driver's seat, she was thankful the Cadillac rode so well, but a few things were lacking. For one, the radio was an old AM original. Not that she would mind listening to some of the more retro stations, particularly country music, but she had a feeling once Sleeping Beauty woke up, she might not be such a big fan. *There I go making assumptions again*, she thought. *Melanie could like any kind of music and might surprise me.* Milo had been surprised already that morning. The simple dress, the long, yellow braid down her back, almost no makeup—all caught her off guard. By far, the woman beside her was not the glitzy and glamorous woman she found in the alleyway in the short, black cocktail dress and high heels.

Another problem with the car was it was a gas guzzler. As she filled up the twenty-five-gallon tank, she was glad her payoff would be substantial because the drive would be expensive. *We'll make up for it by staying in cheap hotels,* she thought, already knowing there would be a fight over that news, but she wasn't willing to give the woman a choice. Sleep in the hotel or sleep in the car.

Seeing a sign for Phoenix sixty miles ahead, Milo contemplated if they should get gas again. The needle showed they were down to a quarter tank, but the problem with Interstate 10 was the long stretches of freeway without many cities. The last thing she wanted was to run out of gas and have to hike.

The final problem with the Cadillac was the lousy heater, although she was thankful it was only October and not July because the car didn't have air conditioning either. Even though Arizona was a warm state, the early mornings in fall were cold. Melanie had even shivered a few times in her sleep. Milo tried to get the heater to work harder but with little success, and the cabin stayed chilly. At least the sun was finally up, and hopefully the car would get warmer.

Seeing a sign for a large gas station, Milo changed lanes to take the next exit, and Melanie raised her head. "Where are we?" she asked with a yawn as she glanced around. "Looks like we're in the middle of nowhere."

"We kind of are," Milo said. "Although the city of Phoenix is coming up soon."

Melanie shifted on the seat. "Thank God for that," she said. "My butt is numb, and I need to pee."

Milo pointed to the large orange and brown sign high in

the sky. "I'm taking us to one of these big truck stops where the gas is cheaper," she said. "You can pee there."

"Thank you," Melanie said. "How is the driving? I can't believe I fell asleep."

"You've been asleep for about two hours," Milo said with a smile.

Glancing over, she saw Melanie's eyes widen. "Two hours?" she asked. "Milo, I'm so sorry."

"It's fine," Milo said with a chuckle. "Although you snore."

Eyes even wider, Melanie shook her head. "That's not true. I do not snore," she said, sounding only half convinced.

Pulling up to one of the pumps, Milo grinned at her. "You're right," she said. "You were quiet as a mouse." Unfastening her seatbelt, she started to get out to fill the tank. "Go ahead inside to find the restroom. I'll park when I'm done here and come find you."

Walking through the sliding glass doors, Melanie was both impressed by the size of the gas station's store and thankful to see the large, overhead sign pointing to the restrooms. She couldn't believe she had slept for two hours while Milo drove them halfway across Arizona. *Some copilot I am,* she thought as she used the facilities. *I should buy a couple of magazines or something to flip through while we travel so I at least stay awake.* Then she remembered that she didn't have any money and sighed. *Assuming Milo will let me have some cash.* They were supposed to discuss the topic of Melanie having her own money on the drive, and now that she was awake again, it would be a good time to settle a few things. Milo might be in charge of the trip but she wasn't allowed to make all the rules.

Washing her hands, Melanie looked in the long mirror over the row of sinks. In the reflection, she noted there were two other women in the room. One was brushing her teeth at the furthest sink, and another was only two sinks over with a toddler who she tried to get to wash her little hands. Neither paid any attention to Melanie. *And why would they?* she wondered. *I'm nothing but another person stopping to use the restroom.* They would have no way of knowing the last time Melanie traveled across the country, it was in a private jet. She wasn't exactly dressed like a billionaire's wife anymore.

Focusing on her own reflection, she turned her head left and then right, feeling a little naked with so little makeup. Somehow it made her look a little younger though. Fresher. *I wonder if Milo likes it?* she thought and frowned. *But why would she even notice?* Once again, the random ideas about the woman driving her across the country confused her. *How many more clues do I need to get the message she isn't interested in getting to know me?* With a shake of her head, Melanie turned off the water. Milo could be looking for her already and staring into the bathroom mirror trying to find meaning in everything wasn't going to solve any of her problems.

After drying her hands, Melanie wandered back into the store area of the gas station, more than a little amazed at the selection of things. Everything from toiletries, to t-shirts, to car parts. A regular one-stop shop. Keeping an eye out for Milo, she wandered the aisles until she reached a wall of colorful brochures. The display advertised any number of things—small local attractions like a hotel room where Elvis slept, to helicopter rides over the Grand Canyon. Pulling out one of the many brochures relating to the majestic national landmark, Melanie was surprised to see Phoenix was only a short blue line away from it. The national park was another place she hadn't visited, and a part of her wanted to see the famous grandeur. Plus, the pictures of the little cabins on the front of the glossy, color pamphlet looked quaint and inviting. *Maybe a little on the rustic side*, she thought. *But I'm on an adventure, so why not visit the national park, see the famous views, and stay there tonight?*

As she considered how to broach the subject with her grumpy traveling partner, Milo appeared at her shoulder. "There you are," she said. "Did you use the bathroom?"

"Yes," Melanie said, turning to face her. She held up the Grand Canyon brochure. "I want to stay in one of these cabins tonight."

Milo simply stared at her as if Melanie had spoken in a different language. "No," she finally said, plucking the pamphlet from her hand. Without even looking at it, Milo stuffed the thing back into one of the slots on the wall. "Not going to happen."

"Now, wait a minute," Melanie said, pulling it back out and showing Milo the little map. "It's just up the road."

"No, actually, it's not," Milo shot back. "Don't be fooled by that picture on the back. The Grand Canyon is at least three hours away."

Melanie was quiet for a moment while she considered what Milo said. "Have you ever even been to the Grand Canyon?" she asked, deciding three hours out of a week of traveling to see something beautiful was worth the effort.

She watched Milo grit her teeth. "No, I haven't," she growled. "And I'm not going to today either. We are going to El Paso, Texas. Case closed."

Hearing the words, Melanie froze at the mention of the giant state. "We're going to drive through Texas?" she asked softly. "You never told me that." Feeling a trickle of dread, she started to shake her head. Texas was the last place in the world she wanted to go, and Milo would have to tie her up and drag her there before she would step one foot in the state again. "I won't go there with you."

. . .

Scratching her head, Milo realized Melanie had lost her mind. One second, she said she wanted to go to the Grand Canyon of all places, and then she claimed to be unwilling to travel through Texas. *And from the look in her eyes, I can tell she's not bluffing*, she thought. Still, there wasn't any way around it. She chose the route to avoid any chance of bad weather further north. Even in October, the Grand Canyon could be under a foot of snow. Unfortunately, Melanie sounded like she was tricked by the announcement. "What do you mean I didn't tell you?" Milo said, pointing to a giant USA roadmap painted on the wall of the store. "I told you we were taking Interstate 10. The freeway goes right through the middle of Texas."

Color coming to her cheeks, Melanie pointed at the map too. "How was I supposed to know that?" she snapped. "Look at all those blue lines. I didn't know which one was the ten or I would never have agreed."

"Agreed?" Milo said, feeling her face getting flushed. "You're making it sound like I asked you. I'm the one doing the driving, and we will go where I choose."

Shaking her head, Melanie held up the Grand Canyon National Park brochure again. "Not only are we not taking your way, but we're instead going here." She lifted her chin. "Or I'm not getting back in the car, and our deal is off."

Doing her best to keep her voice down, else they alert the entire truck stop of their disagreement, Milo stepped closer. "And then what would you do?" she said with a glare. "Hitchhike?"

Not flinching from Milo's look, Melanie took a step closer too, until she had to crane her neck to see into Milo's face. "If I have to, then yes," she said. "I'm pretty sure one of these truckers will be happy to earn all that money." Unable to believe the woman's stubbornness, Milo could only stare into the woman's beautiful, but quite angry, blue eyes. Melanie didn't blink.

She heard someone clear their throat nearby, breaking the standoff. "Excuse me," an elderly, gray-haired man with a cane said. "If you're done looking at the brochures, I'd like a peek."

Breaking the staredown with Melanie, Milo looked at him. "Sorry," she mumbled, stepping back to let him through. "We're done."

Melanie turned to the older man. "Have you been to the Grand Canyon?" she asked and was rewarded with a broad smile.

"I have," he said, pointing to the brochure in her hand. "Just came from there. I've been a lot of places in my life, but that was one of the most marvelous things I've ever seen."

Milo closed her eyes, unable to believe she heard his answer. *Now Melanie will never let this go,* she thought, and when she peeked, she saw the woman looking right at her. "That's what I thought," she murmured, a smug smile on her face. "I can't wait to see it."

The man nodded. "A good time to go," he said. "No snow to worry about yet and a beautiful drive up through Flagstaff."

"I see," Melanie said, as Milo watched her move closer to the giant map on the wall. After searching for a second, she pointed at Flagstaff, Arizona. "And what blue line is this going through there?"

Milo shook her head, knowing she was losing ground every second, and answered before the stranger could. "Interstate 40."

"And?" Melanie said with a tilt of her head.

Knowing to accept defeat when she had to, Milo sighed. "And yes, it will take us in the direction we need to go."

Chapter Fifteen

Riding with Milo as they made their way north of Flagstaff, Melanie wished she could think of a way to get the woman to talk to her. Ever since the stop for gas and the argument in the store, she hadn't said a word. The silence made Melanie uncomfortable and having Milo mad bothered her more than she would have expected. Usually, when she would get into a fight with Monty, how he acted afterward didn't faze her. He could sulk around all he wanted; she didn't care. Even when he first courted her years ago, she hadn't really taken the man's feelings into consideration. If he bought her something she found too gaudy or impractical, Melanie would turn her nose up at it, no doubt frustrating him. She didn't feel concerned. Monty was wealthy, powerful, and wanted a trophy wife. Melanie had no problem with that arrangement, seeing no reason to involve emotions in the decision. Riding beside Milo, Melanie wondered at the lack of respect she and her husband had for each other. *What am I doing married to a person I am not sure I even like and certainly hardly even talk to?* she wondered, narrowing her eyes. *But even more interesting, why do I suddenly care?* Everything felt so confusing.

Not until after stopping at the South Rim Station to pay the park fee did she refocus on their surroundings. As Milo followed the signs to the Grand Canyon visitor's center, she watched out her window, loving how the thick stands of evergreens and rocky scenery looked more stunning the further north they traveled. The only issue was the car's heater, or more precisely, the lack of one that worked. As they climbed higher in elevation, the outside air temperature dropped. Melanie had no idea how low, but there was frost in places along the road's edge. Without a word, Milo had given up her coat for Melanie to use across her lap. At first, used to being pampered, she took the offering, but slowly Melanie felt selfish keeping it with the temperature dropping. When Melanie could see her breath, she knew Milo had to be freezing. "You should take back your coat," she said, and Milo shook her head, not saying a word. "Damn it, Milo, you don't need to be so stubborn." As much as she hated to give up the warm coat, Milo didn't need to suffer. "It's cold, and I can see goosebumps on your arms. Take your coat."

"I'm fine," Milo said. "Keep it."

Melanie frowned. "No," she said. "You're not fine. It's freezing cold, and you're only acting this way because I talked you into going to the Grand Canyon."

Barking out a laugh, Milo glanced at her. "Talked me into it?" she asked. "Is that how you see it?"

"Well, I persuaded you then," Melanie said, feeling a hint of remorse at how manipulative she had been. "I am sure it will be worth taking the time." Milo didn't reply and Melanie sighed. "Okay, I wasn't totally fair to you, but this trip is likely my one shot at seeing it. Aren't you excited to see the landmark too?" When Milo still didn't respond, Melanie let out a frustrated breath. "You are so obstinate, Milo—" She stopped, intending to use Milo's full name but realizing she didn't know it.

When Melanie stopped midsentence, Milo glanced over a hint of alarm on her face. "What?" she finally asked. "Is something wrong?"

Melanie tilted her head. "Nothing is wrong. I just don't know your last name," she said, and Milo narrowed her eyes.

"It's Milo," she said. "Why?"

Melanie was surprised. "Wait," she said. "Milo is your last name? What's your first name?"

Glancing at Melanie again, Milo frowned. "I don't understand why you're asking," she said. "Just call me Milo."

"Oh, come on," Melanie said, glad the woman was at least talking again. "Is it bad or something? Do I have to guess?" She tapped her chin with her forefinger. "Let me see... What do you look like...?" Then she laughed. "Is it Bertha?"

Shaking her head, Melanie could see Milo actually fighting a smile. "Hey, Bertha's a good name," she said. "My great grandma was named that. But no, it is not."

"Well, then what is it?"

Shaking her head, a look of resignation on her face, Milo sighed. "Elizabeth," she said. "Okay? Happy?"

Smiling, Melanie nodded. "Very," she said. "It's nice to meet you, Elizabeth Milo."

After finding a parking space and a quick trip to the visitor's center, Milo followed Melanie down a wide, well-maintained path toward an overlook. The woman's excitement was contagious, and as much as she wanted to pretend seeing the Grand Canyon wasn't a big deal to her, she was excited too.

When Melanie first brought up wanting to go to the Grand Canyon, making the detour was the last thing Milo expected to agree to that morning. Somehow the woman had outmaneuvered her with the help of some stranger, and there they were, about to reach the famous Mather Point. According to the info at the visitor's center, in a minute they would see one of the most breathtaking views of the park. Milo wasn't so sure standing at the rail along the canyon's edge with a dozen other people to see the famous view from the South Rim could be special. Picking some spot heavy with tourists was not how she expected to see the majestic landmark for the first time. *Although I honestly don't know what I was expecting*, she thought. If she was truthful with herself, pretty much everything felt upside down and out of control since Melanie came into her life. *And why is that? How can she have such an impact?* They arrived before she could analyze what it was about the woman that knocked Milo off-kilter. "Oh, Milo," Melanie whispered as she went to the rail. "Can you believe this?"

Joining her, Milo was suddenly speechless as she looked at the vista. She had seen pictures of the Grand Canyon in her travel books and thought she knew what to expect, but real life changed everything. Gripping the rail while she stood beside Melanie, Milo looked out at the view of different hues of browns, tans, and rusty reds. It was impossible not to find the landscape awe-inspiring as she thought about how the majestic scenery was something slowly carved over centuries. Because it was growing late in the day, long shadows from the slowly setting sun added even more depth and texture to the mosaic of colors. While she stood there trying to take it all in, she felt Melanie touch her hand. As if by instinct, Milo intertwined their fingers. Somehow, in the midst of so much beauty, holding Melanie's hand seemed the most natural thing in the world to do.

"Thank you for bringing me here," Melanie murmured. "I know you didn't want to, but I hope you see what I see."

Unable to help herself, Milo nodded. "You were right,"

she whispered, not wanting to spoil the moment. "This was worth a detour." Others around them appeared as amazed as she felt, and many held up cellphones to take pictures. Families took turns taking photos of each other in front of the canyon. A few couples framed selfies or asked other tourists to photograph them. Watching, Milo suddenly wished she had a camera to capture the moment too. Maybe even have someone take a picture of her standing with Melanie. Then, realizing what she was thinking, she froze. *Have I gone crazy?* she wondered, feeling Melanie's warm hand clasped with hers. *A memento of Melanie and me? Like we are some sort of couple?* Knowing her thoughts were beyond foolish, she pulled her hand away from Melanie's and looked at her watch. "We need to go."

"Oh," Melanie said, clearly surprised at the abrupt transition. "Already? We just got here."

"We did what you wanted," Milo said, ready to join a few others starting the walk back to the visitor's center parking lot. "It's getting late, and I don't want to try driving these curvy mountain roads in the dark."

Melanie didn't take a step. "That wasn't the plan," she said, stubbornness in her tone. "We are staying the night up here. No more time on the road today."

Milo stepped aside to let others pass before walking to Melanie. She didn't intend to make a scene but allowing Melanie to make the plans had to stop. Immediately.

Melanie could tell by the look on Milo's face that the woman was getting angry. It was such a transition from the hand-holding a second ago, she wasn't quite sure what happened. *And now she wants to leave after five minutes,* she thought, frustration mounting. Indeed, the detour was for Melanie. *But this is so beautiful. And I could see by the look on Milo's face that she loved the view too*. The woman was so stubborn she wouldn't admit how she felt. *That probably explains the hand-holding too.* Milo acted like she had been burned, and her entire attitude changed. *Can this woman be any more confusing?*

Before Melanie could challenge her, Milo pointed. "Listen," she started. "You got your way, and now I'm going to get mine. We need to get back to Flagstaff at least so we can jump on your Interstate 40 first thing in the morning."

Lifting her chin, Melanie wasn't ready to give in. "How far is that?" she asked. "I don't have any way to tell time, but it felt like it was far."

Milo scowled. "It's about an hour and a half," she answered. "But will be more if I have to do it in the dark." Biting her lip, Melanie thought about what Milo had explained. Ninety minutes wasn't bad, but knowing what she did about Milo, they would stay at some low-end hotel chain. Part of the reason to come to the Grand Canyon was to stay overnight and absorb more of the grandeur of the place. *Maybe even find a nice spot with a view of the canyon to wake up to,* she thought. *Surely, they have them.*

Finally, she crossed her arms. "No," she said. "I don't want to do that. I want to stay here tonight."

"What do you mean 'no'?" Milo growled, stepping closer. "Why do I keep getting the idea you don't understand the purpose of this trip?" Pausing, Melanie considered the woman's statement and began to think she was acting foolish. Even if she did appreciate the view, Milo evidently didn't want to be at the Grand Canyon with her.

Everything was about getting to New York and earning her money. "I understand the purpose of this trip," Melanie shot back. "So you can get rid of me and get your big payout to start your own adventures."

Milo looked surprised and shook her head. "You make it sound like you don't even want to go home."

Heat rose to Melanie's cheeks. "Of course, I want to go home."

Milo looked hard into her eyes. "Are you sure?" she asked, and their stare held for a beat. A million thoughts ran through Melanie's head as she considered what Milo asked her. *Well?* she thought. *Do I?* Feeling more upset and confused by the second, Melanie finally looked away into the distance. She took in the beauty of her surroundings and tried to understand her feelings.

After another moment, she nodded. "I do want to go home," she repeated. "But I want to stay one night here." When Milo didn't answer, she glanced back. Milo's hazel eyes stared at her, but there was no way to read what the woman felt. *And maybe I don't even want to know,* Melanie thought. *Maybe my guess she only wants to be rid of me is correct.*

Milo narrowed her eyes. "And then you promise to cooperate?" Milo finally asked, and Melanie sighed, never liking the feeling of giving up control but knowing she had no other choice.

"I promise."

Chapter Sixteen

Melanie immediately took control of the situation and marched them up the path to the visitor's center. Knowing when she was beaten, Milo went with the flow. She still couldn't understand how she ended up not only at the Grand Canyon but now spending a night there. At the speed they were going, it would take them forever to get to New York. And that would cut into the time she had planned to enjoy on her own during a leisurely drive back. *But am I not enjoying myself?* she wondered. *Didn't I find the view as majestic as I would have alone?* To be honest, Milo wasn't sure if she would have stopped there on the way back. She had considered the park too touristy, but in the end, the extra delay was worth the detour. Admitting that fact to Melanie was a different story altogether.

Back at the visitor's center, Milo entertained herself strolling the displays of how the Grand Canyon was carved by something as simple as flowing water while Melanie asked the desk about places to stay. As Milo wandered back to the main doors, Melanie was lost in conversation with the volunteer behind the counter. After looking at a map with their heads together, plenty of pointing and drawing, plus a phone call, Melanie finally smiled. Milo overheard her thanking the woman. As she walked in Milo's direction, she beamed. *Why do I feel like this will be something I don't want to hear?* Milo thought as the beautiful woman approached her. *Although anything that makes her eyes light up like that might be worth it.*

"I have just the place," Melanie said, falling into step beside Milo as they headed for the exit. "It's up the road a little bit, but I have a map." She held it up for Milo to see like a prize that would lead them to buried treasure. "Are you ready?"

Milo snorted a laugh. "That's a loaded question," she said. "But as ready as I'm going to be."

"Don't be grumpy," Melanie said, swatting Milo's arm with the map. "The place I found is one-of-a-kind."

"Whoa," Milo said, slowing down. "What do you mean by one-of-a-kind?"

Melanie tilted her head, giving Milo an impatient look. "I know you understand what I mean by one-of-a-kind."

Frowning, Milo stopped. "Just how much is this one-of-a-kind going to cost me?"

"Now, Milo," Melanie said, playfulness returning to her tone. "Keep an open mind. I promise it'll be worth every penny if the woman behind the counter was telling the truth. Let's go see."

With a shake of her head, Milo followed Melanie to the car. As she started to climb in, her stomach grumbled. They hadn't eaten much the entire day, and she suddenly realized she was ravenous. "I don't suppose this place you're dragging me to would have a restaurant?"

Melanie's eyes twinkled. "They do," she said. "And room service."

Milo paused as she was putting on her seatbelt. "Oh, hell no," she said. "This place is way beyond our budget."

"Since when did I agree we had a budget?" Melanie said with a laugh, but when Milo met it with a glare, she sobered. "Don't worry. I promise in the end you'll get plenty of money for your hard work."

Letting out a frustrated breath, Milo started the car. *How do I keep getting talked into things?* she wondered, leaving the parking lot. Slowing at the first intersection, she looked at Melanie. "All right, Magellan, which way do I turn?"

Melanie bit her lip as she looked at the map, running a finger over where the volunteer had drawn in orange highlighter. "Well, if we're here now..." she said, frowning.

Trying not to laugh at how adorable Melanie looked while concentrating on the map, Milo held out a hand. "May I look at your precious map?" she asked, unable to hide a grin.

Melanie gave her a glare but then relented. It took Milo a few seconds to orient where they were on the map, but then she saw the circled building. The place looked less than ten minutes away, but she didn't like the name. El Tovar Hotel. It sounded fancy and even worse, expensive. Glancing up from the map, she was about to tell Melanie they weren't going. Then her eyes met the woman's hopeful blue ones, and she sighed before putting on her blinker to make the turn.

Although she wasn't quite sure what to expect from the few pictures in the brochure at the visitor's center, the hotel had even more character than she had imagined. From the outside, the El Tovar Hotel looked like a grand Midwest mountain lodge crossed with a Swiss chalet. As Milo parked the car, Melanie clapped her hands. Initially, she thought a quaint, rustic cabin would fit the setting best, but when the volunteer described the turn-of-the-century hotel's unique charm, Melanie knew she had to go there. "We're staying here?" Milo asked, and Melanie nodded.

"Yes," she said. "Isn't it fabulous? And they said they have rooms available when I had the woman at the visitor's center give them a quick call."

As she got out of the car, Milo growled. "Of course, they do."

Melanie followed suit. "Come on now," she said. "Doesn't this look like the perfect place to sit on the rim of the Grand Canyon?"

Milo grabbed their stuff. "If you say so," she said, still grumbling as she took one bag in each hand. Although she seemed perfectly capable of easily carrying both, Melanie paused. She wasn't sure what to do, but the last thing she wanted was for Milo to feel like her porter.

She held out a hand. "I can take mine," she said, pointing to the pink and polka-dotted suitcase. "It rolls."

"I've got it," Milo said. "Let's just get this over with."

Melanie rolled her eyes at the woman's attitude as they started walking toward the entrance. "Even you have to admit this place looks fun," she said, but Milo didn't comment. Beginning to second guess herself, Melanie pushed them through the front doors only to stop. Together they paused as they entered the large reception area. The sloped ceiling of dark-stained wood rose over a great room with matching hewn logs making up the walls surrounding a wood floor polished to a golden shine. A fireplace filled one corner and was lit to help warm the grand space. Armchairs were in groups scattered around the room where tourists sat visiting. Melanie watched as Milo let her eyes drift around the room.

Finally, the woman gave a curt nod. "It'll do."

Melanie raised an eyebrow. "It will do?" she asked hiding

her relief Milo liked the hotel. "Now you sound like me. Don't forget I'm the one who usually lives in the lap of luxury."

Her eyes still scanning the room, Milo gave her a half smile. "I guess you're rubbing off on me."

Feeling an unexpected pleasure at the words, Melanie hugged Milo's arm. "Let's go check in," she said, turning toward the long reception desk.

A young man dressed in a suit with a name badge on his lapel greeted her with a smile. "May I help you?" the hotel receptionist asked.

Reading the badge, Melanie returned the smile. "Thank you, Devon," she said. "Someone from the visitors center just called and asked if you had any rooms."

"Ah, right, Grace called," Devon said, turning to the terminal beside him. After a few taps of the keys, he nodded. "Yes, we did have a last-minute cancellation. Very lucky for you. This balcony suite has our best canyon view." Melanie was delighted. Enjoying a cup of coffee in the morning while taking in the scenery sounded perfect.

After a smug glance at Milo, Melanie returned her attention to Devon. "That sounds wonderful," she said. "And the second room?"

The man paused, a look of confusion in his eyes. "I'm sorry," he said. "I misunderstood when Grace called because we only have one room. Only the suite."

"How many beds?" Milo asked from behind her.

Looking a little flustered at the bluntness of Milo's question, Melanie watched the hotel receptionist swallow hard. "It has one king bed. But it also has a couch."

"That'll work," Milo said. "How much is it?" Melanie braced herself. She already knew the answer and expected Milo was about to blow her top. Hopefully, the woman would do it quietly and not make a scene.

Devon cleared his throat. "Five hundred and twenty-five a night plus tax." Melanie watched Milo out of the corner of her eye. The woman stood there with her lips in a tight line.

She repeated the number back. "Five hundred and twenty-five dollars. Plus tax. For one night." Melanie held her breath. After a beat, Milo set down the duffle bag and suitcase and reached in her back pocket to pull out her wallet. "And let me guess, you won't take cash."

"No, ma'am," the man said. "Only credit cards."

Milo handed the receptionist her credit card. "Of course."

"Thank you," the young man said, all smiles again. "Let me call you a bellman."

Even as Melanie rushed to look out the large sliding glass doors that faced the canyon, Milo couldn't get past the immediate problem with the room. Although there was plenty to like—a fireplace, a giant television, a king-size bed behind glass paned French doors, and the promised couch. A very small couch. *A glorified loveseat at best,* she thought, wondering how exactly she would cram her six-foot frame onto it. *I think the floor will be better.*

Melanie glanced over her shoulder at her. "Milo, you've got to come to look at this," she said. "It's breathtaking. Not quite as good as Mather's Point, but almost as beautiful." She paused, clearly noticing Milo's unhappy face. Milo watched her scan the space as if searching for the problem until her eyes landed on the tiny couch. "Oh." Her eyes drifted to Milo's. "You can have the bed," she said. "I can sleep on that. I'll fit."

"No," Milo said. "This place was your idea. You can have the bed, and I can sleep on the floor."

"The floor? No," Melanie started, but Milo held up her hand.

"Not open for discussion."

113

Melanie closed her mouth, apparently considering if she should continue to argue. *But hopefully she won't,* Milo thought. *Because it would be nice to merely relax tonight.* "Well, at least come look at the view," she said, and after putting down the luggage, Milo joined her. "What do you think?"

Milo shook her head in disbelief. Even in the fading daylight, the view was spectacular, just like the room. "I think this is the nicest place I've ever stayed in my life," she said before snorting a laugh. "Of course, it's also the most expensive, but I can honestly say I've never been in a place like it.

"Well, I'm glad you approve," Melanie said. "And you know what I want to do before it gets completely dark?"

Milo looked at her. "What?

A smile lit up Melanie's face, and Milo couldn't keep from feeling her heart tug at the look. *She's so happy,* she thought, already knowing whatever the woman asked, she would give it to her. "I'd like to have a glass of champagne while I'm wrapped in a blanket on this balcony," she said. "I'm going to call room service. Will you have some with me?"

Milo tried not to process what it might cost to have someone bring them a bottle of champagne. "Champagne? Is that what you want to drink?"

"Yes, when I celebrate something as amazing as this view, I do."

With a sigh, Milo looked out the window, seeing the canyon's beauty. "Then let it be so," Milo said, deciding tonight she would go with the flow. *Let it be special,* she thought. *I'll never have a room like this again, and certainly not with Melanie Sotheby.* "And order whatever you want to eat." *And I better remember to call my credit card company to ask for them to raise my limit.* "While you do that, I'm going to try the shower."

Melanie laughed. "I can guarantee it's bigger than the one

in your apartment," she said as she walked toward the phone on the nightstand. "What would you like to eat?"

Milo paused on her way to the bathroom door, lifting her gaze to look at the ceiling as she pondered the question. "A really big steak," she said. "Medium rare." Then she went to take a shower.

Chapter Seventeen

By telling room service to bring the champagne immediately and not wait for the food, Melanie already sat on the room's balcony enjoying a glass. Unfortunately, the drink was going straight to her head. Possibly because she hadn't eaten all day, or maybe simply the higher altitude, but it was happening. *Probably a combination of both*, she thought, but even after only one glass, she felt fantastic. Milo was smiling too as she sat wrapped in her coat, looking skyward. Following her gaze, Melanie sucked in a breath. The night sky had darkened to an almost blue-black, covered in stars. "I've never seen anything like it," she whispered, taking in the magical canopy. "There's so many."

Milo slowly nodded. "Me either," she said. "Seeing all those stars helps me."

Melanie still looked skyward. "How so?"

"I realize we are small compared to the universe," Milo said before adding quietly. "And maybe I shouldn't worry so much." Trying to take the multitude of what she saw in, Melanie could understand what the woman meant. There was so much beyond the trivial things she concerned herself about. Like trying to find the perfect pair of shoes to go with another twelve hundred dollar dress she didn't need. *But there's more to life than that,* she thought, surprising herself. Shopping was her existence, or at least it had been. The last few days put everything into a different perspective. *And what is Milo worried about?* She leaned closer to the woman, wanting to ask her for more, but suddenly Milo changed the subject.

"It's freezing," she said, clearly wanting to avoid any deep conversation tonight. "You want to go back in?"

"Do we have to?" Melanie asked with a shake of her head. "I know it's cold, but this is so lovely. So quiet. With the stars and it's just..." Her voice trailed off. *It's just I don't want this moment to end. Especially with her.* A part of her wanted to explain sharing the experience with Milo was a big part of what made it special.

"The view of a lifetime," Milo finished for her, starting to stand.

"Wait," Melanie said, raising her empty glass. "I want to propose a toast to tonight."

After a beat, Milo settled back in her chair. "You know, I don't really drink champagne," she said. "Except maybe once or twice at a New Year's Eve party. I don't remember it tasting this good."

Melanie laughed. "Don't look at the hotel bill in the morning." For a moment, Milo's face darkened, and Melanie was afraid she had crossed the line. Then the woman threw back her head and laughed, making Melanie's eyes widen. The sound was authentic and deep and the last thing she expected. *Is it the champagne affecting her too?* she wondered. *Or is she finally letting down her guard with me?*

After another minute, the woman sobered, shaking her head. "You are going to be the end of me," Milo said, lifting the champagne bottle and pouring more into each glass.

"Or I'm good for you," Melanie murmured, and Milo stopped pouring, holding the bottle in midair for a moment.

Slowly she set it on the table. "Why would you say that?" Milo asked quietly.

Suddenly embarrassed about her bold statement, Melanie shrugged. "It seemed like you needed a change in your life, and fate brought me into it."

Milo furrowed her brow. The moment went so long that Melanie felt like she had to say something when suddenly the woman nodded and raised her glass. "You may be right."

Following suit, Melanie raised hers. "Then let's toast serendipity," she said, and after a pause, Milo clinked the glasses together and both sipped. The moment held, and Melanie wanted to reach out to touch her. *And do what?* she wondered, unable to deny how drawn she was to Milo.

Before Melanie could act, there was a knock at the door. "Finally, the food is here," Milo said, sounding slightly relieved as she got up. "I'll answer it." And Melanie was left alone under the stars.

As she laid her knife and fork on the empty plate, Milo knew she might be in trouble. She hadn't felt so good in a very long time. *Five years?* she wondered. *And why exactly is that the case?* Before they sat on the balcony and drank champagne, Milo enjoyed a long hot shower lathering with soap that likely cost more than she spent on soap in a year. The water had streamed down like rain, relaxing her tense muscles. Then there was the champagne, which she considered a girly drink, but currently the alcohol was kicking her ass. Especially since they had ordered a second bottle and drank most of it too. The food was incredible as well. The steak was cooked exactly how she liked it, and the baked potato tasted perfect—flakey and hot. All were things she could claim were the reason she felt so wonderful, and they were a part, but not all. The largest part was because she sat across from a woman who made her heart beat faster. Milo had girlfriends in the past, even one she believed she loved. *But the chemistry was never like this*, she thought. *I don't even know what to compare it to.* When Milo went to jail, her girlfriend deserted her. Ever since she was out, she hadn't taken the time to try to meet anyone. *And then fate dropped her into my lap.*

As if feeling cozy too, Melanie yawned. "Sleepy?" Milo asked, a beat before the reality there was only one bed suddenly came rushing back. *Calm down,* she told herself. *I'm going to sleep on the floor.*

"A little," Melanie answered. "It's been a long day." Then she paused before touching the back of Milo's hand. "A long, wonderful day."

Trying not to let the heat from Melanie's touch distract her, Milo gave her a half smile. "Good," she said. "Because tomorrow we are not taking any detours."

Shaking her head, Melanie sighed. "Okay, okay. No more detours," she said, then met Milo's eyes. "But I need you to know something, Elizabeth Milo. No matter how this end, you have changed my life. For the better. Thank you."

Unable to help herself, Milo covered the woman's hand with her own and relished the warmth of her skin. "You're welcome," she said and felt heat blooming inside her in a way that scared her. She needed to throw the brake, or she might make a complete ass of herself. *Just because the woman is grateful for you taking her on an adventure doesn't mean that she wants anything other than friendship*, she thought. *Calm down.*

As if to prove Milo was right, Melanie leaned across the table to give her a friendly peck on the cheek before pulling her hand away. "I think I'll shower and then try to get some sleep," Melanie said, getting up from the table and stretching. "I'm exhausted."

"It's an amazing shower," Milo said. "I think I'm going to lay down. I want to start early in the morning again."

Melanie rolled her eyes. "You want a lot of things, so we'll see," she said with a little wave and then disappeared into the bathroom. Surprisingly not frustrated by Melanie's unwillingness to cooperate, Milo stacked the dishes and set them in the hall to be picked up. When she turned around, all she could see was the bed. It seemed to loom even more prominently than before. Then she glanced at the hardwood floor, with only a small area rug. *It will have to do*, she thought. *I've slept on worse*. Then she pulled one of the pillows from the bed, a decorative blanket from the couch and lay down. She tried not to think about Melanie in the shower and closed her eyes as if she could force herself to sleep.

As she slipped into the terrycloth robe the hotel provided, Melanie's good mood continued. A hot shower was exactly what she needed. After washing her hair with the lodge's fabulous smelling shampoo and shaving her legs with a complimentary razor, it was the first time she felt genuinely bathed since she stepped out of the limo. Wrapping her hair in a towel, she suddenly realized there was a problem. In her excitement to shower, she hadn't brought anything into the bathroom to put on for sleeping. Her suitcase was still in the other room. With no choice but to go get something, she hoped she wouldn't wake Milo if the woman was already asleep. Yet when Melanie crept into the main room, she saw one small light still burning and Milo on the floor.

"Milo," she said, louder than she intended and the woman flinched. Melanie covered her mouth. "I'm sorry. I didn't mean to startle you, but you are not sleeping there." Walking to the bed, she grabbed a pillow to put on the couch. "You sleep on the bed, and I will sleep here. It's no different than your apartment."

Milo rolled onto her back and looked at Melanie. "I refuse," she said. "I don't mind sleeping on the floor."

Putting her hands on her hips, Melanie could not believe how stubborn the woman could be. "I mind," she said. "Please get on the bed."

With a sigh, Milo climbed to her feet. "I'll try the couch."

"You're too tall for that, and you know it," Melanie said. "Why do you always have to be so difficult?"

Milo raised an eyebrow at her. "I'm the one who is difficult?"

"I'm not," Melanie replied in a sweeter tone. "Just because I always get my way doesn't mean I'm difficult. It just means I'm skillful."

Milo shook her head, moving past her to the couch, but a smile played on her lips. "Skillful," Melanie heard Milo mutter under her breath as she plumped the pillow on the couch and looked prepared to lay down. Not giving up, Melanie plucked the pillow off the couch and tossed it on the bed. Watching it land, a possible solution struck her—they could simply share the large bed. *Am I crazy?* she wondered. *I don't even sleep with Monty. But this is different, right?* Not ready to explore her line of thinking, she could see no better alternative. "Milo, I have an idea," Melanie finally said. "The bed is big enough for the both of us, so I think we should sleep in it together."

Milo froze where she stood by the couch. "What did you say?" the woman asked without looking at her.

"I'm saying if you stay on your side of the bed, I'll stay on mine," Melanie said, forcing herself to sound more convincing than she felt. "And everybody gets to sleep on the bed and be comfortable." For a second, Milo didn't say anything and then her shoulders slumped as if in defeat. Not sure how to read the body language, Melanie moved closer, looking into her face. Milo's eyes were closed. Melanie touched her arm. "Why does that upset you so much?"

Milo sighed and opened her eyes to meet Melanie's. "Because I have to be honest," she said. "I'm attracted to you, Melanie. No matter how hard I try, I find it's impossible not to be."

"Oh," was all Melanie said, trying to get her head around what Milo had confessed. "Okay."

Rubbing a hand over her face, Milo stepped away as if needing space. "You're sexy, and stubborn, and damn it," she said. "And there's something about you that draws me."

"I didn't realize," Melanie whispered, her heart racing, and an unmistakable tingle ran through her body at the confession. Milo was attracted to her, and it was both thrilling and scary at the same time. A part of her wanted to admit she felt it too, yet another part threw off warning signals. There hadn't been time to decide what her feelings meant. Milo was a woman, and although that didn't necessarily matter, she had never considered being attracted to a woman before. She stared into Milo's serious hazel eyes. "But what are you saying? I can't trust you if we share a bed?"

Milo threw up her hands. "Of course you can trust me," she said. "I won't move an inch, but I don't want you to think I tricked you."

Oh, Milo, I'm not sure who is tricking who, Melanie thought, but instead of explaining, she put on a smile. "We will be fine," she said. "Now, let me get to my suitcase, and then we can both go to sleep."

Chapter Eighteen

Relaxed and incredibly comfortable, Milo didn't want to open her eyes. She never remembered her bed being so soft or her blankets so warm. Plus, there was a sweet smell in the air around her, like flowers, but subtle. With a sigh, she started to nestle down deeper when suddenly, something moved in her arms. In an instant, the real world came rushing back. Somehow, against all her plans, she was in bed snuggled under the covers and holding Melanie. The night before, even after Milo's big confession, the woman insisted she get into the bed with her. Knowing Melanie wouldn't take no for an answer, she obliged. Her intention was to let Melanie fall asleep and then return to the couch where she belonged. *Apparently, I fell asleep too*, Milo thought, not daring to move and risk scaring Melanie. *So, what do I do now?* There was no way she could slide her arms from around her, and at any second, the woman could wake up. When she realized Milo was touching her, there was no telling what she would do.

As she saw it, there were two options. Milo could wait and let Melanie keep sleeping, hopefully moving away without ever noticing. The other was waking Melanie and explaining it was an accident. Wavering back and forth, the sudden tension in Milo's body made the decision for her. Melanie's even breathing stopped, and she could feel the woman holding perfectly still. "Milo?" she whispered, making Milo swallow hard.

Here we go, she thought, bracing herself. "I'm awake," she answered, more than a little surprised Melanie hadn't sprung out of bed yelling yet. "I promise, this wasn't intentional."

"Okay," Melanie said softly. "Is it time to get up?"

Based on the lightness of the room, Milo thought it was morning already. "Yes," she said. "I'd like to get started." Suddenly rolling toward her, Melanie looked into Milo's face. The woman was rosy-cheeked, and her eyes were sleepy but still bright blue.

Amazingly, she smiled rather than freaked out. "Good morning," she said. "Can I order breakfast from room service first?"

Tempted to give in to her charms, Milo hesitated before smiling. "No," she said. "But nice try."

"Hmmm," Melanie hummed, and Milo had to grit her teeth to not react to the sexy sound. *It would be so easy to kiss her right now,* she couldn't help but think. *And what would she do if I did?* Milo didn't like the different reactions that came to mind. Getting out of the bed immediately was the best thing. Starting to extract herself, Milo was surprised when Melanie grabbed her shoulder. "Wait." She bit her lip, and her eyes lingered on Milo's mouth. "I remember what you said last night, and I'm not sure how I feel about it, but..." Her words trailed off for a second, but then Milo saw something come into her blue eyes. "Would you kiss me if I asked you to?"

Her heart racing, at first Milo didn't know how to react. *Is this a test?* she wondered. *Or an experiment?* Things could get so complicated if she kissed Melanie, but then instinct took over. "It's probably a bad idea, but I would," she answered.

Melanie took a long time before she replied, and Milo considered letting the question go and getting up. Even when she moved away, Melanie didn't let go of her shoulder. "Then kiss me," Melanie finally said.

Throwing caution to the wind, Milo lowered her face until their lips met. Melanie's kiss was everything Milo could have ever imagined. Warm, soft, and inviting. It was hard not to want more, but after a moment, Milo pulled back. "Well?" she asked, and Melanie's answer was to put her hand behind Milo's neck and pull her down again. That time the kiss held more heat, making Milo feel her entire body tighten. She wanted her, and if they kept kissing, she might do something Melanie wasn't ready for yet.

When Milo lifted her head again, Melanie sighed. "You're an amazing kisser, Milo," she said. "I think I could do this all day."

Milo swallowed hard, not sure how to respond. As if her concerns were on her face, Melanie laughed. "Don't worry. I won't ruin your driving plans."

"It's not my driving plans I'm worried about," Milo said before she could stop herself. "You have no idea what you do to me."

Melanie touched her cheek. "No, I suppose not," she said. "But that gives me something to think about in the car, now doesn't it?"

As they continued to head east, Melanie watched the landscape change from mountainy to flatter with fewer trees. Although, to be honest, she wasn't seeing much of it as her mind kept returning to the kisses. Milo's mouth fit perfectly with hers. The woman's lips were soft and warm, but a cautiousness let her know Milo had been restraining herself some. *And if she hadn't?* Melanie wondered for the hundredth time. *Where would things have gone?* That was the big question. She had to admit, the kiss had made heat form in her stomach, with a tightness low on her body that wanted to try more. The physical reaction to being intimately close to Milo surprised her. *When was the last time I was turned on with nothing but a kiss? Ever?* Even thinking about what happened was arousing her in ways she couldn't quite explain.

"Melanie," she heard Milo say softly. "We need to talk for a minute."

Turning from her gaze out the passenger window, Melanie hoped the blush she felt from thinking about Milo wrapped around her didn't show. "What about?" she asked, guessing that after riding a few hours without speaking, the woman would want to address the elephant in the room. *Or, in this case, the backseat,* Melanie thought, suppressing a smile, not sure Milo would understand her humor.

In answer, Milo surprised her by pointing to an oncoming freeway marker. "That is what I want to address," she said, and Melanie squinted to see what Milo referred to on the green sign. Then she saw words that bothered her greatly. They were nearing Albuquerque, New Mexico, which was fine, but the next city listed was Amarillo. As in Amarillo, Texas. The city was still three hundred miles away, but there could only be one reason Milo pointed it out. She wanted to go there.

Looking at Milo, she saw the woman kept stealing glances in her direction. "Are you saying there isn't another way than to go through Texas?"

"Well..." she started, and Melanie could see the reluctance on her face. "Honestly, not really." She sighed. "It's too soon to start north and risk hitting snowy weather. We need to keep going on the I-40 a little longer."

Melanie looked at her hands, thinking through the information. "I understand," she said, then raised her gaze. "You probably think I'm being foolish about this."

Furrowing her brow at the statement, Milo shook her head. "I don't think that," she said, then hesitated. "Or at least I don't now."

Loving the fact Milo was always painfully honest, Melanie had to laugh. "Oh, before this morning, you thought I was crazy?" she asked. "Everything changes with a kiss?"

Watching her, Melanie saw the woman blush. "No, I'm not saying that exactly," she said. "I was thinking through what you said in Phoenix and didn't want to take you into Texas without a discussion." Melanie studied Milo's face for a beat before unhooking her seatbelt and sliding across the wide seat until she was beside the woman. Clearly surprised, Milo looked at her for a second before refocusing on the road. "What are you doing?"

Finding the belt for the middle seat, Melanie clicked in before snuggling against Milo's body. "I want to sit beside you," she said. "Is that okay?"

"Are you cold?" Milo asked, sounding confused and something else. *Excited?* Melanie wondered. *Do I have that kind of effect on her?*

"Yes, this heater sucks," she admitted. "But that's not the only reason." When Milo didn't respond, Melanie leaned her head softly on the woman's shoulder. "If we go to Texas, I need your support."

Trying to keep the car on the road as her body melted from the sweet cuddle from Melanie, Milo didn't know what to think. First, the request for kisses in the morning, followed by her moving closer in the car, gave off all kinds of signals. More than anything, Milo wanted to make sure she didn't misinterpret them. *What other way could she mean it?* she wondered, still unable to grasp that a woman like Melanie Sotheby could be interested in her. *Talk about being out of my league.* There was plenty for Milo to think about later, but at the moment, she wanted to understand Melanie's dislike of Texas. "Is this something you can talk about?" Milo asked the woman beside her. "Or should I just leave it alone?"

Melanie sighed. "I can talk about it," she said. "And don't think something horrific happened to me because this isn't like that."

Loosening her tight hold on the wheel, Milo let her body relax a little at the news. To be honest, she had been thinking the worse. "Okay," she said. "So, why do you hate Texas?"

"Oh, that's a long explanation, but mostly because I was raised there in a dusty, smelly map-dot town in the middle of nowhere," Melanie answered. "And I swore when I left, I would never go back. People laughed at me for saying that. They made fun of my dreams and said I was foolish to think I could make something of myself." She gave a wry laugh. "But I showed them."

Milo nodded. "I think I follow you," she said. "But have you been back?"

"Only twice," Melanie replied. "Once when my daddy died and then again when my mother passed away." She lifted her head, and Milo could see out of the corner of her eye that Melanie stared hard out the windshield, almost as if seeing into the past. "I don't know why I bothered, though. They never wanted me, mostly because I wasn't a boy, but also because I was unexpected. My parents had me late in life, so I never remember them as anything but old."

Hearing the tinge of hurt in Melanie's voice, Milo gently slipped her arm around the woman. She was rewarded with a sigh as Melanie rested her head on Milo's shoulder. "Do you have any family left there?"

"Yes," was all Melanie said for a long time, but Milo didn't press. She could tell the woman had a lot to process, and they had nothing but time. Not until they were on the other side of Albuquerque did the woman sit up and answer Milo's original question. "A sister," she said in a matter-of-fact tone. "But we don't talk." Milo thought about what she said. She didn't have siblings, and her parents lived in San Diego. Although they took the news hard when Milo went to jail, everyone still talked to each other. *What would that feel like?* she thought. *To not be wanted because you're not a boy. To not talk to your sister.* Clearly it hurt Melanie a lot if she hated Texas enough to avoid it at all costs. If the woman honestly didn't want to cross that border, they would find a way around it. Before she could offer the idea to Melanie, the woman squeezed her arm. "We can go to Amarillo if that's the best route. Do we have to spend the night there?"

"We don't have to," Milo said. "We can drive straight through and sleep in Oklahoma."

"Oklahoma," Melanie said with playfulness back in her voice that Milo was glad to hear. "I never thought I would be happy to sleep in that state but thank you."

"You're sure?" Milo asked. "There are smaller roads we could use. The route will take a lot longer, but it's not impossible."

"I'm sure," Melanie said, nodding. "You can stay on the interstate. But let's not stop, okay?"

Milo pulled her in a little tighter. "We will stop for gas before the Texas border," she said. "Then it's pedal to the metal until we reached the other side. Deal?"

"Deal," Melanie answered, resting her head on Milo's shoulder again.

Chapter Nineteen

Snuggled against Milo, Melanie rode with her eyes closed, neither asleep, nor entirely awake. Simply riding along after the stop they made in Tucumcari, New Mexico for gas and, on a whim, buying a colorful Native American woven blanket. When she asked Milo for it, the woman had only hesitated a second. "You'll need that when we turn north," she had said. "Go ahead and get two."

Riding along now, she wasn't cold but had it over her and Milo's lap for comfort more than anything. Traveling through Texas, she needed all the reassurance she could find. When they were half an hour into the state, she felt Milo put a hand on her leg. The contact seemed to burn through the blanket, and Melanie held her breath. Whatever the woman intended, no matter how innocent, had her feeling tingles all over. "Melanie," Milo whispered. "Are you awake?"

"Mmm hmmm," was all she could muster between the sleepiness and the arousal, and she heard Milo chuckle.

"I'm not so sure I believe you," she said. "But I need to turn on the radio. The weather is turning ugly fast, and I would really like a local forecast." A little alarmed at not only

Milo's request but the tone of her voice, Melanie's eyes popped open. Looking through the windshield into the fading daylight, there wasn't much to see other than flat land. Rain had started a slow patter on the glass. Even for late in the day, the sky was too dark.

Trying to ignore the warning signs ingrained in her from her childhood, Melanie nodded. "Okay," she said, letting Milo reach past her to turn on the small AM radio in the dash. The thing crackled to life with nothing but static. Melanie leaned forward to take the dial. "Let me try." As Milo put her hands back on the steering wheel, Melanie slowly twisted one of the knobs, but it only made the static louder. Trying the other, she first landed on a preacher shouting bible verses, reminding her far too much of how she grew up. Church every Sunday, and prayers over dinner and before bed were the least of it. Her mother always had a bible verse ready when Melanie screwed up. Quickly turning the dial, the next station was classic country and western music with all the guitar twangs and sappy melodies of life gone wrong.

Finally, she found a weatherman, and his first words made her hand freeze. "...and there's a tornado watch for Oldham and Potter counties. Local officials ask everyone to take proper precautions and find appropriate shelter."

"Oh God," Melanie whispered, as one of her worst fears was coming true. In North Texas, thunderstorms and tornados were a serious threat. Although she never saw an actual funnel touch down as a kid, she heard plenty of horror stories. Her chest tightening with anxiety, she looked out the windows and saw they were in the middle of absolutely nowhere. There wasn't a building in sight. Melanie fought back her panic. "Do you know what county we are in?"

Milo shook her head. "No idea without looking at the map," she said. "And I'd rather not stop. We should keep rolling and get past all of this."

KC LUCK

"Okay," Melanie said, but she wasn't convinced getting away from the storm would be so easy. She knew from having nothing else to listen to as a teenager that AM stations could broadcast for hundreds of miles, but her instincts told her they were in danger. Squinting her eyes, she continued to scan the horizon, but the darker the sky became, the more impossible it was to see. All she did know was rain had started pounding the windshield, and the wipers were doing a pathetic job of keeping up. Even if they didn't need to take shelter from tornados, they did need to stop somewhere. There was no way Milo could see. "Do you know how far the next town is?"

"I don't know that either," Milo answered. "Not for sure. I think it was a place called Vega, but I can't think where it was on the map. I expect it's not much of a town." Melanie understood. When she was a kid, her hometown was on the map, but had nothing to offer a lost traveler. There were no hotels. Hardly even a restaurant unless they wanted to brave the only greasy spoon diner. All the memories made Melanie shiver. *It's because we are in Texas*, she thought while her stomach ached. *This state has it in for me.*

Although making sure to show nothing but confidence, Milo was worried. The rapid change in weather caught her off guard. A native of southern California, her world was predictable. Seventy-five and sunny. When it did rain, cities were paralyzed, but even the hardest rain shower in LA didn't compare. She simply wasn't used to what was happening around them. The wind threatened to push the big car off the road, and only because the interstate was straight as an arrow was she able to stay in her lane. The Cadillac's old suspension didn't help. With each gust, the vehicle rocked. Hearing the radio announcer mentioning tornados, Milo was sure they were in the wrong place at the wrong time.

When Melanie asked what county they were in, Milo didn't outright lie, but she had a pretty good guess. The answer wasn't pretty. If the weather forecast was correct, they were smack dab in the center of the danger zone. Finding shelter was her only focus. Unfortunately, with the dark skies and pounding rain, seeing anything beyond the car's weak headlights was quickly becoming impossible. She had no idea what to do and realized if anyone had experience with tornado warnings, it was Melanie. "I can admit it," Milo said, swallowing hard but keeping her voice calm. "I don't know what to do next. Keep driving? Find a bridge to get under?"

For a moment, Melanie appeared flustered, as if she was overwhelmed by the situation, and then a look came over her that Milo had never seen. The damsel in distress act disappeared and she was all business. "No. Never that. If you see any turnoff, take it, even if it's dirt, because out here it will probably eventually lead to a farm or a ranch."

Milo nodded, slowing the car so she could see something like that coming up while praying no other vehicles came racing up behind her. After a few minutes, a dirt road shot off to the right. "Here?" she asked, and Melanie nodded.

"Take it," she said. "But go slow. These dirt roads can have serious potholes." Slowing to turn right, Milo understood. The last thing they wanted was to blow a tire or, even worse, break an axle. They needed the car to be drivable for another seventeen hundred miles.

Gripping the wheel, Milo eased the old car onto the side road that she realized was quickly growing muddy. "Are you sure?" she asked. "We might get stuck if this rain keeps coming down."

"We're okay," Melanie murmured, still leaning forward with a hand on the dash to stare out the windshield. Milo couldn't be sure if she was saying the words because they were true or it was wishful thinking, but she kept going. Suddenly, the woman grabbed her knee in a vice grip. "I see something."

Not sure if the announcement was good or bad, Milo's mouth went dry. "Something as in what? A tornado?"

Melanie started waving as if to make Milo go faster. "No," she said. "A barn I think."

Following her gaze, Milo made out the faintest outline of a large structure in the dark. "I see it," she said and pushed on the gas.

"Hurry," Melanie said, not taking her eyes off the windshield.

As if to reemphasize the woman's words, the radio announcer started his spiel again. "The weather advisory urges anyone outside of appropriate shelter to seek it immediately. Tornados have been spotted across Potter County."

"Shit," Milo said, daring to make the Cadillac go faster as it bumped and bounced over the rutted and muddy surface. The barn loomed in the distance, and she had no idea if there was a way for them to get inside, but deep down, she believed it was their only hope.

Melanie never professed to know much, but she did know she didn't want to die tonight. Not out in some North Texas patch of brown dirt especially. She left the state with all intentions of never returning, and to die there would be an insult. Continuing to look out the windshield, she watched the barn grow larger. There was no way to know if livestock filled the thing, or if it was empty, or quite possibly abandoned altogether, but it would work as a port in the storm. It was a hell of a storm too. The Cadillac's wipers were no match against the pounding rain. Wind rattled the entire car, making Melanie worry the convertible's cloth rooftop would blow off entirely. The old luxury car wasn't designed for a tornado. If they were caught and a funnel hit them, it would be game over.

Thankfully, Milo was confident behind the wheel, and if the woman was afraid, she didn't show it. It was precisely the backbone Melanie needed, and for a brief second, she wondered how Monty would handle the situation. *Probably be a blathering idiot,* she thought. *Although he would never be the one driving across this godforsaken plot of land.* Strangely, Melanie didn't have regrets about being where she was with Milo. Maybe she should have been in her giant four-poster bed in the mansion on Long Island instead of facing a storm, but fate placed her in Texas with a woman in a classic car in the middle of a tornado warning.

As they reached the barn, Melanie noticed the doors were shut. *Please let them be unlocked,* she thought as Milo rolled to a stop. The woman acted like she was ready to get out, but Melanie grabbed her arm. "I'll do it," she said, already sliding across the bench seat. "You be ready to drive in."

"Are you sure?" Milo asked. "It's pouring."

Thinking of all her hours spent in the rain back on her family farm, Melanie almost laughed as she remembered her father's saying—you're not made of sugar, you won't melt. "I'll manage," she said and climbed out of the car.

The wind grabbed the car door, yanking it out of her hands and making her wrestle it closed. Milo helped by reaching across the seat and grabbing the handle. "Be careful," she yelled a second before the door slammed. Melanie had every intention of being careful but also efficient. There was no way in hell she was letting the storm win. Running to the barn's tall double doors, she nearly wept when she saw the hasp for the lock was empty, and she could open the doors. With all her strength, feeling a splinter from the barn's old wood scrape her palm, Melanie grappled the first door open. It slid back on its rails with a screech, for a second seeming as if it wouldn't open far enough, but Melanie threw all her five-foot-two frame against it. Slowly, the door gave, and she stepped aside as Milo drove through. In a flash, the woman was out of the car and helping her close the door.

With the howl of the wind dampened and feeling at least somewhat more protected, Melanie slumped against Milo's sturdy frame. "Tell me everything will be okay," she whispered. "That we are okay."

Milo wrapped her arms around Melanie and held her close. "I promise," she said before kissing her on the top of her head. "Come on. Let's get in the car and try to rest. We can sneak out in the morning."

Chapter Twenty

Spooning front to back, the backseat of the Cadillac fit them surprisingly well. Although Milo had to bend her legs, it worked to coil around Melanie's much smaller body. Trying hard not to let the closeness between them distract her from the danger of the situation and Melanie's need for comfort, Milo lay still. The woman shivered whether from being chilled because of the rain or from fear, Milo wasn't sure, and she did her best to soothe her. With an arm curled around the woman, keeping her tight against her body, Milo wished she could do more. At least they had the blankets to fight off the cold and help provide some calm.

"Talk to me, Milo," Melanie whispered. "Tell me a story or something. I'm so scared."

Blinking with surprise at the unexpected and challenging request, Milo racked her brain for a topic. "Well," she started. "I'm fresh out of stories, I'm afraid." She hesitated, unsure if it was the time or place to make confessions. "But I can explain why I went to jail."

Melanie was quiet for a moment before pulling Milo's arm harder against her. "Yes," she said. "Tell me that one."

Checking in with herself one last time to ensure she truly wanted to talk about her stupidity, Milo took a deep breath. "I was twenty-three," she said. "And fresh out of college with a great job prospect lined up."

"What did you go to college for?" Melanie asked. "What degree I mean."

Milo chuckled. "Brace yourself," she said. "But I paid a lot of money to the state of California's higher education system to get a degree in English Literature."

"Really?"

"Hey, don't sound so shocked," Milo said but didn't take offense. The way she looked with short hair, muscular physique, and blue collar job, seeing her as a scholarly type well versed in literature was a stretch. "I had high aspirations of becoming the next great American novelist. Or at least an editor for some big publishing house."

Quiet for a moment, Melanie seemed to be genuinely considering what Milo said. "You know, when I think about it, I can absolutely imagine that," she finally said. "Now that I know you more. I would love to read something you've written."

Milo sighed. "Don't hold your breath," she said. "I lost my notebooks when I went away."

"What? Why?"

Recalling the past, Milo felt a hard tug of regret. "My girlfriend at the time didn't see a point in keeping them," she said. "My parents came and picked up some of my personal effects but never thought to ask for those." She sighed, deep with remorse. "So, they were lost."

As if sensing the pain Milo felt to her core over that loss, Melanie rubbed a thumb back and forth over Milo's hand. "I don't know what to say," she whispered. "I kept a diary when I was a teenager. I wrote all my innermost thoughts, poems, even my dreams in it. My mom read it and found out I hated living in Texas and all the things I wanted to do." She let out a wry laugh. "After grounding me for my 'disrespectful thoughts' toward the family and community, she made me watch as she threw the diary into the burn barrel the next day." She snuggled into Milo. "That was hard to deal with, but in your case, I am sure it was beyond devastating."

Taking a deep breath, Milo forced down the hurt she thought she had dealt with years ago. "I try not to think about it."

"Do you still write?" Melanie asked, and Milo shook her head.

"No. I haven't written anything since before I was locked up," she said. "I was afraid to be vulnerable in jail, so I never put my thoughts on paper." She shrugged. "And since then, I've simply not felt the desire to be creative."

Even though the story had only just begun, Melanie already felt sad for Milo. She knew what it felt like to have a person's lifelong dreams fall apart. Although looking back, hers were more on the improbability side so she should have known better. Still, after enough people told her how beautiful she was, the fantasy of being a supermodel set in. When she moved to New York and never looked back, she was confident everything would go as planned. It hadn't, and even though she landed on her feet and married a wealthy man, it still hurt to know she would never be what she wanted. But in her mind, Milo still had a chance at her dream. *It doesn't matter if you've been in jail to be a writer*, she thought. *Or maybe even an editor if you did it freelance*. There was plenty to talk about on the subject. *But not tonight*. Instead, she waited patiently for Milo to continue.

Milo was quiet for so long Melanie thought maybe she had fallen asleep—a feat that seemed impossible in Melanie's mind as the wind continued to rattle the barn around them and rain pounded on the shingles. As if reading her thoughts, Milo snuggled a little closer. "Sorry," she said. "I got lost in my memories."

"That's okay," Melanie said. "And if you don't want to continue, I understand. Some things are too personal to share." She hesitated. "Especially since we've only known each other for less than a week."

Milo hummed as if thinking through what Melanie said. "Yes, they are personal memories," Milo said. "But I feel very connected to you, and maybe it's time I share." Suddenly, a loud boom of thunder made Melanie jump. Listening to Milo had distracted her from their situation, but her heart pounded again.

She felt Milo kiss the top of her head. "We're okay," she said softly. "Just some thunder."

Melanie swallowed hard but then nodded. "You're right," she said. "Keep telling me your story. It helps, and I want to hear the rest."

"Okay," Milo said. "Although I'm having trouble finding the words."

"Well, you are twenty-three and fresh out of college and ended up with a felony on your record. Connect the dots for me."

Melanie felt Milo take a deep breath. "Right, thank you. That makes it easier," Milo said. "So, I have a cousin. Mickey. And he was kind of my best friend for a few years." She shook her head, but Melanie could hear the amusement at the memories in her voice. "And wow, did we do stupid stuff when we were together. Super juvenile."

"I think we all did some stupid stuff growing up," Melanie said with a smile, remembering some of her exploits of skipping school to go smoke cigarettes and sneaking out at night to toilet paper houses.

Adjusting a little on the seat, Milo settled in before continuing. "I think you're right," she said. "But we never really were caught, and in the end, it was all good fun. Eventually though, we grew apart when we started high school. I didn't hear from him until after I'd gone to college, and he went into the Army. Then we started emailing back and forth and renewed our friendship. He was going to get married to a nice girl he met in Italy, and I was graduating with a bachelor's degree. Everything looked good."

A sliver of unease crept into Melanie. "That does sound good," she said, not sure if she should press for more, but wanting to know what happened too. "And then?"

Again, Milo was quiet for a long time, but Melanie was patient. "A few days after I graduated, he came home on leave for a week," Milo finally said. "We planned to meet at a restaurant for dinner, but he came by the house my girlfriend and I were renting because he said he had a surprise."

Melanie's stomach clenched, knowing somehow it was the surprise that led to the disaster in Milo's life. Pressed against Milo, she felt the woman's body tensing from the memories. "It's okay, Milo," Melanie whispered. "I'm listening."

Milo let out a long breath. "Of course, I went along with him. After all, I just graduated and felt I warranted a surprise. We went outside to the curb, and there was a sparkling, silver convertible Corvette. It looked brand-new with the top down. My dream car."

Milo remembered the car like it was yesterday. The thing was exactly like she described a few times in her emails. For some reason she didn't put together how unlikely it would be for Mickey to have one in his possession. She remembered what he said. "Want to take it for a spin?" She recalled the big smile on his face. "It's beautiful, right?" he said.

"It's gorgeous," I said, walking around the vehicle to take it all in. I could already imagine cruising down Sunset Boulevard in style.

Mickey had nodded and said, "Let's go."

"I climbed behind the wheel," Milo said. "And Mickey got into the passenger seat, and we drove away." Milo recalled how the engine purred and the feeling of being surrounded by power. "The desire to go fast was impossible to resist." She sighed. "Remember, I was twenty-three."

Melanie closed her eyes and thought of her past. "I remember being twenty-three," she said, trying not to think about the sacrifices she made at that age to become the woman she was now. "You drove too fast?"

"Oh yeah," Milo answered. "Once we got on the freeway, I took that baby up to a hundred and ten. Blasted through traffic, nearly causing accidents. Then a cop saw us, flipped his emergency lights on, and wanted me to stop." Milo's chest tightened, reliving the decision that was a life changer. "But instead, I thought I could outrun them."

"Oh, Milo," Melanie whispered against her arm.

"Don't worry, it's probably not what you're thinking." Milo let out a small laugh, but there wasn't any humor in it. "It's more of a twist ending. No one got killed, and I didn't hit anything if that's what you're worried about."

"I was a little," Melanie said. "Keep going. I need to know the ending."

Milo nodded. "I shot off a freeway exit hoping to get lost downtown. Of course, by then they called in reinforcements, and it wasn't long before the much more experienced drivers of the LAPD boxed me in." She clenched her fists, remembering how she thought it was all in good fun at first. "I was laughing, not understanding what I had done, and I pulled over. Things got serious fast."

"I'm sure they weren't amused," Melanie said. "Cops

rarely are." Thinking back, Milo remembered how afraid she was when the police pulled their guns and screamed for her to get out of the vehicle and on the ground. "It was right out of a TV show. Surrounded and cops pointing guns at me. Everybody was yelling. But I did what they said."

Melanie shook her head. "I can't imagine how scary that was for you," she said, and the tenderness in her tone helped Milo push down the anger at all of it building up.

"They handcuffed us, read us our rights, and threw us in the back of two different squad cars," she said. "By then I was a little pissed. I thought their actions were extreme, and I was angry over how they treated us." She swallowed. "But when they took us to the station and put me in an interrogation room, I was terrified. All I knew is I wanted to get out of there without having anything on my record that would ruin my career." Sudden tears stung her eyes. "I was worried about being in trouble for reckless driving." She clenched her teeth to hold back the pain that burned in her chest before she could say anything more. "I was worried about reckless driving, Melanie, and how I was going to explain it to my girlfriend and parents."

"But what happened?" Melanie asked softly.

"It was a stolen car."

Chapter Twenty-One

Exhausted but thankful the storm passed them, and it was finally daylight, Melanie once again rested her head against Milo's shoulder while the woman drove them east. The same caring woman who held her in the backseat all night even after the wind died down and the thunder rolled off to places far away. The strong woman who let them out of the barn and navigated the muddy road to get back to the freeway. *She must be as tired as I feel*, she thought. *But never a complaint. How lucky am I to have her help me? And not just last night, or when I was attacked, but for all of it? Still...* She frowned, remembering there was the money to consider. Melanie agreed to pay Milo a lot for getting her home well before she knew anything about the woman. *Has her motivation for helping me changed?* After hearing her story, Melanie understood more about why the money was important. Thinking of Milo's confession made her sad. *Such an unfair outcome.*

While they had stayed in the barn, Milo went on to explain more about her trial and the deal she made to avoid a grand theft auto charge. The fact she was the one driving, ran when the police wanted her to stop, and the high value of the Corvette all hurt her case. As much as her attorney tried, Milo was still sentenced as a Class C felony.

"It wasn't so much the two years' jail time that hurt in the end," she had said. "It's the background checks for every good literary or teaching job I'm even slightly qualified for. People can't or won't hire an ex-offender, especially a felon."

Laying there in the dark, Melanie had resolved to help Milo as much as possible. She couldn't change her past, but there were ways to help her future. *If she'll let me,* Melanie thought, tilting her head to look at Milo in the early morning light. It was one thing to earn a hundred thousand dollars doing a job, but Milo seemed too proud to take money as a gift. *I'll figure out something.*

Unable to stifle a yawn, Melanie smiled apologetically when Milo glanced at her. "Sorry," she said. "I'm trying to be a good copilot and stay awake, but I think it's a losing battle."

"It's no problem if you sleep," she said. "I'm fine."

Seeing the dark circles under Milo's eyes, Melanie shook her head at her. "No, you're not fine," she said. "How far to the next town with a hotel?"

Milo frowned. "We're still in Texas," she said. "For at least another couple of hours. We're not even to Amarillo."

Giving a little laugh at the irony, Melanie stared out the windshield. "Then stop when we get there," she said, seeing nothing but freeway for miles. "There are some hotels right off the interstate."

"You're familiar with Amarillo?"

"Oh yes," Melanie answered, unable to keep the contempt out of her voice. "I went there as a teenager whenever I could get my dad to loan me the car. It was the closest town with a real shopping mall." Memories of screaming fights with her father flashed in her mind. The stubborn old man who couldn't even come close to understanding how important designer jeans were to a sixteen-year-old girl. Because visiting was usually an all-day trip, the excuses were always the same—chores to do on Saturday and heaven forbid she miss church services on Sunday. Her mom was no help, always deferring to her husband. In some ways, Melanie was madder at her mother for not standing up for herself at least occasionally. "Actually, there was a time in my life I wanted nothing more than to visit Amarillo, Texas." She sighed. "Go ahead and stop. It seems fitting."

"Okay," was all Milo said after a minute, waiting to see if Melanie would go into more detail. Where some people would ask questions, she preferred to let a person tell the story on their terms.

Melanie surprised her by laughing. "Milo, you're such the strong and silent type," she said. "Don't you want to know anything about how I grew up?"

Milo shrugged. "Only if you want to tell me," she answered, and Melanie went back to resting against her shoulder. It was precisely where Milo liked her to be, and although stopping was the intelligent thing to do, she thought she could drive for hours with Melanie beside her. "But I'm listening."

"I know you are," Melanie murmured. "And after what you shared, I guess it's only fair to tell you a little about me."

"I'd like that."

She felt Melanie settle in. "Well, in a nutshell, my parents never understood me," Melanie said. "And I know that's very cliché, but in my case, it's true. It was as if I was some foreign being to them. We simply did not speak the same language." She shook her head against Milo's shoulder. "I was always getting grounded for staying out after curfew. I can't imagine what they would have done if they ever found out I put on makeup on the way to school and changed clothes to something risqué in the girl's bathroom. And of course, my sister was completely different, so I was also living up to a standard. I can't tell you the number of times my mother would say, "Why can't you be like Chelsea?

Seeing signs for Amarillo ahead, Milo looked for a good exit to try. "And your sister is still in Texas?"

"Last I heard, yes," Melanie answered. "She probably still lives in the same little town. Five kids and a husband who works at one of Texas's biggest turbine wind farms. Those certainly changed things."

"Is that what those windmill things are we see?" Milo said, nodding toward the horizon.

"If you mean those white alien-looking towers, then yes," Melanie replied. "They weren't there when I was growing up but now cover large parts of Texas. My small town has changed because of it. They actually have a few stores now, although certainly nothing like Amarillo. But don't get your hopes up about Amarillo either. It's not New York or Los Angeles." Milo felt Melanie lift her head, and she pointed at a large green and white hotel sign near the first exit ramp. "Let's try that one," she said. "I don't remember it from growing up, which might be for the best."

Following her advice, Milo signaled, thinking of the cities she had visited in Texas. "Did you ever have a chance to go to Dallas growing up?"

"Only once," Melanie said in a soft voice that made Milo glance at her. A faraway look was in the woman's eyes, and there was a hint of something. *Hurt?* Milo thought, wishing she hadn't asked the question.

Melanie relaxed against her again. "When I was seventeen. My parents had to go there for something to do with our farm, and they took me along," she said. "Probably to keep an eye on me." She shook her head. "Boy was that a mistake. I never had more fun than I did that night."

"And why was that?"

"Because I took off and went bar hopping," Melanie answered. "I met a guy visiting from New York City who took me all over town in a fancy sports car. He was at least twice my age, probably more, but I didn't care. I felt like a grown-up."

Pulling into the hotel's parking lot, Milo could already guess the trouble Melanie must have been in. "I bet your parents were upset," Milo said. "How long were you grounded?"

"I wasn't grounded," Melanie continued in a voice that no longer sounded like she was hurt but instead angry. "When I finally wandered back to the hotel at five a.m. my parents were gone. All that was left behind was a note."

Turning off the car, Milo felt a sense of foreboding and took Melanie's hand. "What did it say?"

"Don't come home."

Melanie remembered seeing the note on the cheap wooden table in the hotel room as clear as day, written on a piece of the stationery hotels all used to include back then. Not her father's writing, but her mother's, which somehow made the message harder to take. "Don't come home."

"What did you do?" Milo asked, her voice gentle, and Melanie squeezed the woman's strong hand, but not for reassurance. She had no regrets about the time she spent out exploring the city's nightlife all those years ago. It changed her life entirely and gave her the chance to follow her dreams. In some ways, the sudden freedom was the push she needed to take the chances she might never have otherwise.

"Called the guy I spent the night with," she answered. "He gave me his number and said to call him if I ever made it to New York City." At the memory of his surprised voice, Melanie laughed. "I don't think he ever expected me to contact him, but he didn't leave me hanging. He took me back to New York and let me live with him. At least until I landed a job waiting tables at a diner, all while I was continuing to try for modeling gigs." Suddenly Milo yawned, and even with the faded bruises, the blush on her cheeks afterward was so adorable that Melanie kissed the back of her hand. "Am I boring you?" she said smiling, and Milo shook her head.

"Sorry about that," Milo said. "It's not your story, it's just..."

"Just that you were up all night keeping me safe," Melanie finished for her. "Let's go inside."

Milo smiled. "Not sure how I get credit for that," she said, unfastening her seatbelt while Melanie slid across the seat toward the passenger door.

"Well, you do," Melanie said, getting out of the car and following Milo into the hotel. She wasn't more than a dozen steps into the foyer when she noticed the beautiful young woman working behind the long counter. Even Milo hesitated when they reached the desk, and the receptionist looked up from the paperwork she was working on. Melanie could be looking at a perfect image of herself twenty-five years ago.

The receptionist smiled. "May I help you?" she said, looking first at Milo and then at Melanie. The young woman blinked, the smile faltering. "Auntie Melanie?"

"Hello, Christine," Melanie said to the niece she hadn't seen since her mother's funeral eight years before. It was all she could do to not feel self-conscious about her plain, wrinkled dress and lack of makeup. *And I'm sure my hair looks like a rat's nest*, she thought. *Oh well, not like I have had much choice.* "It's nice to see you."

Christine's eyes flicked to Milo and then back to Melanie, confusion clouding her large blue eyes. "What are you doing here?"

"Stopping on the way back to New York," Melanie said, deciding to keep the facts simple. "And now we need a room."

Furrowing her pretty brow, the young woman seemed even more perplexed. "Why not just go stay with Mom?" she asked. "Andy went to Austin for school, so none of us live at home. There is lots of room."

The idea of seeing her sister made Melanie lift her chin. "We're just passing through," she said, and when Milo glanced at her with a questioning look, her resolve slipped a bit, only to rush back as she remembered her attire. "There's not enough time."

Thankfully, before Christine could discuss it further, another customer came in the front doors, snapping the young woman back into business mode. "Very well," she said, focusing on Milo. "Do you have a reservation?"

"No," Milo answered. "We do not."

Christine checked her computer. "That's fine," she said. "We have two rooms available on the third floor. Is that okay?" Melanie watched Milo, not sure how she wanted the woman to respond. Sleeping beside Milo felt good but explaining it to her niece wasn't appetizing. *Especially when I can't even explain it to myself,* she thought, raising her hand to interrupt.

"That will be perfect," she said, not missing Milo's glance in her direction. She could only hope the woman would understand and not contradict her.

After a beat, Milo nodded. "Yes," she said. "Two rooms."

Chapter Twenty-Two

Riding in the elevator with their luggage as they went to the third floor, Milo wasn't sure what to think about Melanie's decision to have two rooms. Melanie was especially quiet, and they had yet to discuss anything that happened in the lobby. To Milo, it warranted a conversation, even if only because they were on a budget. Whether Melanie liked it or not, sharing a room was always her plan. Yet, Milo had sensed there was more to the woman's sudden decision than wanting her own space and had not contradicted her in front of her niece. *Meeting her was indeed a twist,* Milo thought. *Amazing how much they look like each other, even with the age difference.* Growing tired of the awkward silence between them, she considered commenting on the likeness, but then the elevator dinged as they reached their floor. Without a word, Melanie hurried out with her roller bag as soon as the doors opened, and not until they reached their rooms directly across the hall from each other did the woman face her. "I'm not sure how to explain why I wanted two rooms..." she started before hesitating. "It's just that we're in Texas, and well..."

"You're nervous because I'm a woman," Milo said. It wasn't a question, only a fact.

Color rose to Melanie's cheeks. "Not entirely," she replied. "You can't imagine how confusing all of this is for me."

"It's fine," Milo said, ignoring the sense of loss she felt to her core. Theirs was a temporary arrangement, and even if things weren't inevitably going to end soon, they had no ties to each other. Milo needed to remember that fact. "You can do what you want for tonight. Luckily, the rooms weren't too expensive."

For a moment, Melanie looked like she wanted to reply but only nodded as she put her keycard in the lock. "Okay," she said. "Thank you." Then she was in her room and left Milo alone in the hall. The impulse to knock on Melanie's closed door and search for more explanations was strong, but she let it go. *Now is not the time,* she thought, unlocking her door. *And honestly, I doubt there ever really will be one.* It wasn't likely they would be trapped in a car ever again.

Pushing inside the hotel room, her eyes scanned the beige walls, ordinary hotel furniture, and a double bed in the middle. Like a million other hotel rooms. About as far from the beautiful and unique lodge in Arizona as a place could get. The memory of waking up with Melanie in her arms suddenly came to mind, but Milo pushed it away. Their morning together felt like forever ago, and it might as well have been. She didn't need to waste time thinking about things that happened in the spur of the moment and meant nothing.

Instead, she focused on the immediate decision in front of her—sleep or shower first? The need to close her tired, burning eyes ranked high, but the thought of slipping between the sheets after getting clean was even more tempting. Tossing her duffle bag onto the armchair in the corner, she pulled off her t-shirt as she walked into the small, overly bright, white bathroom. The vision of steam filling the room as hot water pounded her skin nearly made her swoon, and she cranked the shower lever to the highest heat. Stripping off the rest of her clothes, Milo waited as long as she could before stepping in. Sighing with pleasure, she relished the feel of the water running over her. It was even more blissful than she hoped, but as she soaped her hair and body, thoughts of Melanie crept back. Somehow, she couldn't go more than a few minutes without thinking of the attractive woman who traveled with her. *No, I'm not traveling with her,* she thought. *I'm hired to drive her home. Nothing more.* Resolving to keep the facts straight in the future, she scrubbed harder, willing all images of Melanie to be washed away.

In less than sixty seconds after the door closed, Melanie knew she had made a mistake. Feeling the quiet of the space settle in around her, her apprehension quickly mounted. Not only because Milo wasn't there, but the sterile feel of chain hotel rooms set her on edge. *Why did I say yes to two rooms?* she wondered. *I don't want to be here alone.* Part of it was a knee-jerk reaction not to confuse her niece about the relationship between Melanie and Milo. Although Monty never joined Melanie at either of her parents' funerals, Christine would likely remember that her aunt was married to a wealthy man. Learning she planned to share a room with a woman, a rather butch looking woman, too, might raise an eyebrow. All the more so when Christine relayed the information to her mother. *But since when do I care what anyone in my family thinks?*

Yet, for some strange reason at that instant, she had cared when the question about having two rooms came up. "But how did that make Milo feel?" she asked the empty room as she moved closer to the bed and plopped on the edge. From the silence in the elevator and the woman's words in the hall,

Melanie didn't have to guess. Milo was hurt by what she had decided. *But maybe the separation will be good for us,* she thought before glancing at the nondescript furniture. She felt her stomach tighten. *Or at least maybe for Milo.* Staring at the commercial-grade brown carpet, Melanie had no problem admitting she didn't need to be separated. *So, what do I do about it now?*

While she tried to think of the best way to apologize to Milo, the phone in her room rang. After jumping at the sound, Melanie instinctively hurried to answer it. The call could only be from Milo across the hall. "Hello?" she answered, ready to hear a calming, confident voice, but instead there was a hesitant one.

"Auntie Melanie?" Christine said. "Are you all right?"

Melanie frowned. "Of course, I am," she answered, for a second not sure why the young woman would ask her such a thing, but then connected the dots. Considering her rumpled attire and the dark circles under her eyes, Melanie did not look like the woman her niece had met before. In her niece's position, Melanie would question if she was all right, too. "Thank you for checking, Christine. But I promise I'm okay. I ran into some bad luck a few days ago, and the woman I'm with is helping me."

There was a pause on the phone. "Okay," Christine said. "Well, I called Mom." Melanie rolled her eyes, once again cursing the culture of small towns and their tendency toward gossip but let her niece continue. "And she wants to know how long you are in Amarillo."

Irritation growing, Melanie switched ears with the handset before answering. "As I said at the desk, I'm passing through," she said. "There's no time for a visit." *Not that I want one*, she thought. She might have broken her vow never to set foot in Texas again, but she would not relent on visiting her hometown. "I'm on my way back to New York."

Again, there was quiet on the phone, and Melanie guessed Christine had a million questions starting with why she was driving across the country with some stranger instead of taking a plane. "I think you should reconsider not visiting," her niece said, in a voice much more serious than before. "It's important."

"Why?" Melanie asked, ready to be done with the conversation.

"Because it will mean a lot to Mom," Christine said. "She has stage 4 breast cancer and wants to see you."

Pulling her head from under the stream of hot water, Milo thought she heard a knock on the door to her hotel room. It was faint, especially over the sound of the shower running, but somehow she knew Melanie was outside in the hallway. *I could ignore it,* she thought, thinking of Melanie's decision in the lobby. *And later say I was in the shower if it comes up.* Then the knock came again, and with a sigh, Milo knew she couldn't disregard it. If Melanie needed something, she would be there for her.

Turning off the water, Milo grabbed a towel to dry off. "One minute," she yelled. There was no way she was rushing to the door dripping in a towel. Things had been awkward enough simply riding up three floors in the elevator, and she had no doubt Melanie would prefer Milo to be at least somewhat dressed. Still only half dry, but not wanting to take time to find clean clothes in her duffle bag, she threw on what she wore earlier and answered the door. "What's wrong?" she asked after taking one look at Melanie's pale face. The fact the woman had her polka-dotted suitcase with her registered a split second later.

"Can I come in?" Melanie asked softly, and Milo stepped aside, giving the woman space to enter and time to explain why she was there. After coming in, Melanie stopped in the middle of the room and faced Milo. "Is it okay if I stay with you?"

Sensing there was something going on beyond just their relationship, Milo didn't hesitate. "If that's what you want," she said. "I don't mind."

"Thank you," Melanie said, dropping the handle of her suitcase before stepping closer to wrap her arms around Milo's waist and rest her head against her chest. "I need you." Reacting on instinct, Milo put her arms around Melanie and held her close. Not sure what happened but knowing the woman in her arms needed comfort instead of questions, she quietly stood there. Minutes ticked by without a word before Melanie lifted her head. "Milo, why are you all wet?"

Milo smiled. "I was in the shower when you knocked."

"Oh," Melanie said, taking a step back. "Do you want to go finish?"

"Maybe just put on clean clothes," she replied. "Will you be okay for a minute?"

With a sigh, Melanie nodded. "Yes," she said before looking away, almost as if she was embarrassed to say the next sentence. "But when you're done, I have another big favor to ask you."

Feeling a sense of unease, Milo considered asking to hear it before changing clothes but then respected Melanie's hesitation. *This must be a serious request*, Milo thought, quick to pick up her duffle bag and go into the bathroom. It took her less than two minutes to finish towelling her hair dry and change into a tank top and loose basketball shorts to sleep in. When she returned to the hotel room, Melanie had moved to sit on the end of the bed. If Milo didn't know better, she would think the woman was engrossed in the unoriginal piece of artwork on the wall. Only after Milo stood there a minute did she look at her. Melanie's gaze flicked over her body for the briefest of moments before meeting her eyes. "You really are amazing," Melanie said. "I hate to keep putting you through this."

Milo furrowed her brow. "Putting me through what?" she asked, and Melanie gave a little laugh.

"Oh, you know, dragging you to the Grand Canyon, hiding from tornados..."

"I don't mind," Milo admitted after a moment, surprising herself. Still, if she was sincere, everything so far had turned out to be good. The Grand Canyon was majestic and telling her story in the car had felt very liberating. But Melanie's next question might be different. It was time to stop dancing around the subject. "What do you want to ask me?"

Melanie held her look, and Milo saw a flicker of indecision, but then it was gone. "I want you to take a detour tomorrow," she said. "And take me to see my sister."

Chapter Twenty-Three

During the two hours of backcountry roads with nothing to see in the landscape around them but barbed wire fences and white wind turbines in the distance, Melanie was lost in her memories. As a teenager, the trip to Amarillo was always long, especially since she was eager to get there. On the flip side, the ride home was sheer torture as the miles dragged and there was nothing positive for her to look forward to about getting back to the farm. Milo had the radio on low, and the AM station picked up popular music from the eighties. Songs that only reinforced how she remembered her wild teenage years.

One thing was for sure—her family definitely never owned a Cadillac, and Melanie asked to have the top down on the vintage convertible. If she was forced to go to her hometown again, she intended to arrive in style. "Well, that's new," she said when she saw the large, ornately carved 'Welcome to Grand Pickett' sign announcing her town. The last time she visited, the only thing to mark the boundary was a small green highway marker put there as required by the department of transportation.

The car cruised past it. "Grand Pickett?" Milo asked. "Interesting name."

Melanie glanced at her, not sure if she was being sarcastic, but found only curiosity on her face. "It's named after the landowner who first settled here in 1868," she said. "Rumor was Ol' Mister Pickett was a distant cousin of the famous soldier at Gettysburg, but who knows." She watched as they passed patches of rundown, single-wide trailers with neglected cars in the yard. "I never understood the 'grand' part. There's nothing grand about this town." Still, as they drove further, Melanie saw more things that were new. Buildings had cropped up, giving Grand Pickett more of a downtown. There were a couple of restaurants that actually looked inviting, some fashion stores with merchandise other than fishing tackle and camouflage vests in the window, and even a small five-room motel.

Milo slowed to a stop at the blinking red light that marked the center of town. "Which way?" she asked, and Melanie pointed to the left.

"Not much past the city limits," she said. "My sister was smart enough to live closer to town than my parents. The house I grew up in was too far to walk into town easily."

She remembered how trapped she felt as a kid, with no place to go to get away from her parents and nothing interesting to do. Unlike the present, she used to read books. Any book. With television time strictly restricted, not that they had much reception anyway, she escaped into the exciting world of the rich and powerful between the pages. Thinking of Milo's bookshelf, crammed with so many titles, she had not felt the urge to read one. Reading was a part of her past that she ignored along with everything else. A large farmhouse came into view, painted a light yellow with white porch rails and matching shutters. Orange leaves were starting to fall from the towering oak tree in the front yard.

"This is it on the right." Milo dutifully pulled the long Cadillac over but left the engine running.

Melanie appreciated that the woman was smart enough to recognize she might change her mind at the last second and need to flee. "Do you want me to wait here?" Milo asked. "Or come with you?" Not entirely sure, Melanie reached for Milo, needing a moment of contact before she faced someone she knew resented her. Milo took her hand, and just as she hoped, the warm touch gave her courage.

Making Milo come so far from their original route, Melanie felt like she at least needed to say hello to her sister. "You can stay here," she said. "It will only take a minute, and she might not even be home."

"If I'm not mistaken, she is home," Milo said, looking out the windshield. Melanie followed her gaze to see a woman, thin as a reed, in a sleeveless, faded green summer dress walking around the side of the house toward them. A simple white scarf with tiny yellow flowers tied under her chin covered the top of her head, and her steps were slow, but Melanie could already see the steel in her blue eyes.

"I was wondering if you would come," the woman said as she approached the car. "Christine called ahead and said that you might." Milo noticed the woman had a much stronger Texas drawl than anything she heard in Melanie's voice. *Because over the years, she has worked hard to lose it*, Milo thought. *Just another thing she would have wanted to shake from her past.*

"Hello, Chelsea," Melanie said. "I honestly wasn't sure either."

The thin woman looked down the road as if studying something in the distance before slowly nodding. "Well, y'all come inside," she said after a moment. "I was clipping roses in the backyard, but now I'm too tired."

Melanie didn't make a move. Milo could almost feel the emotions coursing through her. She still didn't understand exactly what was wrong between Melanie and her sister, but she sensed there was more than what Melanie had told her.

"At least come in for a glass of lemonade," the woman said. "You drove this far, and it's too hot to stand out here."

Unfastening her seatbelt, Melanie sighed. "But we can only stay for a few minutes."

As Melanie got out of the car, Milo joined her, and they followed her sister through the smattering of oak leaves across the lawn to the house. The broad porch with a bench swing at one end and two rocking chairs at the other made Milo think of settings described in books she had read over the years. She had never visited any place like North Texas and would have found the whole thing fascinating if it were under different circumstances. Unfortunately, tension filled the air. Nobody said anything as they walked through a mudroom that led into the farmhouse's kitchen.

If Milo was impressed by the porch, the kitchen made her eyes widen. The room held a warm personality of its own with a high ceiling, wood cabinets painted a soft blue and a small butcher block island in the center. The appliances were modern, but the polished, worn wood floor, slightly faded Formica countertops, and well-used kitchen stools gave the space a pleasant lived-in aesthetic. She had no problem imagining a family cooking dinners, getting ready for the day, or simply visiting around the island. It felt like a place Milo would have liked to grow up.

As Melanie's sister made her way to the refrigerator, she glanced back over her shoulder. "I would hope you would at least have the manners to introduce us," she said. Milo watched as a bit of color rose to Melanie's cheeks. She wasn't sure if it was from embarrassment for not having thought to make introductions or irritation at her sister's tone. *Or maybe both*, Milo thought.

While her sister set the pitcher of lemonade on the small island, Melanie waved her hand in an unnecessarily grand gesture. "Chelsea," she said. "I'd like to introduce you to Elizabeth Milo. She is from Los Angeles and is helping me out."

Chelsea's eyes flicked to Milo and held. Not sure what to expect, Milo patiently looked back. "It's nice to meet you Elizabeth," Chelsea said, pausing as if sizing Milo up. "I'm glad you have been there for my sister."

Milo gave a slight nod. "It's nice to meet you, but please, you can call me Milo," she said, not quite sure she liked the scrutiny. "And it has been my pleasure to help Melanie, although it is a business arrangement."

Chelsea looked from Milo to Melanie and back as if appraising the situation. "Oh, I see," Chelsea said before taking glasses from the cupboard and setting them on the island beside the pitcher. "A business arrangement."

Slowly, she started to pour the lemonade, but Milo noticed her hand shook, and Melanie stepped forward to take the pitcher. "I'll do this," she said. "Please sit down."

Without argument, Chelsea took one of the stools along the island's edge. "Thank you," she said. "I'm still getting my strength back."

Because of the age difference, the two sisters never really got along growing up. When they were still under the same roof, Melanie felt as misunderstood by Chelsea as she did her parents. Being so much older, Chelsea married and moved out while Melanie was young, which was part of the resentment. Chelsea had escaped. Still, Melanie hated seeing her sister so weak. No one deserved cancer, and if she was being honest, her sister especially didn't. Chelsea was a good person and had always been well-liked by everyone. Unlike Melanie's poor choices in men, she married an honest man and raised a family. She and her sister had lived entirely different lives, but she realized for the first time that didn't make her sister's life any less worthy.

"When did you find out?" Melanie asked as she poured the lemonade for the three of them.

Accepting the glass Melanie slid to her, Chelsea studied the rim. "Six months ago," she answered. "I noticed something was causing me pain whenever I lifted my right arm above shoulder height." She looked at Melanie, meeting her eye, and there was a mixture of emotions there. Sadness, for sure, but also anger. "A trip to the doctor here and then another to a specialist in Amarillo, and the news was all downhill from there."

Unable to help herself, Melanie felt a tug of sadness because even though they were nearly strangers, Chelsea was still her sister. "And what is your prognosis?" Melanie asked as she handed a glass to Milo before taking a stool across from Chelsea.

"Not great," Chelsea said. "We're still in a wait-and-see mode, but I have another test coming up next week. Then we will know if the cancer is receding or advancing."

Not sure what to say, Melanie was quiet as Milo took another stool. Their eyes met, and Melanie saw nothing but compassion in Milo's eyes. *She seems almost more moved by this news than I am*, Melanie thought. *When did I get so hardened?* Her sister had not been the one who abandoned her, and she was not to blame for the choices Melanie made. No more than Melanie was to blame for anything that Chelsea had done with her life. *Maybe it's time to put all that hurt behind me.*

"So why are you here?" Chelsea asked, interrupting her

thoughts. She saw her sister glance at Milo. "Why are both of you here?"

That was a good question. Christine's confession had caught Melanie off guard, and it had surprisingly shaken her. She even rushed to Milo for comfort and slept in her arms for another night, needing to feel protected again. *But why?* she wondered. *Was it a glimpse at my own mortality that upset me so much? Or is there a connection I've denied all these years?* Looking at her sister and seeing the hollowness of her cheeks and the dark circles under her eyes, Melanie's feelings were all over the place. The ones full of sympathy both surprised and confused her.

Melanie picked up her glass. "I'm not sure, but when I learned about what was happening and that you said you wanted to see me, it seemed like the least I could do."

"Who said I wanted to see you?" Melanie's sister asked.

Melanie blinked. "Your daughter," she answered at the exact second she realized that the two women had been set up by her well-meaning young niece. One who had no idea of the history between the two sisters. *Or lack of history*, Melanie thought. They hardly knew anything about each other. *And yet, she's my family.*

As she caught Chelsea's gaze, whatever new emotions Melanie felt were not reflected back. "Well, I think Christine has overstepped," Chelsea said with a frown. "I'm sorry you came all this way for nothing."

Chapter Twenty-Four

Watching the two women sitting across from each other, Milo could not help but see the similarities between them. Even with Chelsea's illness making her look frailer and the fact that she was several years older did not hinder the strong resemblance. The set of their jaw, the slope of their nose, and the beauty of their blue eyes. Any physical similarities did not alleviate the tension in the air though, and Milo wished she was better at making conversation. The two sisters seemed at a standstill.

Finally, Melanie put her hands on the island as if she was going to stand. "I see," she said. "I didn't mean to barge in."

"You didn't barge in," Chelsea corrected. "You didn't know any more than I did what Christine was up to." She pointed at the lemonade. "Enjoy your drink and don't rush off."

Settling back into place, Melanie picked up her glass of lemonade. "True," Melanie agreed before taking a sip. "And I imagine her heart was in the right place."

Chelsea nodded. "Yes, she's a good daughter and my

cancer has been hard on her," she said, then gave a little laugh. "And of all of my children, she reminds me the most of you."

"Me?" Melanie asked, sounding surprised, although Milo could easily see the physical similarities. "Why?"

"Oh, definitely you and for lots of reasons," Chelsea said. "Not only does she look so much like you, but she has high aspirations." She played with her glass. "Grand Pickett is not big enough for Christine."

Melanie tilted her head, and Milo guessed she was trying to decide if there was any condescension in her sister's tone. If there was any, Milo didn't hear it. After a beat, Melanie glanced over. "I think my sister is trying to point out how much I wanted out of this town," she said. "But then, I didn't have a choice but to leave after what Dad and Mom did." Milo watched the two women's meet eyes again. "We never really talked about that—how you felt when they came back from Dallas without me."

"No, we never have," Chelsea agreed, a wistful tone in her voice as she ran a finger down the side of her glass. "I guess because I always felt guilty."

The answer caught Milo by surprise, and by the wide eyed look on Melanie's face, she was too. "You felt guilty?" Melanie asked. "I never knew that. I thought you agreed with them."

"No, of course not," Chelsea said with a shake of her head. "You probably don't remember, but I was a parent myself by then. When Mom told me what they did, I couldn't believe it. No matter what any of my children do, I would never abandon them."

There was silence in the room, and Milo kept her eyes on Melanie to see how she would respond. After a moment, she saw the slightest glimmer of tears. "I wish I'd known that sooner," Melanie said softly. "It would've made such a huge difference."

"Would it?" Chelsea said, making a quick swipe at her eyes

before lifting her chin. "You were off to New York to find your fame and fortune. And I was left here in Grand Pickett."

Melanie's eyebrows went up. "But wasn't that what you always wanted?" she asked. "To live in this small town and raise a family?" She waved a hand at the kitchen. "You and Joel married right out of high school and bought this house. I never doubted that it was what you wanted."

"It was," Chelsea said with a smile, and Milo liked seeing how her eyes lit up. "I wouldn't trade what I have for the world. My family is everything to me." She shrugged and looked down at her hands. "But sometimes, late at night when I couldn't sleep, I would stare at the ceiling and wonder where you were and what you are doing."

Melanie was shaking her head with what Milo was sure were a dozen emotions. The woman had been so adamantly against going to Texas. Hearing what her sister said would be a lot to take in. "I just can't believe it," Melanie said in a whisper.

"It's true. I was afraid to reach out to you after so much time passed," Chelsea said. "Now that I see how short life can be, that is my big regret."

Milo watched Melanie slowly reach across the island to take her sister's hand. "But I'm here now," she said. "And we have lots to talk about."

As she held her sister's hand, unable to miss how frail her bones felt, Melanie's head spun with all she heard. Nothing could have come out of her sister's mouth that would have surprised her more. A confession that she felt guilty about what happened to Melanie was almost beyond comprehension. Over thirty years had passed, and they never once spoke about it. The short visits when Melanie returned for her parent's funerals were filled with other family members. They never sat down and talked. *And if I hadn't met Milo and gone on this trip, we never would have,* she thought with a surprising ache in her chest. *I would never have known.*

As she looked across the island at her sister, Melanie saw the woman wiping her eyes. Chelsea glanced at Milo and gave her a slightly embarrassed smile. "Well, you've certainly brought on quite the reunion," she said. "I guess you're helping more than just my sister."

Milo gave her a gentle smile. "I'm glad we took the time to have a glass of lemonade in your kitchen."

Before anyone could say anything more, the house's back door opening made everyone look in that direction. Suddenly a man with jet black hair peppered with gray came wandering in. He carried two small, white sacks that Melanie thought might come from a pastry shop. "Babe," he called before he noticed Melanie and Milo were with Chelsea. "Oh, sorry, I didn't realize we had company."

As his eyes settled on Melanie, she gave him a big smile. "Hello, Joel."

"Well, hello, Melanie," he replied, coming closer and putting the sacks on the island.

Not making the same mistake twice, Melanie gestured toward Milo. "Joel, let me introduce you to my friend Milo," she said. "We are on our way to New York but ran into Christine in Amarillo and decided to come to visit."

"Well, that's good timing," Joel said with a smile. "Because I was wrapping up my night shift and decided to swing by Beulah's bakery shop on the way through town. A few pastries to have as a treat." He put his arm around Chelsea's shoulders. "I bought the lemon bars you like so much."

Melanie felt a little tightness in her chest at the caring in the man's eyes. She wished for a moment she married someone who would look at her like that, but then a thought struck her. She had seen it, but not from Monty or any of the other husbands, and letting her eyes drift, she met Milo's gaze. The look was in them at that very moment, and it was all she could do not to reach for Milo's hand. Suddenly, she wanted nothing more than to feel the woman's arms wrapped around her. *But that can't keep happen*ing, she thought, and it made her a little sad. *Even with this detour, our trip will be over eventually, and the closer I get to her, the more confused I feel.* As if hearing her thoughts, Milo looked away but not before Melanie saw the hint of what looked like sadness in her eyes.

"Well, let's not have these go to waste," Chelsea said, drawing Melanie's attention away from her thoughts about Milo. Her sister stood and went to the cupboard to take out four small plates.

Melanie started to slip off her stool. "Let me help with that," she said, but Chelsea shooed her away with a hand.

"Don't get into that habit," she said with a hint of humor but also some sternness in her eyes. "For the most part I can take care of myself." Taking the bags, Chelsea put a lemon bar on each plate.

"You really don't have to share," Milo said, accepting the treat Chelsea held out to her.

"Of course, we do," Joel said with the warm and welcoming smile that Melanie remembered. He was a good guy, and she had always been glad Chelsea married someone so kind.

Someone different than our father, she thought, taking her serving of the lemon bars from her sister. "Thank you," she said as she banished any memories from her childhood. "These are my favorite too."

As Melanie took a bite, Joel stopped with his fork in midair. "Hey, how long are you in town?" Joel asked. "I can text Brady and tell him to bring a couple more steaks if you two want to stay for an evening cook out. I don't work tomorrow."

Melanie glanced at her sister to see if she had a reaction to his unexpected invitation. After a moment of hesitation, Chelsea smiled, nodding. "I think that is a great idea," she said, turning to Melanie. "Unless you are truly in too much of a hurry."

Melanie wasn't sure what to say. Never in a million years had she thought things would go how they were. When she had the sudden desire to visit her sister, she didn't know what she envisioned. *A short hello?* she thought. *Or to be relieved if she wasn't home?* The idea of reconnecting over lemonade wasn't even on her radar. *And now we are talking about a family barbeque?*

Before she could answer, Milo spoke up. "A grilled steak sounds fantastic to me," she said. "We're not in that big of a hurry." Melanie noticed the woman staring right at her. *Like she's giving me the go ahead to delay our trip a little longer,* she thought. *But do I want that?*

Feeling a flicker of panic, almost like she was a little trapped, Melanie thought of refusing but then had to admit she didn't hate the idea. A little more time with Chelsea could be good.

Still uncertain, she forced a smile. "It would be great to see Brady again."

With a laugh, Joel clapped his hands together, and joy was written all over his rugged features. "Oh, it's not just Brady and his wife anymore," the man said with a twinkle in his eye. "Haven't you heard? They had a son back in January. Brady Junior." He wrapped an arm around Chelsea and pulled her a little closer. "We're grandparents." He shook his head. "And that little devil is quite a charmer."

"I had no idea," Melanie said, feeling a tug of remorse that something so magnificent could happen and her not hear about it.

As if feeling the same, she noticed her sister studying the

lemon bar on the plate in front of her. "A lot was going on, and I didn't know how to reach you," Chelsea finally said. "The attorney handled calling you in the past for the funerals—"

Melanie held up a hand. "I understand," she interrupted. It wasn't like Melanie ever reached out with contact information. There was never a reason. She smiled at Joel and Chelsea. "I would love to see all of them and having a baby to play with will make the barbecue even more fun."

"Really?" Chelsea asked, and Melanie nodded.

"Yes, I can't wait to see everyone," Melanie said, and to her surprise, she meant it.

Chapter Twenty-Five

Driving the old Cadillac through the small town of Grand Pickett, Milo was taken in by its simple charm. She knew Melanie hated growing up there, but something about the close-knit feel of the place appealed to a part of Milo. It was radically different than what she felt in Los Angeles, even growing up in Culver City. There they had neighborhoods which sometimes led to camaraderie between families, but here she could tell just by the interactions of people walking along the sidewalks in front of the storefronts that everyone knew each other well. *Which could be difficult*, she thought. *There wouldn't be any privacy.* She realized very little could remain hidden behind closed doors. *I wonder what that would be like?* Glancing over at Melanie in the passenger seat, she assumed it was something Melanie hated. Her defiant teenage years were likely the talk of the town at some points, and that would be hard on anyone.

Passing in front of a small grocery store, Melanie gave a little laugh. "What?" Milo asked with a smile, surprised at her sudden humor.

Melanie pointed. "I spent a lot of hours standing in that

parking lot," she said. "It's where the boys with trucks would stop on Friday nights." Melanie's smile grew. "They would line up with their parking lights on, drink cokes, and pretend they were cool."

Seeing Melanie's face light up at a good memory, Milo slowed. "Pretend to be cool?" Milo asked, trying to envision what that would look like. Boys wanting to be men strutting around in jeans and cowboy boots, proud of whatever vehicle they could lay their hands on. The luckier ones even having the means to fix up a classic, and Milo guessed the Deville she currently rode in would have been a big hit.

"Well, I suppose considering this is Grand Pickett they were cool," she said. "At the time I definitely thought so."

Milo was suddenly curious. "Did you have a steady boyfriend?"

"Of course," Melanie answered with a sly smile. "The star quarterback of the high school, and we were like celebrities."

Milo raised her eyebrows. "There's a high school here?"

"Not here. An hour long bus ride," Melanie said. "All the small towns in the area send kids there." Melanie flipped her hair. "And I was a shining star if I say so myself."

Milo thought about what she said for a second and could easily envision Melanie, gorgeous with her big blue eyes, long blonde hair, and sexy petite figure, standing out amongst average teenagers. "That does not surprise me."

Melanie reached across the bench seat and rubbed Milo's leg. "Flattery will get you everywhere," she said, making Milo feel warmth throughout her body even at the casual touch. "But it was one reason I dreamed of becoming a model in New York. Everyone told me I was so special."

"I can believe that," Milo said as she pulled up at the curb in front of the small motel. Although Chelsea and Joel had wanted them to stay in a couple of the empty bedrooms, Melanie declined. They would stay the night in Grand Pickett after the barbecue and sleep at the local motel. Milo shut off the car. "Let me go get us some keys." A part of her guessed Melanie wouldn't want to broadcast to the entire town that she was back by being seen at the motel. Especially considering how she was traveling and who she was with.

Melanie ran her hand up Milo's arm, clearly understanding Milo's intention. "You're good to me," she murmured, making Milo's pulse pick up.

She swallowed hard. "I'll be right back."

Milo went inside and was greeted by a heavyset woman behind the counter. Before Milo could say a word, she held up her beefy hand. "If you're looking for a room," she said. "I won't waste your time. We are booked up indefinitely. There's some construction happening at one of the wind farms nearby, and every room is doubled up with workers."

Rubbing the back of her neck, Milo frowned. "Anywhere else you recommend?"

"I'm afraid you probably won't find any place to rent in any of the nearby towns," she answered. "I would have to recommend Amarillo."

Sitting in the car with the top still down, Melanie looked around, still taken aback by all the changes that had happened since she grew up in Grand Pickett. Although it was still tiny by any standard, there was much more to see and do. When she lived there, only the grocery store and a sporting goods shop offered anything interesting. Melanie had made the most of it. She wasn't lying to Milo when she said she was a star growing up. Ever since she could remember people remarked on her beauty. All the boys wanted to date her in high school, and all the girls, or at least most, were jealous. *It didn't help that I had such a high opinion of myself because of it,* she thought. She wouldn't say she was a mean girl, but with her two best friends at the time, she did have to admit she looked down on others. Still, her oversized self-esteem from high school gave her the confidence she needed to survive those early years in New York. *Back then, I never stopped believing I was the most beautiful woman in the room.* She felt a sudden wave of sadness wash over her. *And I haven't felt that way in a very long time.*

Suddenly, she saw two women walking on the sidewalk chatting and headed in her direction. It took her less than a second to recognize one of them was a girl from her pack when they were in high school. Not one of her two closest friends but someone on the outskirts. *Someone I wasn't always nice to,* she thought and averted her eyes, hoping to go unnoticed. She wasn't so lucky, because when they were a few steps away, the girl she remembered let out a gasp.

"Oh my God, is that you, Melanie Kowalski?" she asked before correcting herself. "Oh, I mean...is it Garrison still?"

Knowing she couldn't hide, Melanie turned her face to them and gave a huge smile. "Sotheby," she corrected, forcing cheerfulness into her voice. "It's good to see you, Jeanette." She tried not to think about how things might look, her sitting there in the Cadillac. Even after a shower that morning and putting on a little more makeup, she knew she looked nothing like her normal self. Certainly nothing compared to her usual glamour.

As if thinking the same thing, Jeanette's eyes roamed over Melanie and the car. "What brings you to Grant Pickett?"

"Visiting Chelsea and seeing the new baby," Melanie answered, happy that what she said was at least partially true. She had come to visit her sister and seeing Brady's little one would be a bonus.

Jeanette clapped her hands. "Oh, that little boy is such a sweetheart. He inherited the Kowalski blonde hair and blue eyes," she said. "He's going to be a heartbreaker."

A surprising glow of pride warmed Melanie. "I can't wait to see." Just then, Milo came out of the motel and walked to the car. Melanie saw her take in the scene and pause before getting in. The hesitation made Melanie think she might retreat to the motel, but it was too late. Jeanette looked at her, and Melanie watched her eyes widen. She felt her chest tighten with anxiety. Without a doubt, before the day was over, there would be speculation about what Melanie was doing back in town with a butch looking woman in an old car. *God, I hate this place*, she thought. *It's none of their business who I travel with, yet they will have all kinds of theories.* Melanie wasn't sure what to do next but was ready to leave the scene before any questions started. She met Milo's eyes.

No doubt seeing the panic on Melanie's face, Milo slipped behind the wheel. "Ready to go?" she asked as if the two women on the sidewalk were not even there.

"Yes," Melanie answered before turning her attention to Jeanette and giving her another dazzling smile. "It was good to see you again."

Having some good gossip fodder, Jeanette smiled back. "Likewise," she said. "Maybe we can catch up before you leave town?"

"Maybe," Melanie lied. "Take care." She started to turn to Milo and ask her to go, but Jeanette wasn't done.

"Where you off to?" she asked, and Melanie scrambled for an answer. There wasn't much nearby. Finally, something came to her, and she felt a strange tightening in her throat.

It was the last place she would have thought to go, but it was her only answer. "The cemetery," she said. "I'm going to go pay respects to mom and dad."

After a few more fake "let's catch up soon" comments, Milo was finally able to drive them away from the curb. "Thank you," Melanie said. "For being patient through all that nonsense."

Milo glanced over and saw an irritated look on Melanie's face. "It was fine," Milo said. "Although, even after only being in Grand Pickett a couple of hours, I can see why you would've found it frustrating as a teenager."

"Oh, that's an understatement," Melanie said before tilting her head. "But I'm curious about your observations."

Milo shook her head. "You mean that those two women were all but taking notes on things they wanted to tell others?" Milo said. "I have never seen anything quite like it."

"That obvious?" Melanie asked. "Well, you're right. We will be the talk of the town before the evening is over." She sighed. "I'll have to remember to give Chelsea a heads up."

Milo gave that some thought, and it didn't seem to her that Melanie's sister would care. She radiated an inner strength that would be above local gossip. *Because she's had cancer?* she wondered. *Or was she always able to take the high road?* "I get a sense it will be okay," Milo said. "About your sister I mean."

After a beat, Melanie nodded. "You are right," she answered. "My sister was never bothered by that stuff. Even when I was in high school and getting into so much trouble, she just went on her way. And then married Joel and started a family as if..."

Melanie's words held a trace of something sad as they faded off, and Milo furrowed her brow. Usually she wouldn't press, but the hurt she detected in the woman's words felt like it needed to be addressed. "As if...?" she asked softly. "What?"

Wiping at her eyes, Melanie looked out the window. "Sometimes, I felt like Chelsea disowned me." She paused, making Milo think she might not say more, but then she continued. "That's a harsh word, but I never felt I could reach out to her. Maybe that's when the divide between us truly began." Nodding, Milo slowed the car as she reached for

Melanie's hand. They had driven to the outskirts of the small town, and it felt safe enough. Taking it, Melanie looked at her, and a tear slipped down her cheek. "I felt so alone that leaving without even a look back was easy."

"I'm sure," Milo murmured, unable to find words to help with her level of hurt, but things were much clearer to her now.

"But maybe I was wrong," Melanie said, running her fingers across her cheeks to wipe away the wetness. "Maybe I was wrong about a lot of things."

Milo squeezed her hand. "Maybe," she said. "Do you still want to go visit your parents' gravesite?"

Looking out the window, Melanie didn't answer for a long time. Finally, she let out a long sigh. "Yes," she said. "Turn right at that stop sign ahead and go further out of town, about a mile, to the town cemetery. We buried them side by side there."

Chapter Twenty-Six

Standing beside Milo, Melanie looked at the large, granite headstone shared by her parents. The late afternoon sun cast her and Milo's shadows across the names etched in the stone. They were buried side by side, and Melanie agreed it was how they were in life. After over seventy-five years of marriage, having them together for eternity seemed appropriate. Harold and Jane Kowalski. 'A beloved mother and father at rest' and Melanie couldn't help but feel the irony in the words. Her sister must have picked the phrase, because they didn't relate to Melanie, but then she didn't offer to help with any of the arrangements. *Maybe I should've brought flowers*, Melanie thought. *Although never in a million years would I have believed I would be standing here*. Yet, being there with Milo seemed par for the course. There were many things over the last few days she never thought she would do. *Like kiss the wonderful woman standing beside me*. She suddenly felt like a hypocrite, because being out in the open she was afraid even to hold her hand. *The town gossip will be bad as it is.*

Having seen enough, Melanie turned to the woman beside her. "I think I'm ready to go."

"All right," Milo said, a solemn look on her face while she still stared at the headstone. "They lived a long time."

"That's true," Melanie said. "Because my arrival was a surprise, they were older parents. Sometimes, I was jealous of my friends whose mom and dad wanted to do more with them." She sighed. "Just another one of our disconnects."

Milo nodded. "I can imagine," she said, then hesitated. "But for what it's worth, I'm glad you decided to come to Grand Pickett."

Surprised, Melanie met her eyes. "You're glad?" she asked. "Why?"

Milo shrugged. "From what I can see, it is something you needed." Her eyes softened. "To let go, maybe?"

Melanie frowned, not sure she heard Milo correctly. "Let go?" she said, focusing on the headstone again. *Am I?* she thought, understanding the bridge being built with her sister but not her parents' memory. *Could I find a way to forgive the two of them?* A part of her felt nothing when she thought of her parents. The anger was gone. *As if I have a hollow place in my heart.* She turned to Milo again. "When I came for my father's funeral, I arrived in a limousine. I wore a two-thousand dollar black dress and an elegant string of pearls." Pausing, she waited for Milo to comment, but as so often, she patiently waited. "I wanted to show my mother how far I'd come." Suddenly, there was something in the hollowness inside her—hurt. Tears burned her eyes, making her angry at a memory she hated. "Mother didn't even return my hello. Like she took one look and still wanted nothing to do with me." Melanie remembered how it made her angry then and felt the emotion all over again.

"I don't know what to say," Milo murmured. With a shake of her head, Melanie started for the car. As she passed Milo, she took her hand. *Screw what anyone thinks in this town*, she thought. *I need her.*

When they reached the car, Melanie didn't immediately get in and looked at Milo. "Thank you for being here with me," she said. "And I don't mean just the cemetery, but all of it. Grand Pickett, my sister's home, even the barbecue coming up. I know it was never part of the plan."

"You're welcome," Milo said. "Like I said, it needed to happen. But we have to get back on track after tonight." She hesitated for a moment, and Melanie saw something in her eyes that she couldn't quite read, but then it was gone. "And get you back to New York."

Sitting in a lawn chair in the shade with a cold beer in her hand, Milo watched the interactions of Melanie's family. Not only had Brady and his wife arrived with the baby, but two more of Chelsea's sons were there. She was surprised to see how much they all looked like their father, while the baby, Brady Junior, was as blond-haired and blue-eyed as Melanie and his grandmother. The only one who looked different from the others was Brady's wife, Monica. Her red hair added a nice contrast.

The thing she liked seeing the most was how happy Melanie looked. Whatever walls she had built between her and Chelsea seemed to be slowly cracking. *I wonder how much of it stems from Melanie not arriving in a limousine wearing an expensive dress,* she thought. *Perhaps this time she was more relatable.* As she watched Brady's wife bouncing little Brady Junior on her hip, she saw her hand the baby to a reluctant Melanie.

"Oh no," she heard Melanie saying as she held up her hands to stop her. Monica was not deterred, and before Milo knew it, Melanie was holding the baby boy. As Milo watched her look at the child, a smile lit Melanie's face like she had never seen before, and the sight made her happy. She felt a slight sense of wonder about how everything was turning out. Brady's wife wandered over to sit in the lawn chair beside her. She carried two beers and held one toward Milo. "I thought maybe you were ready for a new one," Monica said with a welcoming smile. "I hope you don't mind my crashing your space, but it seemed like an excellent opportunity to step away and let everyone enjoy Brady Junior.

"I don't mind," Milo replied with a smile of her own, meaning what she said. Although everyone was friendly, Monica especially radiated a warm and open personality.

The woman leaned back in her chair, taking a sip of her beer. "Now, why don't you tell me what you think of Grant Pickett?" she asked, and Milo tilted her head, hesitating before answering.

Her instinct told her that the question was sincere and not someone looking for gossip. "I find it small but charming," Milo answered after a moment. "I can see how growing up here might be difficult though."

Monica nodded. "I can see that too," she said. "I'm actually from San Antonio and only moved here after marrying Brady. We met at the university and thought about settling there after graduation, but he wanted to be near his family."

"And you didn't mind?" Milo asked.

"No, not really. I know from stories that Melanie had a hard time, but Brady loved growing up in Grand Pickett," she answered. "And I do enjoy living here. Even though it's remote and there's certainly not nearly as much to do as in San Antonio, I have my little garden, and we are remodeling our farmhouse." Her face lit up. "Plus, now we have Brady Junior, and I don't think I could be more content anywhere in the world."

Milo envisioned what the woman's life might be like and could see the positives. "That sounds nice," she said. "I live in

Los Angeles, where everything is rushed and congested. Grand Pickett is quite a difference."

"I bet," Monica said with a little laugh. "So, you and Melanie met in Los Angeles?"

Milo raised an eyebrow, once again sensing there wasn't anything behind the question other than curiosity.

Still, she sipped her beer to consider her answer. "Yes. We met by accident in Los Angeles," she finally said. "Melanie needed some help getting back to New York, and she hired me."

"To drive her back in your wonderful convertible Cadillac?" she asked with sincerity in her voice. "What an incredible adventure. I'm jealous."

Liking her enthusiasm, Milo smiled. "Yes, we are," she said. "Although we keep getting sidetracked."

"Like coming here, you mean?"

"Exactly," Milo replied.

As if considering her answer, Monica was quiet, and for a moment they watched the family interacting. "You know," Monica started in a quiet voice while still studying the others. "I am surprised it's a business arrangement to be honest."

Milo sipped her beer to take a minute before responding. "Why?"

"Honestly," Monica said, keeping her voice very low. "I thought there might be more." She finally turned to look Milo in the eye, and there was nothing but kindness in them. "Because of the way you look at each other."

After everyone left, Melanie found herself sitting alone with her sister on the wide, farmhouse porch swing. They had gravitated there as if each sensing they needed some time with only the other. Joel and Milo had slipped away, and Melanie appreciated Milo's understanding. Her excuse of needing to turn in early so they could drive a long day tomorrow was probably only partially true. *She knows how to read me and sense what I need*, she thought. *Sometimes better than I know myself.*

"You looked good holding Brady Junior," her sister said, breaking into her thoughts as they rocked slowly back and forth.

Melanie smiled. "He is quite the charmer," she agreed and felt something unusual in her heart as she remembered what it was like to hold him. She never thought about having her own children, believing she was too busy or even too selfish. Suddenly that made her a little sad.

As if reading her mind, Chelsea slowed the swing. "And you never wanted children?"

"You know," Melanie started. "I never decided not to, but life kind of got away from me. None of my husbands ever wanted them." She shrugged. "So I didn't."

"I understand," Chelsea said, using her foot to start the bench moving again.

"But I will admit," Melanie said softly. "Something inside me woke a little when I held your grandson in my arms."

Chelsea glanced at her, smiling. "I think that's normal," she said. "You realize you are now a great aunt?"

Melanie hadn't considered that fact and let out a little laugh. "Wow," she said, trying not to let herself panic at the idea. "That certainly puts a few things in perspective." *Like what I've been doing all my life with so little to show*, she thought. *I could have at least started a charity.* She shook her head. "Let's change the subject, shall we?"

"I didn't mean to upset you."

Patting her sister's hand, Melanie forced a smile back on her face. "It's fine," she said. "Just took me a little by surprise." The last thing she wanted was for things to be awkward. "Thank you for letting us stay at your house."

"I'm sorry the motel is full," her sister said. "But I'm also glad that you're staying. It's been nice having you here."

"It has for me too," Melanie said, happy she could honestly agree. Although she felt ready to go in the morning, the visit was possibly life-changing, and she knew it. In her heart, she knew tonight would not be the last time she visited her sister. Melanie sighed as they gently swung back and forth while twilight fell around them. "We went to the cemetery."

Her sister's eyebrows went up. "I didn't realize that was in your plans."

"I know. It surprised me too," Melanie said. "It sort of evolved, but I think I'm glad I went."

"You think you're glad?"

Melanie shrugged a shoulder. "I guess some people would say I was able to get a little closure, but I don't think I did." She looked at her hands. "When I looked at their headstone, all I felt was hollow."

"And do you think that will always be the case?" Chelsea asked.

Not sure of the answer, Melanie looked into the front yard and watched a cloud of fireflies twinkling. "I don't know why it would change," Melanie finally said in nothing but a whisper. "I never really knew them when I was growing up under their roof, and they certainly never understood me." She swallowed the lump growing in her throat. "What would be the point of forgiving them now?"

Chapter Twenty-Seven

Driving the Cadillac along the highway into the rising sun, Milo was happy to be back on the road. Not that she hadn't enjoyed her time in Grand Pickett meeting Melanie's family, but a part of her needed to find some resolution soon. While they were sitting in the lawn chairs, what Brady's wife said struck a nerve. Milo did look at Melanie with too much of her heart, and that was dangerous. Melanie had her life in New York City. No matter how long it took for them to get there, the ending would be inevitable. For Milo, it could not be a happily ever after. *At least with the money maybe I'll be able to start over and travel like I planned*, Milo thought. *And keep this time spent with Melanie as just fond memories.*

"You're awfully quiet," Melanie said, breaking into her thoughts. Milo glanced over. She thought Melanie had fallen asleep, but instead, she was gazing at her with the big, beautiful blue eyes Milo was attracted to so much.

She smiled. "Just enjoying the morning," she answered. "I'm hoping we make good time today."

Melanie nodded. "Yes," she said. "Especially with Joel's good advice."

"True," Milo said, thinking back to having coffee with him and Chelsea before they hit the road. He had asked her where they were headed, and she told him they would get back to Interstate 40 in Amarillo. "Go through Oklahoma City," she said, and he had shaken his head.

"There's a lot of construction between here and there," he said. "A major road improvement project will tie you up for hours if you go that way. I suggest looping south a little bit toward Dallas and then cutting across."

Avoiding sitting in traffic made sense to Milo, so they were on the route he suggested. As they passed a road sign pointing in the direction of Dallas/Fort Worth two hundred miles away, she remembered what Melanie told her about the fateful night in Dallas. Apparently having noticed the same sign, Melanie shook her head. "I can't believe I'm seeing signs for there," she said. "Not that I hate the city. It simply brings back so many memories, especially after the last few days."

"We will be out of Texas this afternoon," Milo said. "And then you can start thinking about New York." Her comment was met with silence, and not for the first time, Milo had a sense Melanie was not ready to go home.

"Milo," Melanie said suddenly. "This trip has been all about me." She reached across the seat and took her hand. "But where would you have liked to have gone?"

Milo tilted her head. "What do you mean?"

"I mean, is there any landmark or city you have always wanted to visit?" Melanie said. "That we could pass by somehow."

Milo thought for a while. There were plenty of places she would like to see, and she tried to think what city even remotely nearby would be highest on her list of places to explore. There was Nashville, because she appreciated the excitement of country music and Philadelphia because of the history. Still, when she really thought about a historical and exciting place, only one city came to mind.

Finally, she nodded. "If I were going to visit any place on this trip, it would take us way too far off track."

Again, Melanie was quiet and let go of her hand. "Are you saying that because you wouldn't want to go there with me?" she asked softly. Milo felt a tug in her chest at the question. *Nothing could be further from the truth, but do I tell her?* she wondered. *Do I tell her where I want to go would be even more perfect with her by my side?* They rode in silence for a while before she came up with an answer.

No matter how much it would hurt in the end, Milo wasn't ready for Melanie to walk out of her life. "I would love it if you went with me," Milo finally answered.

"To where?" Melanie asked.

"New Orleans."

Milo's answer could not be more perfect. Not only because Melanie was excited about going to see the vibrant city of New Orleans, but even more, the fact she wanted to go with her. *She's not ready for the trip to be over either*, Melanie thought with a tingle in her stomach. *She doesn't simply want to be rid of me.* "I would love to go to New Orleans," Melanie said. "I think that would be the perfect place to explore with you."

Milo glanced over, a broad smile on her face. "Have you been before?"

Melanie rolled her eyes. "Once," she said. "With husband number two. Although it was during our unraveling stage, and the visit was not pleasant."

Melanie saw Milo frown. "Does that mean you will have negative connotations?" she asked, and Melanie shook her head.

"Not at all," she replied. "Going with you will wipe away all of them." And Melanie meant it. They weren't even there yet, and already she could feel the magic.

"Well, I guess we better find a place to pull over and check the map," Milo said before raising an eyebrow. "Unless you want to do it for us while I keep driving?"

Melanie laughed. "How lost do you want to get?" she asked. "I've never read a map in my life." Then she realized that was the old Melanie speaking and the new one was not the fragile socialite who was worried about doing new things. "Where's the map?"

With a smile, Milo gestured toward the glove box. "There's a US map inside, and it will be enough to give me the general direction."

For a second, Melanie felt a hint of panic. "Do you think it means we will have to go through Dallas?"

Milo frowned. "Unfortunately, it might," she said. "But we could go around. I don't want this to upset you."

Will it upset me? Melanie wondered. Her initial instinct was to avoid Dallas at all costs. *But maybe it's another thing I should face and put behind me.* "I don't know," she said. "Going around will probably take a lot longer though, right?"

Milo shrugged. "I'm not sure, but I know it will probably take all day to get to New Orleans regardless."

Taking a deep breath, Melanie was ready to consider that possibility. "If it makes sense to go through Dallas, then let's do it," Melanie said, reaching for the glove box. In a moment, she had the map open on her lap, and after turning it a couple of times, she had it facing in the right direction. "Where exactly are we?"

Glancing over, Milo pointed at a spot. "We are northwest of Dallas, and the town we just passed was Paducah."

Melanie ran her finger along the lines shooting out of Dallas until she found the name. "Okay, I found it."

"Good, now find New Orleans at the southern edge of Louisiana. It's along the Gulf of Mexico."

Melanie laughed. "I remember where Louisiana is," she said. "I did learn a few things in high school."

Shaking her head, Milo laughed too. "Sorry," she said. "I just don't want to assume."

"It's the blonde hair, isn't it?" Melanie asked, still smiling, while she found New Orleans. She ran her finger between the two spots. "That's quite a ways," she said softly as she realized the only practical path was straight through Dallas. With her finger on the city's name, she hesitated.

She saw Milo glance over, and her eyes went straight to Dallas. "You're sure about this?" she asked, and even though Melanie felt a tightness in her throat, she nodded.

"I'm ready," she said, not entirely sure it was true but knowing it was another part of her journey. *No different than going to Grand Pickett,* she thought. *Or visiting my parents' grave.* She stared at the map. *And maybe it will help me forgive them.*

Sitting along the curb in front of the Sweet Caroline bar, Milo waited to see what Melanie wanted to do. They were in downtown Dallas, and she had been surprised when the woman wanted to go to the bar. Her explanation had been short, and Milo didn't press.

"When I walked in those doors, it was the beginning of the chapter that changed my life forever," she had said. "I want to see if it's still there."

Milo had agreed, and they fought traffic, getting lost twice trying to find the place. Sometimes it was frustrating, and Melanie apologized, but Milo believed it would be worth the trouble. Once they were there, Melanie seemed content to stare out her car window at the bar's front door. Knowing all she could do was be patient while the woman worked through whatever was inside her head, Milo shut off the Cadillac and relaxed in her seat.

After a few minutes, Melanie turned to her. "I want to go inside and have a drink."

Milo nodded. "Do you want me to come with you?

A soft look came into Melanie's eyes. "I want nothing more," she said, and after getting out of the car, they stepped through the door into a darkened room. The bar looked like it had once been stylish but now was worse for wear. Half empty liquor bottles lined one wall in front of a vast mirror behind the long, scratched and faded wooden bar. Melanie sighed. "Well, this doesn't look quite like I remember it."

Without waiting for Milo to comment, she walked right up to the bar. With the place nearly empty, there were several available stools, and Melanie slipped onto one. Glancing over her shoulder, she caught Milo's eye and patted the seat beside her. "Sidle up, cowgirl," she said. "And let me buy you a drink." Relieved to see Melanie's playfulness, Milo smiled as she crossed the floor and took her stool. The aging bartender with a handlebar mustache joined them.

"What will it be, folks?"

"I'll take a lemon drop," she replied before turning to Milo. "What can he make you?"

Milo would have been content with a light beer, but something in the woman's tone made her believe having a proper cocktail would be the only thing that suited the moment. "I'll take a whiskey sour," Milo said. "No bitters."

The bartender nodded. "One lemon drop and one whiskey sour sans bitters coming right up," he said before walking away. Melanie put her hand on Milo's. As always, her skin was soft and warm.

The woman sighed. "You're very special to me, Milo," Melanie said softly. Milo gave the comment some thought.

Does she mean that because I let her go to the Grand Canyon and then took her back home? she wondered. *Or is there more behind the words?* Underneath all the glamour, Milo cared for the Melanie she had gotten to know. *Because there is more for me.* Suddenly, she realized somewhere along the line she had fallen in love with Melanie. *The woman I have to let go.*

The thought made her sad, but she hid it with a smile, trying to lighten the mood. "Well, I feel the same about you."

Melanie gave her a half smile in return. "You might not feel that way if you knew how angry I was right this moment."

Milo raised her eyebrows. "Angry?" she asked. "Because this is where you had your first drink that night in Dallas?"

Nodding, Milo watched Melanie find herself in the mirror. "Yes," she said. "But I'm not angry for the reasons you think I am." Before Melanie could continue, the bartender was back with their drinks. Melanie picked up hers after he wandered away and held it toward Milo. "I'd like to make a toast."

Milo picked up the whiskey sour. "What are we toasting?"

Melanie lifted her chin. "A toast to new, better memories I will have forever," she said, and, not liking the ominous sound of the statement, Milo hesitated for a beat before clinking her glass against Melanie's.

"To new memories," she said, accepting what could not be changed and sipping her whiskey sour.

Chapter Twenty-Eight

By evening, Melanie used an old-fashioned metal key to let them into a small room at the Hotel St. Pierre. They drove straight through from Dallas to New Orleans, and as she flopped onto one of the two queen beds, every muscle in her body felt exhausted. Milo followed, carrying both pieces of luggage, and she put them down at her feet, surveying the room. "Doesn't seem like much," she said, and Melanie rolled onto her side to survey more of the space. The two beds filled most of it with their heavy dark-stained wooden head and footboards. Only a narrow matching nightstand with an ornate, stained-glass lamp on top fit between them. A tall chest of drawers and a quaint writing desk made the room even more crowded.

Melanie agreed it was cramped, but she liked the atmosphere of the room. "Oh, it's not bad at all," she said. "And the location is fantastic." With only a little effort, she had been able to convince Milo to stay in the city's famous French Quarter. Although Melanie didn't remember much from her one visit, she knew driving and parking in the area was challenging. "We can leave the car in valet parking," she had said. "And walk everywhere you want to see."

Milo had agreed at the time but now looked skeptical. "It better be," Milo said in a tired tone reminding Melanie that as exhausted as she was, Milo would be worse from doing all the driving.

She patted the edge of the bed beside her. "Come sit down," she said sitting upright. "You look ready to drop."

Obeying without complaint, Milo plopped down, close enough to brush their hips together sending a tingle through Melanie. The urge to put her arms around Milo was strong, but she resisted for the moment. Something had been off with Milo since the bar, and she wanted to find out why first. For the moment, she would focus on their immediate needs.

Milo rubbed her eyes. "I think I'm more hungry than tired," she said. "But I'm too exhausted to go find anything."

Giving it some thought, Melanie's stomach felt empty too. "Unfortunately, this little hotel won't have room service."

"No, I suppose not," Milo said before her face brightened. "Would you mind if I ordered us a pizza?"

Although unable to remember the last time she had pizza, let alone having it delivered, Melanie nodded. "What kind do you want?"

"Do you like cheese, pepperoni, mushrooms, and olives?" Milo asked, suddenly acting wide awake.

Melanie smiled at the woman's excitement over ordering them dinner. "I like all those, although I'm not sure I've had them together on a pizza."

Pulling herself to her feet, Milo started around the bed for the hotel phone on the nightstand. "I promise, it's delicious," she said. "Maybe the front desk will have recommendations of pizza places nearby."

Letting Milo handle the arrangements, Melanie left the bed, wandering to the bathroom only to stop in the doorway.

"Oh, this is too perfect," she said, taking in the large, white enamel clawfoot tub settled on the black and gray hexagon tiles. A long, hot bath would be heaven on her worn-out body. Looking over her shoulder, she saw Milo hanging up. "Do you mind if I take a bath?"

Milo met her eyes, and Melanie couldn't miss the flicker of something in them before she answered. "That's fine," she said softly. *That was desire,* Melanie thought, pleased to see it back in the woman's eyes. All through the trip, even though chemistry smoldered between them, there seemed to be a constant hot and cold with Milo's passion toward her. *But now something has changed.* Milo seemed distant after their drink in Dallas, and there was no snuggling in the car. Her asking for two beds only proved Melanie's concerns. *But her feelings toward me are still there, and I just saw it.*

For a moment, she considered asking why Milo was pulling back from her, but the tired look on the woman's face made her pause. "I'll be in the tub," she finally said, grabbing the suitcase handle to pull it into the bathroom with her. "Will you let me know when the pizza is here?"

"Of course," Milo answered, her voice huskier than usual, only convincing Melanie further. The thought of her naked, soaking in hot water, had Milo aroused. The steady, confident woman who veiled her emotions so well couldn't quite contain her desire. *And why do I want that? Or even more, what do I do with it?* Melanie wondered while her reactions were all over the place. She knew she needed to figure things out. Soon.

After Melanie closed the bathroom door, Milo dropped her head into her hands. The vision of Melanie soaking in the bathtub threatened to be her undoing. As hard as she worked to keep her thoughts supportive but entirely platonic all afternoon, it wasn't easy. Her emotions continued to betray her. Being in Dallas was the hardest, or at least until the bathtub conversation. During their drink together at the Sweet Caroline bar, when Melanie said Milo was special to her, it was all she could do to play it off as friendly. She could never admit how she truly felt. *And then I screwed it up by letting my want for her show on my face,* she thought with a groan. The hint of color that rose to Melanie's cheeks while Milo all but licked her lips was unmistakable. *Thank God she fled to the bathroom.* Shaking her head, all Milo could do was order the pizza and hope the bathroom also had a shower. Once Melanie was out of there, she would take a cold one.

The pizza order went smoothly, although they couldn't promise to have the order to Milo in under forty minutes. As her stomach growled at the idea of such a long wait, Milo contemplated if she should tell Melanie there was no rush. *Is that a good idea?* she wondered. The mere thought of the woman naked on the other side of the door was enough to make Milo's heart race. Knocking might be too much. Then, she grit her teeth. *I'm being ridiculous. A polite mention the pizza will be late should not be cause for paralysis.* Standing, she went to the door and knocked, but Melanie didn't say anything immediately.

Furrowing her brow, Milo considered knocking again, but then Melanie answered. "Come in."

Milo's eyes widened as she stared at the smooth surface of the wooden door in front of her. "No," she said, trying to keep her voice even. "I wasn't asking to open the door. I wanted to tell you the pizza will be late."

Another few seconds with no answer left Milo thinking she should simply retreat and leave the situation alone. "Milo," Melanie finally said. "Come in."

Her mouth suddenly going dry while her stomach tightened, Milo considered objecting. Opening the door seemed like a terrible idea. Entering the bathroom was even more dangerous to consider, yet every nerve in her body tingled with excitement. *She's probably entirely covered by bubbles*, she thought. *And maybe needs a towel.*

Convinced Melanie wanted something harmless, Milo turned the handle and stepped into the steamy room. "Do you want something?" she asked, relieved but also a little disappointed at the view. The large vintage bathtub dwarfed Melanie's small stature, and only her head was visible.

Melanie watched her. "I do," she said, and there was an unmistakable trace of desire behind the two words. "Take a bath with me." Freezing in place, Milo wasn't sure she could speak if she wanted. *A bath?* she tried to comprehend. *With her?* Milo watched as Melanie's eyes roamed her body. "Are you going to say no?"

Sure it was a mistake, but unable to walk away, Milo did not hesitate. "I won't ever say no," she admitted, stripping off her t-shirt and jeans. As she pulled off her sports bra, she heard Melanie gasp. Milo stopped moving. "What?"

"You have the sexiest body," Melanie said, and Milo couldn't hold back a small smile as she finished removing everything.

"Thank you," she said, approaching the tub to find all but Melanie's head and shoulders buried in white bubbles. "May I join you?"

Melanie smiled with a sultriness Milo had never seen on her face before. "I warn you, the water is hot," she said. "But please get in."

Taking a deep breath, Milo stepped into the water.

Unable to take her eyes off Milo's perfectly toned body, Melanie felt a yearning in her core like she never had. Messing around under the bleachers with boys in high school had excited her and the satisfaction of having them wrapped around her finger was undeniable. Later, when she was with men, starting with the stranger in Dallas all those years ago, there was power in being so desired. All her life, she used her face and body to get where she wanted to be, and the tables never turned. She was always in control. *Until tonight,* she thought. Some men were handsome, sexy, or charismatic, but none made her feel as aroused as she was while Milo slowly entered the bathtub. And her reaction confused the hell out of her.

While Milo's body slipped under the surface, she let out a hum of pleasure. "This feels good," she murmured as her eyes met Melanie's. The usual hazel color seemed to have darkened, and a flush of color highlighted her cheeks. Once again, Melanie realized Milo was truly stunning. The beauty was easy to miss behind the broad shoulders, close-cropped hair, and rugged clothing. Only because Milo let her in had Melanie seen it, and she felt lucky. Under Melanie's scrutiny, Milo's eyes narrowed. "What are you thinking?"

"About how attractive you are," Melanie didn't hesitate to answer. "When we get to New York, I want you to let me arrange a photographer."

Milo blinked. "Why?"

Drawn to the woman, Melanie pulled up her knees and let her body glide through the water until she was close enough to touch Milo's face. Slowly, she reached to run her fingertips along her still slightly bruised cheekbone, then down her jawline, to linger on her lips. "I want him to capture your face as I see it," she said, and Milo took Melanie's hand in hers to kiss the tips of her fingers.

"I don't see it," she said, leaning forward until they were face to face. "You are the one who is attractive." Before Melanie could disagree, the woman kissed her. Erotic flames radiated through her body at the feel of Milo's lips. The touch was tender but with a promise of much more behind it.

Wanting to feel more of the intensity, Melanie cupped Milo's face and kissed her back, harder and with more urgency. A moan escaped from Milo's throat and knowing how much she was exciting the sexy woman made Melanie all the more turned on. Nipping at her bottom lip before kissing her again, Melanie quivered when she was rewarded with the touch of Milo's tongue on hers. In a moment, she knew kisses were not enough. Melanie pulled back to whisper in Milo's ear. "Take me to the bed."

"Are you sure?" Milo murmured, and Melanie answered by leaving a trail of kisses along her neck before sliding away to have room to stand. As she lifted out of the water, the sensual feeling of the suds sliding down her breasts, stomach, and hips made her gasp. She wanted Milo's hands in all those places and more, but just as much, she wanted to touch her in all those places too.

Although she never believed she would want a woman, the burning desire in her for Milo left her breathless. "Yes," she murmured in answer to Milo's question. "I've never been more sure."

Chapter Twenty-Nine

Although her entire body thrummed like a live wire, Milo moved slowly as she lifted herself out of the bathtub. Unable to keep her eyes off Melanie's naked body, an ache started deep inside her. As the woman's blue eyes watched every movement Milo made, there was no way Melanie could comprehend what she was doing to her on every level. Their smoldering chemistry over the last week had finally burst into flames.

As soon as Milo was on the bathmat beside the tub, she started to move closer, but Melanie held up her hand. "Wait," she said, and Milo froze, unsure if she would survive if everything stopped now but forced herself to be patient. "I want to dry you." Melanie reached for a towel and gently, with slightly trembling hands, she slid the fabric over Milo's skin. Starting with her shoulders, Melanie ran the towel down Milo's arms, across her chest, before lingering on one breast and then the other until the nipples grew hard. Milo watched Melanie bite her lip at the sight, but then the woman continued. Using the towel to wipe away the water on her stomach, she paused above the hair between Milo's legs. "I don't know what I'm doing."

Milo swallowed hard. "Don't know as in you're unsure you mean to be touching me like this?" she asked. "Or that you've never explored a woman?"

Looking into Milo's eyes, Melanie lowered the towel until it grazed Milo's upper thighs. "Let's be clear," she said. "There is nothing in me unsure that I want to be touching you right now."

"In that case, I think you are doing great," Milo whispered.

Melanie gave a little laugh. "Please tell me when I'm not."

Slowly, Milo took the towel from her and draped it around Melanie's back until she could pull her closer. Their skin touched, and it was as if a lightning bolt shot through Milo's being. Passion like she hadn't felt in a long time, if ever, flamed to life. When Melanie gasped, Milo knew she also felt the powerful wave of need. Dipping her head, Milo kissed the incredibly sexy woman and was rewarded when Melanie opened her lips to let the kiss go deeper. A growl came from low in Milo's throat, and the need to pick up Melanie to take her to the bed was intense. Only the greatest of willpower kept her most primal instincts in check.

As if reading her mind, Melanie broke the kiss. "I can't stand here like this and keep kissing you," she said. "My legs are so weak I'm afraid I will collapse any second."

Taking the words as a cue, Milo wrapped her arms around Melanie's hips and lifted her small frame easily. "Then let me help you," she said, carrying her to one of the beds.

Clearly loving the sudden show of strength, Melanie cried out with excitement and put her arms around Milo's neck. "This is so crazy," she said. "Never in a million years would I let a guy carry me around like this, but for some reason I love what you're doing."

"Do you?" Milo murmured, taking satisfaction in knowing she pleased her. "I only want to make you happy." As they reached the bed, Milo started to set Melanie down, but the woman didn't let go, and they tumbled onto the bed. Instinctively, Milo took them into another kiss while rolling onto her back to pull Melanie on top of her. In an instant, the woman was straddling Milo, and she felt the wet heat between her legs pressing down on Milo's thighs. Breaking the kiss, Melanie sat up, and Milo didn't think she had ever seen anything so sexy. Blonde hair, wet at the tips, spilling down her shoulders and to the tops of her breasts. Tight nipples gave away the depth of her arousal. Half-closed eyes reflected the need Milo felt.

Melanie ran her hands down her own body as she tilted her head. "I want to make you happy too," she said. "Do you like what you see?"

"Yes," Milo breathed. "Yes, I do."

Melanie had never been more turned on while at the same time more nervous in her life. As she straddled Milo, she felt heat rising from the woman's skin. The sensation ignited a raging passion inside her that she wanted to let loose in a way that would make Milo feel as excited as she did. She hadn't been lying in the bathroom when she told Milo she didn't know what she was doing. Yet her instincts had her wanting to explore the woman's sexy body with her fingertips, with her lips. To trail them along the slope of her broad shoulders, leading to her small, firm breasts and then across her tight abdomen. *I want to know every part of her*, she thought, and the intensifying throb between her legs threatened to drive her wild.

Looking at Milo's face, their eyes held, and there was an intensity in them that made Melanie shiver with excitement.

Although she had an idea, she wasn't sure what Milo would do to her, but she knew it would be like nothing else she had ever experienced. *And not just because she is a woman*, she thought. *But because this is a new level of desire intertwined with passion for me. That's what makes it different.* "I want you," Milo murmured. "But only do what you are comfortable with."

"I want you too," Melanie said. "But I don't want to do it wrong."

Milo smiled with both tenderness and longing. "You can't do it wrong."

Biting her lip, she hesitated. "But I want to make you feel everything I'm feeling," she said. "Just sitting here doing nothing but feel you under me is making me crazy."

"Then touch me," Milo said, and taking a deep breath for courage, Melanie slid her hands up the woman's tight stomach to her breasts, running her fingertips over the tight nipples. The sensation of hearing Milo draw a quick breath at the contact made Melanie feel bolder, and as she explored, she started to move her hips. The friction between their skin made her shudder.

Milo moaned at the new movement, and Melanie leaned in to kiss her, but before their lips met, there was a light knock on the hotel room door. Milo's eyes popped open. "Shit," she growled. "The pizza."

Unable to help herself, Melanie leaned back and laughed at the mixture of surprise and frustration on Milo's face. "Just as I was finally getting up my nerve, I'm interrupted by a delivery boy," Melanie said. "I hope he doesn't expect a tip."

Milo started to lift her off. "I'll get it," she said with a growl, but Melanie pushed her down.

"No, I'll get it," she said, rolling off Milo and pulling the comforter from the other bed to wrap around her. When she opened the door, a pudgy, slightly balding middle-aged man was holding a pizza box in front of him.

Unquestionably surprised by her lack of wardrobe he blinked. "Uh, sorry," he mumbled, as if realizing he had interrupted something intimate.

"It's fine," Melanie said, snaking an arm out from under the blanket to take the food from him. "But I'm afraid I don't have a tip for you."

The man started backing away while he shook his head. "No problem," he said and darted down the hall while Melanie closed the door. Turning to Milo, she found her under the bed covers.

Melanie felt a twinge of disappointment, missing the view of the woman's nakedness, and hoped the moment wasn't over. "I think we embarrassed him," she said, carrying the pizza across the small room.

Milo smiled. "Well, he deserved it," she said. "He did interrupt something."

Melanie slid the pizza box onto the top of the small writing desk and fixed Milo with a look. "Yes, he did," she said. "But if you don't mind, I'd rather eat cold pizza tonight."

Milo pulled back the covers, inviting her in. "I don't mind at all." Dropping the comforter to the floor, leaving her naked again, Melanie climbed into bed.

"Now, where were we?" Melanie said, sliding beside Milo, who rested on her elbow. "I think I was on top of you."

Nuzzling Melanie's neck, Milo nipped at her ear, loving the smell of the woman's skin and the feel of her hair on her face. "I think you're right," she said and took hold of Melanie's wrists while she lay back, easily pulling the smaller woman on top. Lying there, face-to-face, Milo felt a stirring inside her like she never had before. *What is so different about her?* she wondered. Not only a physical attraction, although at that moment she felt ready to burst into flames, but there was more. Every other relationship with women in the past paled in comparison to how she felt toward Melanie.

"Tell me what to do," Melanie whispered, and Milo kissed her.

"Follow your instincts," she said, and after a moment of hesitation, Melanie started to trace her lips along Milo's jaw, leaving a burning trail. Sliding lower, Melanie kissed and nipped at Milo's neck, then the inside of her shoulder, until Milo felt on fire. She felt her body tightening, and a part of her wanted to resist because she was usually the one taking control but stopping Melanie would be a mistake. The last thing she wanted was for the woman to feel like there was something wrong with what she was doing. Still, it would mean Milo would have to be entirely vulnerable, and as Melanie slid her mouth across her nipples, she had to force herself to stay on her back.

Melanie started to suck, at first tentative, but when Milo arched her back to press into her, the woman pulled on her nipples with more confidence. Jolts of pleasure shot through her, and Milo ran a hand into Melanie's long hair while at the same time starting to squirm. "That feels incredible," she growled and spread her legs wide enough to let the Melanie's weight press down against her center.

Lifting her head, Melanie gasped at the contact. "I can't believe I'm making you so wet," she said. "I can feel you against me."

"That's how much I want you," Milo said, and in response, Melanie slid lower until she stopped at the center between Milo's legs.

"You have to tell me if I'm doing something you don't want," Melanie whispered, and Milo knew that as hard as it was to relinquish control, she did want it. If she could only let herself relax, the intensity of any contact might make her climax.

Milo swallowed hard, needing to surrender as much as she could. "Keep going," Milo murmured. "You're making me feel incredible."

As if taking confidence from her words, Melanie slid her mouth to the inside of Milo's thighs, tasting one side and then the other and making Milo start to shake. She wanted to tell Melanie she was killing her with the teasing but worried the woman might stop. That was the last thing she wanted. There was a moment of hesitation, but Milo forced herself to stay still and wait. Then Melanie slid her tongue through Milo's wetness, making her cry out as she touched the tip of her clit. Unable to help herself, Milo lifted her hips, wanting Melanie's mouth tighter against her. Taking the cue, the woman added pressure while starting to slide her mouth slightly back and forth. If there was any concern that Melanie's inexperience would be an issue, it was forgotten.

With the need in her growing stronger with every stroke, Milo closed her eyes and thought of all the ways she would take Melanie. Aching to know what she would feel like when Milo slid her fingers inside her. Almost desperate to hear the sounds Melanie would make as she came in Milo's mouth. All the images were what she needed to let go, and when Melanie intuitively added more pressure, lightly sucking on her, Milo let the wave of an orgasm take her at last.

Chapter Thirty

Sitting outside the famous Café Du Monde, Melanie tried to eat a beignet without white powdered sugar going everywhere. She could not believe she was so hungry. The poorly timed but delicious pizza from the night before was long gone. *And I did burn a lot of calories,* she thought with a satisfied smile. They had managed to stay awake long enough to both eat the pizza and spend at least another hour enjoying each other. The memory of how fantastic a lover Milo was fluttered her stomach. Color rose to her cheeks as she pictured them wrapped up naked in the sheets, spent and drowsy.

"I don't know for certain what you're thinking," Milo said from where she sat across the small, wrought iron table. Her battle with the powdered sugar was not going well either, and it peppered the black surface. The effort was worth the trouble though, as the French pastry was beyond delicious. Added to the flavors of the rich chicory coffee in the hot café au lait, and their day was starting perfectly. "But I can tell it is something good."

Her smile growing wider at being caught red-handed,

Melanie finished the beignet and started to lick her fingers. She moved slowly while keeping eye contact with Milo as she touched each one. Milo's eyes widened. "Now who is thinking something good?" Melanie asked as she finished, pleased to see desire reflecting in Milo's gaze.

"Maybe I'm trying to think of how long it would take me to get you back to the hotel?"

Melanie waved a finger. "Oh, no," she said. "You're going to have to wait. There is a lot to explore, and I know you're excited."

Nodding, Milo finished her coffee. "Fair enough," she said, setting down the mug before reaching across the table to take Melanie's hand. "Thank you for being willing to do this today." Milo brushed her thumb across Melanie's skin, and a tingle ran through her from the warmth of Milo's fingers. *Such magical fingers too*, she thought, a memory of how they explored her body earlier as the first rays of sunlight filtered in through the lace curtains. *I want to learn to touch her like that.*

Not ready to be caught blushing again, Melanie squeezed Milo's hand. "There is no place I would rather be," she replied, meaning it more than she would have ever thought possible two weeks ago. Being with Milo made her happy. It was as simple as that, and she tried not to think about what would happen in a few days when the trip was over. There seemed no good outcome when they got to New York.

Milo glanced at her watch. "If we leave now, we should arrive at the Mardi Gras costume museum right when they are opening."

Smiling to cover her anxiety about the near future, Melanie slid back her chair. "I'm ready," she said, brushing the few stray spots of white powder from her yellow and blue dress. "This will be interesting. I've never been to Mardi Gras, but it looks like a lot of fun."

Milo took her hand as they started to walk past Jackson

Square. "Then I will take you to one," she said, making Melanie pause their steps. "I promise."

Looking into Milo's face, she saw nothing but sincerity. *She really believes we can come back here together,* she thought. "I would like that," she murmured, but her heart knew the chances of their returning for the famous festival were slim. *But maybe not impossible.* Worry filled her stomach. *This is going to get so difficult.* "But you'll have to be patient with me."

After a soft kiss on the lips, Milo rested her forehead against Melanie's. "I didn't mean for that promise to put pressure on you," she said. "But I don't want to go to Mardi Gras with anyone but you." All Melanie could do was nod because, as complicated as it was, she felt the same.

Milo was having one of the best days of her life. New Orleans proved to be as exciting and engaging as she had ever hoped. Having Melanie beside her experiencing and discussing everything from her perspective had been perfect. After shopping the French Market, exploring a historic cemetery to visit the grave of Marie Laveau, the famous and powerful voodoo priestess, and tasting the many delectable treats New Orleans offered, they ended up on Bourbon Street. With daylight fading, the place was a mini festival in motion as people of all shapes, sizes, colors, and genders enjoyed the bright sights and sounds. "This is amazing," Melanie said, holding Milo's hand. "I'm so happy we did this."

"Me too," Milo replied, grinning ear to ear while jazz music rolled out from the different brightly lit bars. A man playing a saxophone on the sidewalk drew a crowd and people tossed tips in the instrument's open case. Others started to dance in the street. Excitement was in the air, and if she had to capture it all in a word, Milo would call the oncoming night magical.

Starting to move her hips to the music, Melanie turned to Milo. "How about a drink?" Melanie said with a smile. "One of those blue, frosty looking things." She pointed as a young couple walked by holding clear plastic cups filled with a vivid blue cocktail.

Liking the idea, Milo nodded. "All right," she said. Happy to oblige, she pecked Melanie on the lips. "Do you want to stay and watch the show?"

"I'll be right here," Melanie said, and Milo ducked into the closest bar.

Walking to the crowded counter, it took a few minutes for one of the bartenders to get to her. "What will it be?" the woman with purple-streaked hair asked.

"A pair of those blue drinks," Milo said with a smile. "I don't know what they're called."

"Blue Bayou," the young man sitting on a stool beside her said, glancing up from his phone. "Vodka and blue curacao."

"Seems appropriate."

The bartender held up two fingers. "You said two?" Milo nodded. "Coming right up." After the woman moved down the counter to make the drinks, Milo stood beside the stranger who scrolled through his phone. Unable to help but see the screen, she swore she saw Melanie's picture swiped past.

Milo squinted, but then the image was gone. "I'm sorry," she said. "This might be the rudest thing I have ever done, but I saw something on your phone."

The young man shrugged. "No worries. I'm just flipping through random stuff."

"That's kind of why I brought it up," she said. "I thought I saw a picture of someone I recognized."

He started to scroll back. "Oh yeah? Tell me to stop when you see them again."

It only took a second. "Stop," Milo said as she stared at the picture of Melanie. The woman was almost unrecognizable with her blonde hair pinned up, excessive jewelry on, and wearing a lot more makeup. Heavy eyeshadow and bright red lipstick that made her look older.

The stranger looked at Milo. "You know her?" he asked, and before Milo nodded, she read the small caption under the picture. 'Melanie Sotheby, $25,000 reward for information.'

Forcing her face to stay neutral, she shook her head. "No," Milo said. "I mean, anyone could know that face, but you know what I mean."

"Well, that's too bad you don't know where she is," the young man said as the drinks arrived. "That's a nice reward."

Milo quickly paid cash for them. "Yeah," she said as she picked up the cocktails and turned to go. "Too bad." Moving as fast as she could without drawing attention to herself or spilling the drinks on anyone, Milo looked for Melanie. She had wandered closer to the street musician and was beaming with enjoyment at the entertainment. *This is going to upset her*, Milo thought. *But we need to get out of here before someone recognizes her if they haven't already*. Thankfully Melanie looked over, and when their eyes met, something must have shown on Milo's face because she watched the woman's smile fade.

It only took a second for Melanie to know something was very wrong. Not sure what to expect, she hurried over. "Milo, what is it?" she asked as the woman handed her one of the drinks.

"Take this and act naturally," Milo said. "But we need to get out of here. Walk with me." Her heart racing at all the sudden urgency, Melanie took the plastic cup and sipped while Milo casually did the same before moving down Bourbon Street. They were headed in the direction of their hotel. "Let's go."

"Hey," someone yelled from behind them, and Melanie started to look.

"Don't," Milo said, enough alarm in her voice to make Melanie blink with surprise. "Don't turn around. Just keep walking."

Melanie felt a trickle of real fear now. "What is happening?" she hissed under her breath.

"I'll explain everything once we get around the corner," Milo said. "Right now, we need to get lost in this crowd."

Biting her lip, Melanie tried to keep up with Milo's longer stride as they weaved their way through couples and groups of people. When they finally reached the next street and Milo started to turn the corner, Melanie had waited long enough. Tossing her drink in the city trashcan, she stopped. Whatever the bad news was, she wanted to face it head on.

"Tell me what is wrong?" she said. "Or I'm not taking another step."

Milo nodded, throwing away her drink too. "Okay," she said. "But please keep walking. I want to make sure we are far enough away."

"From who?"

"Everyone," Milo said, running a hand over her face while Melanie just stared at her. She didn't know what to even ask after that statement. Milo took her hand and started them walking again. "I know it sounds crazy, but while I was in the bar, I saw your picture on a man's phone."

Melanie's eyebrows scrunched together. "My picture?"

Waiting to let traffic pass before crossing the next street, Milo nodded. "Luckily, the photo doesn't look like how you do now. I mean without all the makeup and the fancy hairdo."

"I'm still not sure I understand," Melanie said, and then it clicked. It had been days since she had any contact with Monty or anyone he would know. "Oh my God, he's started searching for me. Is there some sort of reward?"

"There is," Milo said. Melanie frowned, wondering what Monty felt she was worth, but then let it go. *I'll find out soon enough*, she thought, knowing it was time to talk with her husband. *If nothing else but to tell him to call off the hunt.* Another thought struck her, and her heart leaped into her throat—Milo and her criminal record. If someone caught them before Monty knew the real story, it would look bad. Anything could go wrong with a misunderstanding. *And I won't let that happen.*

She was ready to act. "Let's go back to the hotel," she said, walking even faster than Milo. "We need a phone, and the temporary one you bought in Los Angeles is in my suitcase. We will probably need to charge it, but I think it's the safest way to call him."

"Safest?" Milo asked. "What do you mean?" Melanie wasn't sure what she meant, but she had the strangest feeling that Monty might try to have someone trace any calls or use a GPS locator. She didn't understand all the technology other than what she saw on television, but she wouldn't put it past him to use all his resources. "That way, if we need to, we can toss the thing after I talk to him. I don't think I'm ready to have him know my exact location."

They reached their hotel's street. "Do you think we can go back to the room?" Milo asked. "How well did the pizza deliveryman see you?"

Melanie slowed her steps as she thought about Milo's questions. "I can't be sure," she said. "But he seemed flustered, and I know I probably looked different considering I was just out a bath. And what we were doing." Unable to help herself, the memory made her smile. It had been a fantastic night. *And now it's all going to come crashing down*, she thought as her stomach clenched at the idea she would soon be back to her old life.

Chapter Thirty-One

Driving north on Interstate 59, Milo's arm wrapped around Melanie who nestled beside her. The woman had been upset ever since the phone conversation with her husband. Last night, Melanie found the cellphone in her suitcase and called Monty. When Milo suggested she go for a walk to give her privacy, Melanie wanted her to stay. "I need you near me," she said, and Milo did what she asked. Once the call went through, Milo couldn't hear both sides of the exchange, but she got the gist from Melanie's answers and body language. Whatever the man said didn't make Melanie happy.

So much so that after Melanie hung up, she burst into tears. Not sure what to say, Milo wrapped her arms around the woman who rested her head against her chest. They stood together silently for a couple of minutes until Melanie's sobs stopped. "I don't expect you to tell me any details," Milo had said. "But I need to know how I can help."

"Thank you," Melanie said with her face still buried against Milo's shirt. "Thank you for everything." A moment later, she had pulled back, wiping her eyes. "Sorry, but I needed a few minutes to let that all out."

Milo gave a slow nod. "It's all right."

Sinking onto the edge of the bed, Melanie took a deep breath. "Actually, it's not all right," she said. "And there's not much you can do to help, unfortunately." She covered her face with her hands. "Monty wants me to come back right now, and he wants to send a plane." The words made a lead ball drop in Milo's stomach. She knew all along their relationship was temporary, but that did not make hearing the end was coming any easier. Unexpected tears stung her eyes, but she quickly blinked them away.

She would not let her emotions get in the way of whatever Melanie wanted to do. "Do I need to take you to the airport?" Milo asked, swallowing hard.

Melanie shook her head. "I told him I didn't need his help," she said. "But we have to leave early in the morning. He's already impatient."

"We can start tonight," Milo said even though every word hurt her more and more.

"No," Melanie said. "I want to be here with you and have you hold me all night."

That was what they had done. There were no more tears, although Milo could tell Melanie wasn't sleeping. Milo wished she could find words to console her but kept silent. Their magical world together had crashed down, and Milo felt sick about it. The inevitability of returning to her dismal world in Los Angeles saddened her. *It's just something I will live with*, she had thought and then tried to sleep.

Raindrops started to spatter the windshield as she passed an eighteen-wheeler. Driving back under dark skies seemed appropriate. If they drove straight through, they would be in New York City in nineteen hours. Going that far would be exhausting, but Milo was determined to do it. If Melanie needed to go home, she would get her there. Yet as they neared the exit for Sandersville, Mississippi, there was a tall sign for a local diner. Melanie raised her head from Milo's shoulder. "I could really use a cup of coffee and some food," she said. "Can we stop at that restaurant?" Milo considered arguing that they should wait until they had to get gas in another hour, but the last thing she wanted was conflict with Melanie. Milo turned on her signal. Even though the stop would stretch their already long timeline, the break would do Milo good too. After a predawn start and not taking the time to eat or drink, Milo could use some eggs, bacon, and caffeine.

Stepping quickly through the pouring rain to push through the diner's front doors, Melanie knew having them stop was a stalling tactic, but she couldn't help it. Even though she had promised Monty she would be back soon, she wasn't ready. The thought of leaving Milo shattered her, yet Milo had reacted differently. After Melanie explained how Monty wanted her home immediately, Milo seemed to slam the door on her emotions. Suddenly she was determined to drive Melanie to New York as quickly as humanly possible. She had even told Melanie she wanted to drive straight through, but that was crazy. *Or is it?* she wondered as she stood beside the woman waiting to be seated. *Maybe Milo has the right attitude and getting home will be for the best for both of us*, she thought. *Maybe it will help stop the hurting.* She stifled a sob at the image of being trapped in the mansion with Monty again. *What am I going to do?*

Last night, as she lay in Milo's arms listening to the rhythmic breathing of the woman she cared so much about, she tried to answer that question. Although they had only known each other a little while, the thought of having Milo wander out of her life was heartbreaking. Yet Melanie could not see how she could fit into her old life. Her conversation with Monty, though short, made it clear nothing had changed. "Thank God," Monty had said once Melanie said hello. "Where are you?"

"That doesn't matter, does it?" Melanie had replied.

"Baby, baby, baby," Monty cooed. "Don't be like that. I was worried something terrible happened to you." A million different bitchy retorts had come to Melanie's mind, but when she glanced at Milo, she held them back. Mean and quick-tempered wasn't the woman she wanted to be anymore. Forever oblivious, Monty continued. "I want you to come home. Tell me where you are."

Melanie shook her head. "No, I'm not ready," she replied and meant the words to the depth of her soul.

There was a pause on the line. "What do you mean you're not ready?" Monty asked, a hint of suspicion in his tone. "I'll send the plane to wherever you are and have you back where you belong in a few hours max."

"No," Melanie repeated. "I have my own transportation, and I'll be there soon."

"How soon?"

Still looking at Milo, she considered asking the woman how far away they were from New York but realized that could be a mistake. She didn't want to do anything that might tip off Monty that she was not alone. Having him learn about Milo before she got home to explain their business arrangement felt like a very bad idea. "Soon." she finally answered. "I promise."

"All right," Monty said. "But I don't like you making me wait. I need you here."

"It's for the best," Melanie said. "Now call off the hunt for me."

After a laugh, he had agreed he would. "I promise, no paratroopers will come rappelling through your window tonight."

Not until she and Milo were sliding into the booth at the diner did Melanie realize her husband hadn't bothered to apologize. It was as if he didn't feel at all sorry for what he did in Los Angeles. As Melanie looked across the table at Milo, the differences between them could not be more apparent. While some would only focus on the physical contrasts, the true distinction was on the inside. Monty considered her his possession to be treated however he wanted with no concerns. Not about her feelings or opinions or especially not her dreams. *But those all mean everything to Milo*, she thought. *Just like hers matter to me.* A tenderness filled her heart, and Melanie had a revelation as she watched Milo consider the menu. Somewhere over the last two thousand miles, she had fallen in love with Milo.

Glancing up from the menu, Milo noticed Melanie was looking at her, and the expression was especially sad. Considering the circumstances, Milo understood and was sure her face looked the same, although Melanie's eyes held anxiousness too. *Like someone who is trapped?* she wondered. *How can I take her back to New York if she looks like that?* Putting down the menu, she slid her hand across the table, and Melanie clasped it almost desperately. Wanting to know what Melanie was thinking, Milo opened her mouth only to be interrupted by the waitress arriving at their table. "Can I get y'all some coffee?" the woman in the red and white checkered waitress uniform asked.

"Coffee would be good," Milo answered while Melanie pulled her hand back.

"Yes, please," Melanie said in an almost embarrassed tone. Milo had never seen her act so withdrawn, and suddenly she worried she had things all wrong. Maybe the woman regretted her decision to keep going with Milo and was trying to figure out how to tell her.

Milo waited for the waitress to leave. "Melanie, I need you to be completely honest with me," she said. "Do you wish you took Monty up on his offer and went to the airport?" Even saying the words made her sick to her stomach and the idea of a greasy breakfast no longer sounded appealing.

With a pained look on her face, Melanie shook her head. "No," she said. "How can you say that? Do you have regrets?"

Puzzled, Milo frowned. "I am confused," she said. "When you pulled your hand away..."

"We are in Mississippi in the middle of nowhere," Melanie said, glancing around. "And I don't want you to get into trouble." Her eyes welled up with tears. "I promise, that is the last thing I ever want."

"I'm not afraid."

Melanie gave her a sad smile. "Of course, you wouldn't be," she said a moment before Milo heard the door to the diner opening. Whoever it was made Melanie's eyes widen as she stared in that direction. Alarmed, Milo glanced over her shoulder, unsure what she expected, but the uniform of a Mississippi State Trooper made her heart stop. As he glanced around the diner, he was clearly looking for someone. Before Milo could form the thought that it might be a coincidence and had nothing to do with Melanie, the man was headed over.

He slipped off his hat as he approached. "Melanie Sotheby?" he asked in a deep baritone laced with a heavy Southern accent. Melanie stared at him, and for a moment Milo thought she might deny it.

Finally, she slowly nodded. "Yes," she said. "How did you find me?"

"Not entirely sure, but if I had to guess, the folks who sent me after ya were using GPS," he said. "I was cruising my usual route when dispatch clued me in." Milo's heart sunk. After Melanie said Monty promised to call off the search for her, they thought keeping the phone was safe. They were wrong.

"I should have known he wouldn't be patient," Melanie said, resignation in her voice. "So, what now?"

The trooper sighed. "I hate to interrupt your breakfast, but I have instructions to deliver you to the Jackson airport straightaway.

Melanie frowned. "And if I say no?"

"Now, ma'am," the trooper said, turning his hat in his hands. "Don't make this difficult for me." Finally, he glanced at Milo. "Not sure what to do with you, though."

Milo swallowed hard, unable to shake the trickle of fear at having a law enforcement officer staring at her. She cleared her throat. "I'm Elizabeth Milo and—"

Before she finished her explanation, Melanie interrupted. "I hired her to drive me to New York," she said, staring Milo hard in the eyes. "Thank you for everything, but it looks like we are done. I will have Monty contact you about payment later." Surprised by the dismissive tone, all Milo did was nod as Melanie slipped out of the booth. "Let's go. I see no reason to wait."

So shocked she felt numb, Milo watched the woman who captured her heart walk away. The trooper held the door for her, and then she was gone without a look back.

Chapter Thirty-Two

As she boarded Monty's Gulfstream jet, Melanie had the strangest sensation she was walking into a cage. While she waited at the airport with the Mississippi State Trooper, in many ways, she felt like a prisoner. She wasn't sure what the man would've done if she tried to leave but knew it would not end well. Apparently, Monty wanted her home badly if he was willing to go to such extremes. Besides, making a scene might have felt good at the time, but the outcome would end up the same.

A voluptuous, red-haired flight attendant waited for her at the top of the stairs. Long legs under a short skirt with a form-fitting uniform top showing off her more than ample breasts. Melanie had never seen her before, but that didn't mean anything. Monty kept a revolving door of flight attendants, each looking younger than the last.

"Welcome aboard, Mrs. Sotheby," the woman said with a hint of a Southern accent. There was also an underlying tone that immediately put Melanie off. *Is she talking down to me?* Melanie wondered, becoming more irritated by the second.

Then the realization struck her—Monty was most likely screwing the flight attendant. *Shocker*.

Brushing past the woman, Melanie headed toward the lounge. "I need a drink. Gin and tonic," Melanie said as she sank into one of the plush leather chairs. "How long will it take to get to New York?"

"A few hours," the woman answered. A smirk flashed on the attractive flight attendant's face. "So, make yourself comfortable."

Melanie leveled her glare at the significantly younger woman. "What is your name?"

"Lila," the flight attendant said, her smirk turning to a beaming smile. Melanie wondered where Monty had found her. *Pretty face, but not the right body for a New York model,* she thought. *Aspiring actress?* She was certain Lila wasn't a real stewardess. *Let's just hope she knows how to make a decent drink.*

Melanie lifted her chin, not about to be intimidated. "Well, Lila," Melanie said, drawing out the name. "I only need one thing from you, and that is for you to go fetch my drink."

Lila's eyes narrowed. "Coming right up, Mrs. Sotheby," she said but didn't immediately move to fill the order. "By the way, nice dress."

Feeling the insult full force, Melanie was about to shoot back something nasty about Lila sleeping with her husband but paused. There was no reason to give the woman the satisfaction of getting to Melanie. "Thank you," she said instead. "I love the color blue especially." Lila's smirk flickered as if confused by the pleasant answer. *Looks like Monty has found himself a bright one this time,* Melanie thought with a smirk of her own. *His standards are getting lower every day.* Then a thought came to her. *How much would he pay as a reward to help find Lila?* When Melanie eventually asked Milo the amount, the woman hesitated, only to eventually reveal it was twenty-five thousand. *Is that why Lila thinks she can dismiss me? Because my value to Monty is so low?*

Melanie felt anger well up in her chest. For a man with more money than he could ever spend, that was all she was worth to him—less than even his cheapest car. "Drink," Melanie said to Lila, pointing in the direction of the plane's bar. "Now." Without another word, the flight attendant turned on her heel and left. Melanie rested back into the seat and felt the jet make its way to the runway. She was actually going back home and leaving Milo behind. *I didn't even say goodbye*, she thought, imagining how it must have felt to be left sitting in the booth in the diner. *That was so unfair of me.* But in the moment, it was the only way she could act without completely breaking down. Becoming a wreck would have solved nothing. As the plane took off, Melanie only hoped she would have a second chance at saying goodbye. Somehow.

With the radio blasting as loud as the old speakers could handle, Milo raced west in the Cadillac. There was no destination in mind other than to get back to Los Angeles and put the journey with Melanie behind her. She could not stop thinking about how the woman walked out the diner's door without a goodbye. *Not even a glance back*, Milo thought as tears burned her eyes. *Maybe I should have gotten up and followed her. Maybe I should've stopped her before she got into the trooper's car and asked to her face if going back was what she truly wanted.* But she hadn't, and a part of Milo believed rushing after Melanie would've been a mistake. She had made up her mind to go home to New York, and Milo wasn't a part of the plan any longer.

Milo slapped the steering wheel with her palm so hard it stung. Thinking things through, she could not believe how foolish she had been. *She hired me to do a job*, she thought. *I should've stuck to that and never let my feelings become a part.* The irony was she wasn't even sure if she would ever get paid. Even though the trip had been expensive and used up a portion of her precious savings, Milo wouldn't chase the money. There was no price tag on how perfect the trip was, or at least until the last few minutes. For Milo, their miles together had been life-changing, and she had thought the same for Melanie.

Suddenly the car jerked hard to the left, and Milo wrestled the wheel to keep it from pitching into the ditch. The wump, wump, wump coming from the tire let Milo know it was flat. "Great," she said, blowing out a frustrated breath as she stopped on the side of the road. Climbing out, she saw the front driver's side tire was indeed shredded and let out a sigh. "Apparently my luck is just going to keep getting worse." It didn't help that when she opened the trunk to grab the spare, the first thing she saw was Melanie's suitcase. Pink with polka-dots. The roller bag had seemed perfect for her when Milo found it, and she thought Melanie liked the colorful discovery. Milo's shoulders slumped as she looked at the thing. *She didn't even consider taking stuff with her*, Milo thought, pushing it aside to wrestle the spare out of the trunk. *But then, why would she?* Milo needed to face facts—the items in the suitcase weren't really her things. They were cheap substitutions, only intended to tide her over until she could get back home to her own clothes, shoes, and makeup. *Never more than temporary.*

For a second Milo had a sinking feeling maybe she was nothing more to Melanie either. Standing on the side of the road as a few cars passed, she tried to decide what was real and what wasn't. Finally, she shook her head. *No*, she thought. *I don't believe that.* The chemistry was real, and the passion they shared could not be faked. Melanie wanted her as much as she wanted Melanie, and the abrupt separation was not of the woman's choosing. Milo knew the ending would be different if things had gone another way and they made it to New York City together.

Grabbing the tire and rolling it toward the front of the car, Milo was suddenly sure what she needed to do. The tire blowing had been a sign to pause her headlong escape from her hurt feelings and think. *I shouldn't be heading west, getting further away from Melanie,* she thought. *I need to be driving east.* Her heart pounding, she couldn't get the tire changed fast enough. Milo had a place to be—New York.

When Melanie arrived home to the mansion on Long Island, Monty did not come out of his office to greet her. She shouldn't have been surprised. He hadn't bothered to come to get her in his plane or be waiting in the limousine when she landed. *And what would I say if he was?* she wondered. *That I hate him for having me dragged to the airport in Jackson and then transported home like I was some sort of escaped prisoner?* Just the thought made her furious all over again, and rather than go to her wing of the house, she wanted to confront him.

Stomping to Monty's spacious office, Melanie didn't bother to knock on the large glossy black double doors. Interrupting him in his sanctum was normally unacceptable, but she didn't care. They needed to have a talk, and it needed to be right that instant. Turning in his chair behind the giant desk he ran his business from, Monty held a cellphone to his ear and looked ready to snap at whoever dared enter. He paused when he saw Melanie. "I'll call you in a minute," he said into the phone before disconnecting and turning to his wife. "Look who's back."

Melanie glared. "Well, here I am," Melanie said. "Are you happy?"

Monty leaned back in his chair, steepling his fingers. "Your little vacation had gone on long enough."

"My vacation," Melanie spat out, sure she had never been so angry. "You abandoned me."

The man waved his hand dismissively. "You blew that out of proportion," he said. "I've been looking for you for the last three days."

Barking a laugh, Melanie put her hands on her hips. "Considering I've been gone for almost two weeks, how very chivalrous of you."

Monty sighed as if he spoke to a child. "Listen," he said. "I have business to do, and I don't have time to sit here and argue. You're back, and I need you to burn that ugly dress and start acting your part again."

Narrowing her eyes, Melanie tried to guess Monty's angle. "Why are you so concerned about me..." She used her hands to make quote marks. "...acting my part?"

He glared at her tightlipped, and she thought for a second he wasn't going to answer, but then he leaned his elbows on the desk and looked her in the eye. "There's a fundraising gala tomorrow night at the Met, and I am one of the honorees," he said. "I sure as hell couldn't show up without my wife."

"Ohhh," Melanie said as everything fell into place. Monty's trophy wife needed to be available for photographs to make for a good press release. Having her absent, or worse, considered missing, would have ruined things for him. Under those circumstances, there would be a million questions if he dared appear alone. Questions he wouldn't want to answer. "You are such an asshole. That's all you care about." Then she thought of Lila in the jet. "Come on now. If you hadn't made a big deal about looking for me, I'm sure you have several women you could have taken as your plus one."

"Careful, Melanie," he said. "Or one of them will be a permanent replacement."

Melanie tossed her hair. "Oh really?" she said, feeling strangely hopeful he wasn't bluffing. More than ever, she realized she didn't want to be married to him anymore. Although Milo's company helped her understand she wasn't happy with Monty, Melanie finally saw what she meant to her husband. What she was worth. "I have to ask. Are any of your other women worth more than twenty-five thousand? Or am I just on discount?"

"This conversation is over," Monty said, picking up his phone. "Go get cleaned up. You look cheap." Then his call connected, and he turned his chair away from her. Dismissed, Melanie tried to think of something more she could do to pay him back when Monty swung toward her again. He covered the phone's microphone with one hand. "I do have one quick question."

"What?"

"You were with some guy, weren't you?" he asked, a sneer on his face. Clearly, he took satisfaction in dragging her back from someone else.

Unable to help herself at the thought of Milo, Melanie smiled, and it lit up her face. "No," she said, tilting her head as the memories of where she was flooded into her. "I wasn't with some guy."

She saw Monty scrutinizing her, narrowing his eyes as if studying her glowing smile. "Really?" he asked. "Well, that's good."

Melanie laughed. "I'm glad you think so because actually, Monty." She paused for dramatic effect. "I was with a woman. A confident, sexy, wonderful woman."

Chapter Thirty-Three

Sitting in the Cadillac in the slow morning traffic moving over the Brooklyn Bridge, Milo's body ached with exhaustion. Other than one short stop for a few hours of sleep at a rest area outside of Baltimore, she drove straight through. Her quest to get to Melanie gave her the fuel she needed to make the trip, but as she saw the New York City skyscrapers in the distance, she started to have doubts. *How will I possibly find her?* she thought. *It's not like I can look up her address on the internet and knock on the door.* She had a feeling Monty Sotheby chose to keep their information entirely confidential. The best Milo could hope for would be to reach some executive assistant. A gatekeeper. Someone who might relay a message to Melanie that Milo was in New York.

As traffic crept along, she considered her options. Finding a place to stay in the city seemed priority number one. Although she had never been to New York City, she was aware it was one of the most expensive places on earth. *I'll have to find some cheap dive*, she thought as traffic reached a complete standstill. *I don't know how long this will take.* Milo was determined not to leave until she had a chance to stand face-to-face with Melanie again. All the moments they shared along the way had to mean something. *I need to hear goodbye from her lips.* If Melanie said she didn't want to see Milo again, then that would be the end of it. But she needed to hear the words.

Suddenly a cellphone started ringing, and it took a moment for Milo to realize the sound came from the floor. After a beat, Milo understood Melanie left her purse with the throwaway phone inside. The same damn phone Monty used to track them. Her heart raced at the idea Melanie was calling her. Putting on her flashers, she reached across the seat to grab the purse off the floor. Fumbling to get the phone out and hoping Melanie wouldn't hang up, she finally put it to her ear. "Hello?"

A second passed, and she was sure Melanie had dropped the call when a man's voice surprised her. "Am I speaking to Elizabeth Milo?"

Leery and disappointed, Milo considered hanging up. *But if this is a connection to Melanie, I need to cooperate*, she thought. "Yes, this is Milo."

"Hello, Milo," the man continued. "Let me introduce myself. My name is Monty Sotheby, and I apparently owe you a hundred thousand dollars." Milo's eyebrows went up at the same time cars started honking behind her. Traffic was beginning to move, but she left her flashers on and continued the phone call. People could wait.

"That was the agreement."

The man chuckled. "Although you only partially fulfilled it," Monty said. "But all things considered, I will pay you the full amount." Milo bristled at his mocking tone but held her tongue and listened. "Where can I send the money?"

"Actually, I'm in New York City," Milo answered, and there was a long pause on the phone.

Monty cleared his throat. "I see," he said with no more laughter in his voice. "I thought you lived in Los Angeles?"

The change made Milo smile. "I do," she said. "But I was inspired to finish the trip."

"Inspired," Monty repeated. "How interesting. Well, in that case, let me have you as my guest."

Cars started to creep past as angry drivers yelled obscenities at her, but she ignored them. She tried to understand what Monty suggested. "Your guest?"

"Yes," he answered. "Come stay at the mansion. Can you find your way to South Hampton?"

Even though Monty's offer had warning signals firing in Milo, she would go anywhere if it meant seeing Melanie. "I can," she answered as the skies opened and rain started to splash her windshield. "What's the address?"

Waking with a start to the sound of thunder rattling her bedroom window, Melanie opened her eyes. A lingering memory of Milo and hiding in the barn made her heart race, and then she felt the splitting headache. Squinting, she knew the pain was to be expected. She spent most of the night drinking after a series of nasty confrontations with Monty. The number of gin and tonics she consumed had been considerable.

Rolling on her side to look at the nightstand, it was already close to noon. Not entirely unusual for her during her old life with Monty, but in the last few days, she grew accustomed to early mornings with Milo. *Milo,* she thought, and her heart clenched. *Where is she now? Driving back across Texas?* As memories poured in, they made Melanie so sad she closed her eyes to go back to sleep. There was no reason to get up. She didn't have the energy to face another day trapped in the house with Monty.

The night before had been horrendous. Monty had never been meaner, and Melanie responded by being just as nasty. At one point, she went to call a cab, ready to leave and go back to Los Angeles, to Milo. His threats had held her back. Monty was very clear if she left, he would make sure she didn't see a single penny of his money. With an ironclad prenuptial agreement, Melanie knew he wasn't bluffing. She would have very little to take with her if she insisted on divorce. Only one good thing came out of the evening. Monty promised he would pay Milo the whole hundred thousand dollars. "I'm only going to give her twenty-five thousand," Monty had said. "That was the amount of the reward."

"This is not about your stupid reward," Melanie had spat at him. "I hired her to drive me to New York after you deserted me." Eventually, Monty relented when she threatened to make her trip public. He would contact Milo the next day and wire her the entire amount. Then he had called Melanie disgusting and left her to many more gin and tonics. As she sat alone in the dark in one of their unnecessarily large living rooms, Melanie tried to determine precisely when her life went so wrong. And how the time she spent with Milo had felt so right. *So many regrets*, she thought. *But losing her is the hardest of all of them.*

Finally, Melanie had found her way to her bedroom, and only a drunken stupor helped her stop feeling like her life meant nothing. The problem was the same things haunted her when she woke. A million what-ifs raged through her, yet Melanie had no idea how to change her life. Even if she was in love with Milo, leaving Monty was too scary to contemplate. *I can't deal with this right now,* she thought. *Sleep really will be better.* Starting to roll over and bury her head in the covers, the weather outside did not agree. The storm did not relent as rain pounded and the wind whipped around the side of the house.

Once again thunder boomed, and the sound felt so close that it shook the room. She opened her eyes and pushed back the covers knowing it was ridiculous but needing to check the sky. Going to the window, she heard the rain smashing against the glass as she pulled back the curtain. A flicker of movement caught her eye, and Melanie looked to see someone coming up the mansion's long driveway. Blinking to make sure her eyes weren't tricking her, Melanie felt her heart stop. The car was unmistakable, and she covered her mouth with her hand as she watched it driving closer. It was Milo's silver Cadillac.

Trying not to be intimidated by the grandeur of the mansion, Milo parked the Cadillac in the long circular driveway. After taking two deep breaths to calm her racing emotions, she ran through the rain to the towering double front door. Before she knocked, it was opened by a handsome man in a plain white dress shirt and black slacks. She wasn't sure if he was a butler or what but would expect no less considering the size of the mansion. "You must be Elizabeth Milo," the host said, confidence in his tone. "I'm Kyle, one of Mr. Sotheby's assistants. He asked me to watch for you." Opening the door wide, he stepped out of the way to let her in. "Let me escort you to his office."

"Thanks, Kyle," Milo said, walking into the giant foyer. She was about to say more when she heard her name whispered. Turning to look, Melanie stood in one of the doorways shooting off the entryway. When their eyes met, the woman covered her mouth with her hands, tears running down her face. Although going to Melanie was her first instinct, Milo wasn't sure what to do in the presence of Kyle, so she waited to see what would happen next.

"How? It's impossible—" Melanie said, shaking her head. "I can't believe you're here." Then, as if suddenly free from a spell, the woman rushed toward her, and instinctively Milo opened her arms. Holding Melanie tight, she could feel the woman shaking against her chest.

Unable to help herself, Milo kissed the top of Melanie's head. "It'll be okay," she murmured into her hair.

She heard Kyle cough. "I will go get Mr. Sotheby," he said softly, and out of the corner of her eye Milo watched him leaving in a hurry. No doubt an awkward confrontation was about to ensue, but for the moment, she let herself lean in and enjoy the feeling of having Melanie in her arms.

Finally, the woman lifted her head and looked into Milo's eyes. "You shouldn't be here," she said. "I love that you came for me, but..." Milo didn't know what to think as Melanie's words trailed off. A sinking feeling filled her stomach.

Before she could ask for clarification, someone who could only be Monty Sotheby strode into the foyer, his expensive shoes clicking on the marble surface. "Well, isn't this cute," he snarled. "I invite you to my home, and you attack my wife?"

Breaking away from Milo, Melanie whirled on the man. "She did not attack me, and you know it," Melanie snapped. "But I don't understand why she's here although I know you had something to do with it. Are you taunting me?"

Monty shook his head. "You always think things are about you," he said. "But this time sweetheart, it's not. I asked Miss Milo to come by the house to be our guest, but now I can see that was a mistake." He came closer, holding out his hand with a piece of paper. "Here's the check of what I owe you." He took Melanie by the hand and started to pull her away. "Let's go. You need to start getting ready for tonight's gala. I've hired a makeover SWAT team to come and fix you up again." He waved at her appearance. "I want glamorous, from a full hairdo down to your painted toenails. Everything must be perfect for tonight."

Melanie jerked her arm away but otherwise did not resist. "Go to hell," Melanie snapped, and Milo wasn't sure what to think as Monty's face grew red.

He pointed at Milo. "Oh, and by the way, Melanie," he

said. "Your special friend here? Turns out she's a felon. Do you realize you put your trust in the hands of someone who is an ex-convict?"

"It's not like it sounds," Melanie snapped, and Monty laughed but the sound was mean, and Milo knew in an instant the man could be cruel.

"You always were the naïve one." He glared at Milo. "You can go. Our debt is settled."

Before Milo moved, she looked at Melanie. "Is this what you want?"

"It's not really up to her," Monty snapped, but Milo ignored him and held Melanie's gaze.

"If you come with me, we can make this work."

At that Monty shook his head. "You've got to be kidding me," he said. "Obviously you haven't met the real Melanie. She would never live without all these creature comforts." He waved a hand around at the beautiful portraits and antiques in the foyer. "Can you give her this?"

Milo tried to ignore him, keeping her gaze on Melanie. "Come with me," she whispered. They stood staring at each other for a long moment, and then Melanie shook her head.

Chapter Thirty-Four

Dressed in a ridiculously expensive maroon evening gown, matching heels, gaudy gold jewelry, and a clutch purse, Melanie felt like she had come full circle. Riding in the back of yet another limousine beside Monty in his tuxedo as they made their way to the ever-important gala, she watched raindrops run down the tinted window. Although they had yet to arrive, she already knew at some point in the evening Monty would humiliate her. As she was getting dressed, she had the realization it was one of the ways he controlled her. *One of many*, she thought. *So why am I putting up with it?* A part of her knew the answer—fear. Fear of change. Fear of the unknown. Fear of ending up alone. What surprised her the most though, was she hadn't always been afraid. *Where is the brave seventeen-year-old girl who put her back to Texas and risked everything in New York City? How did I lose her?*

"Yes, Melanie's with me," Monty said into the phone he had been on since they got in the limo. "She's back where she belongs." He glanced in her direction. "Wait until you hear what she was up to." Monty chuckled. "I should have her head examined."

Melanie turned from the window to glare at him. As he ignored her, she genuinely looked at Monty for the first time. Inside the fancy clothing, all she could see was a chubby, balding, greedy little man who always got what he wanted. *And this is who I want to spend the rest of my life with?* she wondered. Suddenly an image of Milo's face popped into her head. She could see the kindness and strength in her loving eyes. *When I was with her, I was brave again.* "What have I done?" she whispered, her heart aching.

Monty pulled the phone from his ear. "What?" he snapped, and she shook her head. There was nothing left to say to him, and as the limo slowed for traffic, she finally realized she had made the worst possible mistake. When Milo said, 'we can make this work' Melanie hadn't believed it. *I think I do now*, she thought, her stomach twisting with panic. *But what if I've lost Milo forever?* Suddenly she had to reach Milo before she went back to California. Somehow, she needed to convince Milo that she did want to try. *I need to contact her.* Calling the throwaway cellphone was the only possibility, but the number was on Monty's phone. He would never give it to her, and while they sat there not moving in the limo, Melanie did the bravest thing she had ever done—she grabbed his phone. The last thing she saw before dashing out of the limousine with her clutch purse and into the rainy night was his shocked face. Then she was running as heavy drops splattered her, high heels nearly tripping her as she raced down the wet sidewalk.

"God damnit! Stop," she heard Monty yell behind her. "Get back here." Only, she didn't stop. As she ran, a part of Melanie knew he was only upset about his phone. *And not about me*, she thought. *Never about me.* Suddenly, she didn't care. Someone yelled over the phone in her hand, but Melanie didn't break stride as she hung up the call. She had to find a place to use the phone. Hoping Monty and the limo were still stuck in traffic, she ducked into a corner grocery store, not unlike the one in Los Angeles. Hiding down an aisle so Monty couldn't see her from the street, she scrolled the recent calls on his phone. All had contact names except for a two-one-three number. It had to be the throwaway cellphone. With a shaking hand she dialed it.

As hard as she searched, Milo could not find Melanie in the storm. The rain was too heavy, and the night was too dark. Even when she called out to her, the wind whipped her words away and there was no answer. Spinning in circles, Milo started to despair. *Maybe she doesn't want to be found?* Milo wondered. *After all, she rejected me.* Still, a part of her wouldn't ever give up. In her heart, she knew Melanie loved her. If she could just find her again. As she ran down the sidewalk trying to look in every shop and restaurant, Melanie was nowhere. As she become more frantic, a phone started ringing in the distance. It was not very loud but distinct, and she whirled in all directions trying to pick out where it came from. "Melanie," she yelled into the stormy night. "Where are you?"

Before she located the phone, the sound stopped. Frustrated, she looked at the sky and let out her emotions in a guttural yell. The cry of anguish shook her to the core, and suddenly she felt the surface of the hard mattress beneath her. Wrapped in the threadbare sheets of the cheap hotel room bed, she struggled to sit up. Rubbing her face with her hands, she tried to force away the grogginess. The last thing she remembered was opening the door to her room and then crashing on the bed. *How long ago was that?* she wondered, noticing the thin curtains were dark with only the glow of city streetlamps casting any light. Looking at her watch, Milo was shocked to see so many hours had passed. *I needed sleep. All the driving plus having my heart broken left me worn out.*

Numb from Melanie's denial, she had been operating like a zombie as she left the Sotheby mansion and drove back into the city. Stopping at the first hotel sign she saw Milo didn't even balk at the high price tag. She had her check for a hundred thousand dollars in her pocket, so money didn't matter for the moment. What mattered was finding a place to lick her wounds and get some sleep. As she sat there trying not to think of Melanie, she recalled remnants of the dream and wondered about the phone ringing. *Did it ring here?* she wondered. Then a thought struck her—what if someone called the phone still stuffed in her pocket? *That would explain why it sounded so muffled.* She pulled it free, and maybe she should have been more excited at the prospect Melanie called her, but Milo wasn't sure that was what she wanted. *How much more can I take?*

Lifting it to her face, she looked at the phone screen and saw someone had left a voicemail. She recognized Monty's number and thought about throwing the phone across the room. *What more can he want from me?* He won. Melanie was convinced she could never leave him. Yet, a part of her needed to know what the message said, and when she pressed the button for voicemail, she didn't hear Monty. "Milo," Melanie said, making Milo's heart race. "I know you probably hate me. You have every reason to, and maybe that's why you're not answering the phone." Milo closed her eyes, relishing the sound of the woman's voice even if she didn't want to. "I want you to be somewhere safe. New York is a dangerous city and… God, I'm rambling." There was a pause, and Milo could tell she hesitated about what to say next. "I made the worst possible mistake, and I am begging your forgiveness. I will be waiting at Parma Nuova restaurant on Third Avenue and East Seventy-ninth. Please come." Then the call was over.

Staring at the phone in her hand, the rawest of emotions ran through her—excitement, sadness, desire, fear. It would be so easy to pretend what Melanie did at the diner and then at the mansion didn't matter, but they did. *Maybe that's the real Melanie*, she thought. *Maybe the entire time she was with me she was pretending to be someone else?* Tossing the phone on the bed, Milo got up and paced the room. It came down to what she wanted. She could take the money, drive back to Los Angeles, and find a way to start a new life. There was no need for the complications of having someone else involved. The best thing would be to cherish the memories of her time with Melanie and move on. Milo didn't know what she was going to do.

In a booth at the Parma Nuova restaurant where she once waited tables decades ago, Melanie waited. Over two hours had passed, and she didn't know how many more glasses of wine she should have before giving up. Eventually the place would close, and she would be stuck with few options. Still, she didn't blame Milo. The urge to call her again was hard to resist, but she forced herself to finally be the patient one. Everything was her fault. She hurt Milo. *Would I act any differently?* she wondered and, after a beat, laughed at herself. *Probably. I'd go back for more. Monty proved I'm a sucker for punishment.*

With a sigh, she took the final sip from her wine glass and considered waving down the waiter for another. Although sitting there getting drunk was likely the last thing she should be doing, her heart was broken, and the future looked bleak. Before she could get anyone's attention, she saw someone come in the restaurant's front door and her heart stopped for a beat. *Please let that be Milo*, she thought, and then Monty stormed up to her table. His face was scarlet, and his cheeks were puffy, and he looked ready to explode. She had never seen the man look so upset, but as much as she wanted to cower away from him, she held firm. Their glares met, and the man shook his head. "Do you realize what you've just done to your life?" he hissed. "You've lost your mind."

Melanie felt a tightening in her stomach but also a fresh resolve in her heart. "I do know what I've done," she said. "I've left you, and I want a divorce."

"Oh, you're going to get a divorce," Monty shot back. "That is certain. Now give me back my phone before I call someone to arrest you."

Melanie raised an eyebrow. "Arrest me?"

"You have my property," he growled, motioning to the phone on the table.

"So take it," Melanie said sliding it toward him, somehow knowing Milo would never call.

Monty grabbed the thing. "I am sick of your antics," he said. "Consider your life ruined."

The last threat was too much, and Melanie pointed a finger at him. "My life ruined?" she spat. "Living a life playing the roles you wanted me to play was never a life anyway. So do what you want, I don't care."

Monty frowned, looking a little confused by her defiant answer. "You really are crazy," he said. "Go try it with your felon and see how long it lasts." With that the man turned on his heel and strode away leaving Melanie feeling more deserted than she ever had. *Except maybe when my parents left me the note*, she thought. *But I was brave then and found my way without a penny to my name.* It was time to be brave again. Squaring her shoulders, she took a few twenties from her purse and tossed them on the table. *I can be that brave again.*

With no plan, Melanie wandered out of the restaurant and into the rain. No coat, no umbrella, and she felt it wetting her hair and running down her face. Somehow, she didn't mind. It almost seemed symbolic of washing away her old life. "Melanie," she heard Milo say from up the sidewalk.

Whirling, she saw the woman she had fallen in love with standing in the rain. "You're here," she murmured as her heart raced. The urge to run to Milo pulled at her, but she resisted. As much as she wanted to be with the woman, she realized it was time to stand on her own too. Melanie would like to spend time with Milo and give their life a try, but finally realized she could survive without her. She was her own woman, in control of her own life for the first time in a long time, and it felt good.

Holding out her hand for Milo to take, Melanie smiled. "Let's talk," she said. "Come into the restaurant with me." After a long pause, Milo nodded, and taking each other's hand, they stepped out of the rain.

Epilogue

Sitting on Chelsea and Joel's back porch in Grand Pickett, Milo watched Melanie and Chelsea cut flowers in the yard and couldn't remember being happier. She genuinely liked Chelsea and Joel, so visiting for a couple of days before going to New Orleans was fine with her. The best part though was seeing the two sisters growing closer. When she saw Melanie laugh at something Chelsea said, Milo smiled. *Just one more of the magical things that have happened over the last few months*, she thought. *My life has changed so much.* Before she found Melanie in trouble in the alley, Milo had been miserable without knowing it. Working a dead-end job. Alone. No real reason to exist, but that had all changed. Melanie was like the sun shining through the window into a dark room, and Milo could admit she loved her.

Monty had threatened Milo would regret taking Melanie into her life, but he was wrong. Although there were moments they didn't see eye-to-eye, their mutual respect helped them navigate any situation. As for Monty, thankfully he was out of their life completely. Although the divorce had started rocky, the billionaire relented when Melanie threatened she would go to the press and explain how he abandoned her on the streets of Los Angeles. In the end, Milo knew the multimillion-dollar settlement helped put Melanie's mind at ease about the future.

As the two sisters crossed the yard, their arms full of beautiful yellow roses, Chelsea smiled at Milo. "Melanie told me you are almost finished with your book," she said. "That's exciting."

Milo smiled back, feeling a thrum of excitement in her chest at the prospect of having written an entire novel. "Yes, it feels good to be writing again," Milo said. "And to almost have it complete is truly a miracle."

"It's not a miracle," Melanie said. "You work hard and are dedicated to the project." She looked at Chelsea. "She won't let me read all of it, but the parts I have read are beautiful."

"Thank you," Milo said, pecking Melanie on the cheek as she got up to hold the door and let the two women take the flowers inside.

"So, what is the book about?" Chelsea asked as she passed by her.

Glancing at Melanie, Milo met the woman's eyes, and she winked at her. "Actually," Milo said after the go ahead. "The plot is straightforward. The story is a sweet romance about two women driving across the country in a Cadillac."

Chelsea paused after setting the flowers on the counter. "Well, that's interesting, isn't it?" she said, meeting Milo's eye. "I don't suppose they wander through Texas?"

"They might," Milo answered, and Chelsea nodded.

"Sounds like something I might enjoy."

In the new silver Cadillac Escalade Milo rented from the airport when they landed in Dallas, Melanie could not help but feel nostalgic for the 1968 vintage car that in part changed her life. *Maybe someday we'll have to find one and have a refurbished*, she thought with a smile. There was a certain amount of flair traveling in it with the top down. The Cadillac SUV just wasn't the same.

"So, you like your place in New York?" Chelsea asked from the backseat. Melanie glanced at Milo and liked seeing a smile on her face. It mirrored how she felt. Although they were still getting to know each other, they decided to share a two bedroom flat in New York on the Upper West Side. It was a big step for both, but it felt right.

Looking at her sister, Melanie nodded. "It's perfect," she said. "You and Joel need to come to visit."

Before Chelsea could comment, Melanie felt her cellphone buzzing in her purse beside her. Not expecting a call, she frowned. *Maybe I'll let that go to voicemail*, she thought, but then something instinctively told her to take the call. Before it stopped ringing, she answered. "This is Melanie."

"Melanie," a man's familiar voice said. "I'm glad I caught you." After a beat, Melanie recognized the caller was a photographer friend of hers, and she couldn't wait to hear his news. "I want to talk to you about those test shots we took of Milo last month." Melanie held her breath, praying he would say something good. "I shopped them around a little bit and found someone who wants to have a full spread. Milo is exactly what they are looking for."

Melanie put her hand on her chest, almost unable to contain her excitement. "That's fantastic," Melanie said, looking at Milo. "We are in Texas and then going to Mardi Gras but will be back in New York by the end of the month."

"That should work fine," the photographer said. "Just give me a call."

Melanie grabbed Milo's arm with delight as she hung up. "They want to take a full spread of photographs of you."

"What?" Milo said with her eyebrows raised.

Melanie all but hopped in her seat. "The photographer," she said. "He wants to see you again. I told you the camera would love you."

She watched Milo shake her head. "I still don't see it," she said. "But I'm not going to say no."

All smiles, Chelsea clapped her hands in the backseat. "Congratulations," she said. "And I'm so happy you have decided to go to New Orleans for Mardi Gras."

"Me too," Melanie replied, rubbing Milo's shoulder lovingly. "We even have the perfect hotel."

Milo glanced at her, eyes twinkling. "It is the ideal place."

Unable to help but blush a little, Melanie nodded. "Yes, it is," she said as Milo pulled them up into the parking lot of the small Grand Pickett cemetery. Looking out the windshield, Melanie's playful emotions sobered. In a few moments, they would be walking along the path to her parent's gravesite. She picked the roses to lay on the headstone with her sister. Ever since the conversation on the porch swing, they had come a long way. Slowly Melanie was letting the hurt go. The time had come to find a way to start making amends with the other parts of her past too. Being abandoned in Dallas was never to be forgotten, but Melanie was willing to start forgiving.

"Are you ready?" Chelsea asked softly, and Melanie searched her heart before she answered. The hollowness she felt before had started to fill with new memories. Every time she held Brady Junior, her love for her family grew. The bitterness she felt was part of the old Melanie, and a new chapter had started in her life.

She looked at Chelsea and smiled. "Yes," she said. "What they did, and all of the other roads I've traveled helped lead me to this moment." She was in the car with two people who she loved and knew loved her in return. Feeling a sense of release, Melanie blinked back tears. "And I wouldn't change a thing."

THE END

Want more?

Sign up for my newsletter (https://landing.mailerlite.com/webforms/landing/r2b5s6) to keep tabs on what I am writing next.

About the Author

Bestselling author KC Luck writes action adventure, contemporary romance, and lesbian fiction. Writing is her passion, and nothing energizes her more than creating new characters facing trials and tribulations in a complex plot. Whether it is apocalypse, horror, or a little naughty, with every story, KC tries to add her own unique twist. She has written over a dozen books (which include *The Darkness Series* and *Everybody Needs a Hero*) and multiple short stories across many genres. KC is active in the LGBTQ+ community and is the founder of the collective iReadIndies.

KC Luck is always thrilled to hear from her readers (kc.luck.author@gmail.com)

To follow KC Luck, you can find her at: www.kc-luck.com

Thank you!

Enjoy this book?
You can make a big difference

Honest reviews of my books help bring them to the attention of other readers. If you've enjoyed this story, I would be incredibly grateful if you could spend a couple minutes leaving a review (it can be as short as you like) on the book's Amazon and Goodreads pages.

Also By KC Luck

Rescue Her Heart

Save Her Heart

Welcome to Ruby's

Back to Ruby's

Darkness Falls

Darkness Remains

Darkness United

Wind Dancer

Darkness San Francisco

The Lesbian Billionaires Club

The Lesbian Billionaires Seduction

The Lesbian Billionaires Last Hope

Venandi

What the Heart Sees

Everybody Needs a Hero

Can't Fight Love

iRead Indies

This author is part of iReadIndies, a collective of self-published independent authors of sapphic literature. Please visit our website at iReadIndies.com for more information and to find links to the books published by our authors.

Printed in Great Britain
by Amazon